A Body is Found

The Adams Round Table
Authors of MURDER IN MANHATTAN

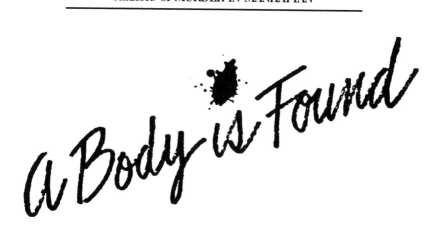
A Body is Found

WYNWOOD™ Press
New York, New York

Contents

About the Round Table

Not so long ago, a three-year-old of my acquaintance was sitting on the floor, whisking his fingers up and down, jabbing at the keys of some imaginary typewriter.

He informed his mother that he was going to become a "writer guy" and as she wondered if it was already time to call in the therapist, he added, "Because I know how to type. And I'm just a sad and lonely guy."

Let's pass on typing and sadness. But if that kid is talking about lonely in the sense of solitary, welcome to the wonderful world of writing for a living. For the profession is the last refuge of the loner, and if you're not doing it alone, you're not really writing.

But when all the pencils have been sharpened and the plug has been pulled on the typewriter for the night, writers, by God, want to stop being slaves of their solitary passion. So what do they do? They go looking for other writers. So that they can all talk about writing.

Not on the "Where do you get your ideas?" level, or the even worse "What do you think of the recurrent symbolic use of the mitre in the work of Ford Madox Ford?"—(to which the only possible answer can be Nothing, Madam, Nothing). No, they want to talk about the nuts and bolts of writing techniques, and that takes other writers who work at it.

Thomas Chastain and Mary Higgins Clark brought together the first group of nine mystery and suspense writers five years ago at a restaurant on the upper East Side of Manhattan. Adam, one of the restaurant's owners, scouted up a large round table and stuck it in the back room for us.

And thus Adam's Round Table.

Over the years, the membership has changed. Some have left, others have joined, but the institution keeps going and still, rain or shine, snow or sobriety, we are at the Bella Vita Restaurant on the first Tuesday of each month, jawing and chewing and arguing and learning.

Always learning.

Once in a while, we seem to get the need to prove that we *are* learning something and so, a few years ago, we did a collection of stories called *Murder in Manhattan*.

This time around, we decided to narrow the focus a bit.

It was our thought that each of us would write a story based on a body being found facedown in New York. The idea was to demonstrate—"Show, don't tell" being one of the Round Table's most cherished rules—that the number of stories that can be built around one single idea is infinite. And also, to have some fun . . . because if writing isn't fun, it is one *fershtunkina* way to spend a day.

So that's what this book is and that's what the Adams Round Table is. What we are *not* is some homogenized, lumpless collection of humankind. We are a thief's dozen now and we love Manhattan and we hate Manhattan, we are conservatives and liberals, churchgoers and the fallen-away, and pets-righters and spiritual vivisectionists . . . and you name it and one of us once believed in it or took it in or had a subscription to it. And as interesting as all of that might be, we try to keep it in the closet and talk only about writing because that's "the guy what brung us."

Some nights we're more successful than others. But we keep coming back and we keep trying and who knows? With luck, we may still be around to greet that three-year-old when he's ready to join the other "writer-guys."

> Warren Murphy
> For the Adams Round Table

P.S. Some of the sharp-eyed might notice that we have eleven members but only ten stories. Member Frederick Knott (*Dial M for Murder, Wait Until Dark*) is a playwright.

A Body is Found

A body is found . . . and the question is not the identity of the victim as is usually the case when a body is found in Manhattan, in an alley, in a crack house, floating in the river, in an abandoned tenement, in Central Park, in the subway. The question is what is the cause of death and, if it was murder, who is guilty of the murder . . .

Thomas Chastain

Admissible Evidence

"—and, Dr. Lyman, would you tell the court please exactly what you found when you arrived at the Harrison residence on Beekman Place?"

"I found the body of the deceased lying on the small terrace out in back of the house."

"The deceased being the victim, Jack Conboy, is that correct?"

"Yes. Although I did not know his name at that time."

"And who else was present?"

"The Harrisons, Walter and Vivian, and Mrs. Conboy."

"How did it happen that you were called to the house that night?"

"I live nearby and I have been Mrs. Vivian Harrison's doctor for several years. I suppose it was for those reasons."

11

"So it was Mrs. Harrison who telephoned you?"

"Yes."

"All right. Now would you describe what happened when you found the body of the deceased on the terrace?"

"I examined him. He was lying on his left side and he wasn't breathing. I couldn't raise a pulse."

"Did you make a judgment as to the cause of death?"

"I made a preliminary judgment that he had suffered a fatal heart attack. The judgment seemed consistent with the facts available to me at that time."

"What facts were those, Dr. Lyman?"

"The physical facts were the condition of the body, the lack of any external marks on the body that might have caused death, and the facts that were told to me by the Harrisons and Mrs. Conboy about what had taken place shortly before Jack Conboy collapsed on the terrace."

"Exactly what were you told?"

"That the four of them had been having cocktails, martinis, in the house when Conboy suddenly lurched up from his chair, said he was feeling ill and needed some fresh air. They said they were all alarmed and followed him when he staggered out to the terrace and collapsed. That's when, they said, Mrs. Harrison rushed to the phone and called me."

"Tell me, Doctor, wouldn't you have thought, under the circumstances, that it would have been more logical for Vivian Harrison to have phoned the 911 emergency number?"

"Objection, Your Honor. Calls for conjecture on the part of the witness."

"Sustained!"

"Dr. Lyman, after you made your preliminary judgment as to the cause of death, did you announce it to the others present?"

"I did. I said it *appeared* the deceased had suffered cardiac arrest."

"What happened then?"

"As I recall, there was a certain amount of confusion among the Harrisons and Mrs. Conboy as to what should be done next. That is, should an ambulance be called? Did a report have to made to the authorities? Could I sign a certificate of death? While this discussion was going on, Mrs. Conboy slipped away briefly. When she returned she announced that she had phoned the police and that they were on the way."

"And did the police arrive soon thereafter?"

"They did. And shortly after that the police called the New York City Medical Examiner, who came and took charge of the body."

"I'm curious, Dr. Lyman. When Mrs. Conboy returned from making her phone call to the police, did she tell the rest of you why she had called the police?"

"She did. She said she didn't believe her husband had died of natural causes."

"Thank you, Doctor. Your Honor, I have no further questions of this witness."

"The defense may cross-examine."

"We have no questions, Your Honor."

"Mr. Dietrich, call your next witness."

"The prosecution calls Detective Donald Granger."

"Detective Granger, when you were called to the Harrison house on the night Jack Conboy met his death, did you find and remove from the house a bottle containing a liquid which was subsequently identified as chloral hydrate?"

"I did."

"I show you this bottle. It is the bottle you found?"

"It has my mark on it. There. Yes, it's the bottle I removed."

"Where exactly did you find the bottle?"

"In a dresser drawer in Vivian Harrison's bedroom."

"Thank you. Defense counsel's witness."

"No questions, Your Honor."

"Very well. The prosecution may call its next witness."

"The People call Dr. Lewis Angstrom."

"Dr. Angstrom, as Chief Medical Examiner for the City of New York, you conducted the autopsy on the body of the deceased, Jack Conboy, is that correct?"

"I did."

"And what were your findings?"

"The complete autopsy report is here."

"We will enter the report into the record of these proceedings, but for now, could you give us the conclusions in your own words, if the defense will agree?"

"The defense has no objections."

"Proceed, Doctor."

"The autopsy showed that the deceased died of a massive ingestion of chloral hydrate, a bitter crystalline hydrate, CCl_3CH—parenthesis OH_2—the potent knockout substance used in so-called Mickey Finns. When ingested in sufficient quantity, chloral hydrate brings on a death that to outward appearances resembles a heart attack."

"Thank you, Doctor. And were you able to form an opinion as to how the deceased might have ingested the chloral hydrate?"

"There were other traces of alcohol in the body. My opinion would be that the lethal amount of chloral hydrate was mixed in with whatever else the deceased drank."

"A martini, for instance?"

"A martini, for instance."

"I show you this bottle, Doctor, removed from the Harrison house by police. Did you test the contents of the bottle?"

"I did. The bottle has my mark on it. The bottle contained chloral hydrate."

"Thank you, Doctor. I have no other questions."

"Your witness, Mr. Maury."

"Dr. Angstrom, would it require any particular mixing process for a lethal amount of chloral hydrate to be concealed in a drink, an alcoholic drink such as a martini, for example?"

"No."

"In other words, if, for example, a martini was mixed and poured into a glass, all that would be necessary would be to add a sufficient amount of chloral hydrate to that glass to make it lethal."

"That is correct."

"I have no further questions, Your Honor."

"The court will take a fifteen-minute recess."

"This court is in session. Mr. Dietrich, call your next witness."

"We call Walter Harrison to the stand. Your Honor, I would like to point out to the court that this witness is aware that he cannot be compelled to testify. The testimony he will give is completely voluntary."

"All right. Proceed."

"Mr. Harrison, you are the husband of the defendant, Vivian Harrison, is that correct?"

"Yes."

"And how long have the two of you been married?"

"For thirty years."

"Has it been a happy marriage?"

"Yes."

"Even though you discovered at one point that your wife was in love with someone else, with the deceased, Jack Conboy?"

"I do not know that for a fact."

"No? Even though you are aware that there exist certain letters written by your wife to Jack Conboy making that fact clear?"

"I have not read the letters."

"You have not wanted to read the letters, is that not more correct?"

"The letters were not written to me."

"I see. Turning to another subject, for how long did you know Edward Crawford?"

"For twenty-eight years, up until his death two years ago."

"You were business partners for those years, is that not so?"

"Yes, we were."

"In your own securities firm, Crawford-Harrison?"

"Yes."

"And how long have you and your wife known Margo Crawford Conboy?"

"For seven years, ever since she married Edward Crawford—five years before his death."

"Your wife, Vivian, and Margo Crawford were close friends, is that not correct?"

"That is correct."

"And you and Edward Crawford were close friends?"

"He was my best friend."

"Were you aware that Edward Crawford kept a diary?"

"No."

"Well, he did. I have a copy of his diary here. On June

eleventh, three and a half years ago, Edward Crawford wrote, and I quote: A rather odd luncheon conversation with Walter today. He asked if I had noticed how that fellow, Jack Conboy, was always hanging around with Margo and Vivian. Walter tried to make the question sound casual, but I sensed that somehow he was disturbed by the relationship between Conboy and Vivian and Margo. Surely he can't think there's anything going on between Conboy and Vivian or Conboy and Margo. Unquote. Do you recall that conversation with Edward Crawford, Mr. Harrison?"

"No."

"No? I see. Now, turning to a later date in the diary. August eighth the same year, Edward Crawford wrote, and I again quote: A curious and somewhat unpleasant evening at the beach club last night. Walter and Vivian, Margo, and I had planned to have dinner there, and at the last minute as we were leaving Walter and Vivian's, after cocktails, Conboy suddenly showed up and Vivian invited him to join us at the beach club for dinner. What made the dinner so unpleasant and, frankly, made me uncomfortable was that Vivian made something of a spectacle of herself gushing over Conboy like some schoolgirl with a crush on him. It was damned embarrassing! Walter, Margo, and I had to pretend we didn't notice anything out of the way, but of course, we did. I could see what an effort it took for Walter to try to ignore the obvious. It was tasteless behavior on Vivian's part. Unquote. Now, I put it to you, Mr. Harrison, do you still maintain you were never aware that your wife was enamored of Jack Conboy?"

"I was never aware, no. Nor am I aware of that fact now."

"Your Honor, I ask that this diary be entered into the record as People's Exhibit 1-C."

"Mr. Maury?"

"No objections, Your Honor."

"I have no further questions of this witness, Your Honor."

"Does the defense wish to cross-examine?"

"We do, Your Honor. Mr. Harrison, do you believe your wife, Vivian Harrison, is guilty of the murder of Jack Conboy?"

"I do not! No!"

"Thank you. No further questions, Your Honor."

"Call your next witness, Mr. Dietrich."

"The prosecution calls Margo Conboy."

"Mrs. Conboy, will you tell us, please, the circumstances of your first meeting with the victim, Jack Conboy?"

"Vivian, Vivian Harrison, and I joined the Arena Tennis Club here in Manhattan. Jack Conboy was the tennis coach, teacher, there. Vivian and I both took tennis lessons from him."

"Did you take your lessons together? You and Vivian Harrison?"

"Yes."

"And you and Vivian Harrison and Jack Conboy became friends, rather good friends, I gather?"

"Yes. I would say we did, yes."

"And when did you become aware that Vivian Harrison had—I would suggest—more than a friendly interest in Jack Conboy?"

"I didn't. At least not during the time the three of us were together, before my first husband was killed and Jack and I married."

"You have heard what your first husband, Edward Crawford, wrote in his diary about the embarrassing display of affection by Vivian Harrison toward Jack Conboy?"

"I have heard it. And I read it for myself in Edward's diary after his death."

"Yet you say you were not aware of her feelings toward Conboy?"

"May I explain? Jack Conboy was a very attractive man. Women were attracted to him. And he was flirtatious in turn. I was certainly aware of that and I know Vivian was, as well. But I thought it was all just an amusing pastime. For Vivian, for me."

"Yet you and Jack Conboy were married some time after your first husband's death. Wouldn't that indicate that you, too, must have been—ah—enamored of him, just as we have gathered Vivian Harrison was?"

"My feelings for Jack developed over a period of time after Edward was killed. Edward's death was a terrible trauma, not just the suddenness of it but the circumstances. I was devastated. It was so senseless."

"Your husband was killed in a hit-and-run accident at the East Bay Bath and Tennis Club on Long Island, is that correct? What do you mean, it was so senseless?"

"The way it happened. Edward, Walter, Vivian, and I were having dinner at the beach club, and when we got ready to leave, Edward insisted on going to the parking lot alone to get the car. On the way he was run down and killed. If the other three of us had gone with him, he probably wouldn't have been hit—or at least we would have seen the car that hit him. That's why I was so devastated. And in the aftermath of the tragedy Jack was always there to comfort me. Gradually, I came to depend upon him and eventually fell in love with him and we were married."

"There is an age difference between you and Vivian Harrison, is there not?"

"Yes."

"You are a decade or more younger than she?"

"Yes."

"And there was that same age difference between Vivian Harrison and Jack Conboy?"

"Yes."

"He was much closer to your age."

"Yes."

"It is possible, is it not, that it was as a consequence of this age difference between him and her that you never really seriously considered her true feelings for him?"

"I suppose so. Yes."

"So that when you did find out, what was your reaction?"

"I was shocked!"

"Will you tell the court please how it was that you became aware of her true feelings toward him."

"Several months after Jack and I were married, he showed me a batch of letters she had written to him."

"Those letters were written to him after you and he were married?"

"Yes."

"I show you these letters. Are they the letters Jack Conboy showed to you?"

"Yes, they are."

"Your Honor, defense counsel has stipulated that these letters may be offered into evidence."

"We so stipulate, Your Honor."

"Proceed, Mr. Dietrich."

"Mrs. Conboy, will you read the opening and last paragraph of the letter I now hand to you."

"Quote: My Darling Jack, I have been despondent ever since your marriage to Margo. I believe with all my heart that you deceived me into thinking it was me you loved. I do not know whether I want to go on living if I've lost you forever. Unquote. The letter ends quote: From the one and only one who truly loves you. Unquote. It is signed Viv."

"And would you read the first line of this next letter."

"Quote: Sometimes I don't know whether I hate you more or love you more. Unquote."

"Mrs. Conboy, there are fourteen letters here in all from Vivian Harrison to Jack Conboy. You have read them all. Are the sentiments expressed in the other twelve similar to those expressed in the two letters you have read to the court?"

"They are."

"Your Honor, the prosecution asks that these letters be entered into the record of these proceedings."

"Since there is no objection by the defense, motion granted."

"Mrs. Conboy, turning to another matter, did your husband, Jack Conboy, ever tell you about procuring a quantity of chloral hydrate for Vivian Harrison?"

"He did, yes."

"Did he tell you *why* the defendant wanted the chloral hydrate?"

"The way Jack told it to me, it was kind of a joke. He said once Vivian was complaining about her husband, about Walter, that sometimes he was so boring she just wished he'd fall asleep and give her ears a rest. He said he told her about how chloral hydrate is used to make Mickey Finns and he thought she'd get a laugh out of it when he gave her the bottle. I don't think Jack ever thought she meant to use it."

"Certainly Jack Conboy never thought she meant to use it on *him*—"

"Objection, Your Honor!"

"Sustained. Mr. Dietrich, please refrain from such comments."

"Sorry, Your Honor. Now, Mrs. Conboy, will you tell us please how your husband was able to obtain the quantity of chloral hydrate he gave to Vivian Harrison?"

"I never asked him. It didn't seem all that unusual to me that Jack would know about things like that. He'd been around, and when he was younger, in college, he'd been a bartender part-time. I would like to add that because I had read somewhere once that chloral hydrate could be fatal, and resemble a heart attack—and that Vivian had such a poison—that I called the police the night Jack collapsed and told them about the chloral hydrate."

"I see. No more questions, Your Honor. The prosecution rests."

"Mr. Maury, your witness."

"No questions."

"In that case, Mr. Maury, would you like a recess before you put your witnesses on the stand?"

"Actually, Your Honor, the defense plans to call only one witness: Vivian Harrison."

"Proceed."

"Mrs. Harrison, you have heard the testimony given in this court. Did you, in fact, give Jack Conboy a martini containing a lethal dose of chloral hydrate on the night he died?"

"I did not! No!"

"And you don't know who might have done such a thing?"

"No!"

"Did you want Jack Conboy dead?"

"No! Of course not!"

"Were you in love with Jack Conboy?"

"It was just a silly flirtation, is all it was."

"And you have cooperated with the investigation of his death in every way you can?"

"I have. When the police questioned me about the bottle of chloral hydrate, after Margo told them about it, I led them to the dresser in my bedroom and gave them the bottle."

"Tell us please exactly what happened with reference to the martinis the four of you drank that night."

"Walter prepared the martinis as he always does, a large pitcher of them. We all had one round. Then each of us returned to the kitchen for a second drink."

"You mean you went to the kitchen one by one and poured yourselves a second round from the pitcher?"

"Yes. As I recall it. Whoever had finished the drink went back to have a second."

"So that, at one time or another, each of you was in the kitchen alone?"

"Yes."

"And it wasn't until after Jack Conboy drank his second martini that he became ill, is that correct?"

"Yes."

"Can you recall the order in which each of you went to the kitchen?"

"I cannot recollect, except that Jack Conboy was the last to refill his glass, as I recall."

"So that anyone present that night might have put the chloral hydrate into Jack Conboy's martini, perhaps even by accident?"

"Yes."

"This court might find it odd to understand why you cannot clearly state who went into the kitchen where the second round of martinis were before Conboy drank his second martini. Do you have any explanation for your inability to reconstruct that sequence?"

"All I can tell you, Mr. Maury, is that at that time when

the four of us were enjoying an evening together, I had no
way of knowing it might later become crucial in a court-
room."

"I ask you now: do you love your husband, Walter
Harrison?"

"Yes. Yes, I do."

"I have no further questions, Your Honor."

"Mr. Dietrich, your witness."

"Mrs. Harrison, we have heard testimony that Jack
Conboy gave you the bottle of chloral hydrate. That's true,
isn't it?"

"Yes."

"As a kind of joke, is that the way you viewed it? So that
perhaps you could slip some of it to your unsuspecting
husband whenever he became too boring and knock him
out?"

"No. It was a joke, but I never planned to use it on
Walter."

"Unless perhaps you wanted to put *him* to sleep permanently."

"Objection, Your Honor! We have no proof that Mrs.
Harrison ever considered such a possibility."

"Objection sustained. Strike the last question."

"Nevertheless, you admit that Conboy gave you the
chloral hydrate?"

"Yes, I have said so."

"And you admit that you wrote a series of impassioned
letters to Jack Conboy after he married Margo Crawford?"

"I have explained—"

"Just answer the question, yes or no."

"Yes."

"And you admit the chloral hydrate was in your possession, in your dresser drawer, until a quantity of it was
ingested by Jack Conboy, causing his death?"

"I—yes."

"No further questions."

"Mr. Maury, does the defense wish to reexamine?"

"No, Your Honor."

"This court is adjourned until nine A.M. tomorrow."

"Members of the jury, have you reached a verdict?"

"We have, Your Honor. We find the defendant, Vivian Harrison, guilty of murder as charged."

"Thank you. The defendant will remain in custody pending sentencing on August fourth. This court is adjourned."

A second body is found . . . nine months later, early in the morning, early in the spring, in the front seat of a car parked on Beekman Place, and . . .

"Lieutenant Patterson, would you tell the court, please, the circumstances of your response to a report of a body in a car parked on Beekman Place on the morning of April ninth this year."

"There was an anonymous call to 911 reporting the sighting of a body in a car near the intersection of East Fifty-first Street and Beekman Place. Two other detectives and I went to the scene."

"And what did you find?"

"We found the victim, a young blond woman in her early thirties. She was slumped sideways in the front seat of her car, a Chrysler Eagle Premier. She was well dressed, in a black cocktail dress, black pumps, and a lightweight velvet coat. There were marks encircling her throat, indicating she had been strangled. The Medical Examiner was notified, and he and a police forensic team arrived shortly thereafter."

"Were you able to identify the victim at that point?"

"We were. A black beaded handbag lay next to the body. It contained a driver's license and credit cards identifying her as a Peggy Kendall with an address on East Sixty-sixth Street. There was also over fifty dollars in bills and coins in the handbag. We went to the East Sixty-sixth Street address, a high-rise apartment building."

"What did you find there?"

"In her apartment we found various papers indicating that the victim worked as a securities analyst for the Sovereign Bank and Trust Company on Park Avenue."

"What else did you find in the apartment, Lieutenant?"

"In the foyer there was a vase of fresh roses with a card reading, quote, my love always, Walter. Unquote. In the bedroom next to the telephone was an address book with a listing for Walter Harrison, at a number on Beekman Place. We were returning there to question Walter Harrison when a call came in over the radio advising us that Walter Harrison had appeared at the precinct and wanted to make a statement regarding the death of Peggy Kendall."

"Did Walter Harrison subsequently make such a statement to you?"

"He did."

"Your Honor, I have no more questions of the witness at this point. But I reserve the right to recall him again at a later time."

"Request granted. Mr. Waller, does the defense wish to cross-examine?"

"No questions, Your Honor."

"Mr. Stanton, call your next witness."

"The prosecution calls Dr. Carl Russell."

"Dr. Russell, you performed the autopsy on the body of the deceased, Peggy Kendall?"

"I did."

"You ascertained the cause of death?"

"Yes. She was strangled by an object that was placed nooselike around her throat and twisted and twisted at the back of her neck, choking her to death."

"This object, the instrument of death, left certain markings on the throat, did it not?"

"Yes, it did."

"I hand you these photographs showing in close-up the marks left on the throat of the victim. Can you identify the photographs?"

"I can. They were taken at the conclusion of the autopsy."

"Your Honor, I would like the jury to be given copies of these photographs so they may study them."

"Mr. Waller?"

"No objection."

"Request granted. Proceed, Mr. Stanton."

"Dr. Russell, did you find any other marks or bruises on the body?"

"No. None."

"So that would lead you to conclude that the victim, Peggy Kendall, was attacked from behind and strangled to death by some kind of nooselike object."

"It—"

"Objection, Your Honor. The District Attorney is leading the witness."

"Overruled. Dr. Russell is appearing as an expert witness. The question is proper. You may answer, Dr. Russell."

"It is my opinion that the victim was attacked from behind and strangled to death, yes."

"Thank you, Doctor. I have no more questions at this point, Your Honor. But again I would like to reserve the right to recall him again at a later time."

"So noted. Mr. Waller, your witness."

"No questions."

"Mr. Stanton."

"The People call Walter Harrison."

"Mr. Harrison, you divorced your former wife, Vivian Harrison, approximately six months ago, is that correct?"

"Objection! No relevancy to this trial!"

"Your Honor, if I'm allowed to continue, I will show relevancy in due course."

"On those grounds, I will allow you to continue. But do not wander too far afield. Objection overruled."

"Mr. Harrison?"

"Yes, my former wife, Vivian Harrison, and I were divorced some six months ago."

"After she was sentenced to a term in prison in Danbury, Connecticut, on the charge of murdering a Jack Conboy. Is that correct?"

"Yes."

"Now, Mr. Harrison, we come to the night of April eighth of this year. Will you tell us please what occurred that night?"

"I gave a party at my house on Beekman Place."

"What was the purpose of the party?"

"To introduce my friends to my new fiancée, Peggy Kendall."

"You had known Miss Kendall for a period of time?"

"Yes. She had worked for our firm for five years, as a securities analyst. Then she left our firm and took another job after she and I began seeing one another."

"When exactly did you and Miss Kendall begin seeing each other?"

"Not until after my former wife, Vivian, and I were divorced. About a month after the divorce."

"And you and Miss Kendall planned to be married?"

"Yes. In June. That was the reason for the party that night, to announce our engagement and the plans for our marriage."

"How did your friends react to your news that night?"

"They almost all seemed, well, happy for me."

"*Almost* all your friends, but not all, is that correct?"

"Yes. All except one."

"And that one was—?"

"The defendant, Margo Conboy."

"Margo Conboy, the defendant. Tell us how you came to know she was not happy about your news."

"It happened in the most—the most—most astonishing manner."

"I know this is difficult for you, Mr. Harrison. Take your time and tell us what happened."

"Right after I made the announcement about Peggy and me, and we'd opened champagne and were having toasts around, Margo came over to me and said she'd like a word alone with me in the library . . ."

"Go on, please."

"We went into the library, and Margo locked the door behind us . . ."

"Would you like a brief recess, Mr. Harrison?"

"I—no, Your Honor. It's all right. Well, after Margo locked the door, she twirled. Her face was blazing, her eyes were glittering, her voice was low but scathing with contempt. I'd never seen her like that, never truthfully seen anyone in such a state."

"And what did she say to you?"

"She demanded to know what I thought I was doing! And did I think she was going to let me get away with it! She was raving and I didn't know what she was talking about."

"She told you then what she was talking about, is that correct?"

"Oh, yes. The words came pouring out of her in a torrent. How she had engineered everything, everything, so we—she and I—could be together, could be married. She wanted to know how I could be so blind as not to know. That she had tricked Jack Conboy into killing her first husband, Edward, Edward Crawford, in a hit-and-run accident to get Edward out of the way. Then that she had led Jack Conboy into marrying her, knowing as she did how Vivian, my former wife, would react. And then, knowing from Conboy about the letters Vivian had written to him and about the chloral hydrate Conboy had procured for Vivian, how she—Margo—had put chloral hydrate into Conboy's martini. That she knew she could arrange it so it would look like Vivian had killed Conboy. Which is exactly what happened, of course."

"Did Margo tell you how she knew where Vivian Harrison kept the bottle of chloral hydrate?"

"Margo was so determined to prove to me she had done everything she said she had, she couldn't stop talking. Yes, she told me."

"And how did she know?"

"She said that one day Vivian opened her dresser drawer to show Margo a blouse she'd bought and Margo saw the bottle. Then, on the night Jack Conboy died, Margo took the bottle from the dresser drawer, spiked Jack Conboy's martini, and replaced the bottle."

"Mr. Harrison, did Margo Conboy have any basis for thinking *you* would want to marry her?"

"A long time ago, right after she and Edward were first married and we all became close friends, Margo told me that she knew she had made a mistake, that Edward was too old for her, too old in a way that was important to her.

She made it clear to me that she would like—well, to have an affair with me. She made it seem simple. She's a beautiful woman and I'll admit I was flattered and attracted to her. But I knew it wouldn't be simple. I told her so. I told her that because of Vivian and Edward, my best friend, there could never be anything between us. I advised her to divorce Edward if she was that unhappy."

"What did she say to that?"

"She said she'd never do that and give up the money, the security, she had with Edward. And that even if she did divorce Edward, she still wouldn't have me. At the time I thought she was just talking, and as the years passed, I forgot all about it."

"At the trial of your wife for the murder of Jack Conboy, you made no mention of the fact that Margo Conboy had once wanted to have an affair with you. Why did you omit that fact from your testimony?"

"I swear that it never occurred to me that there *was* a connection. Vivian was the defendant then."

"On the night of the party, in your library, did you tell Margo Conboy that you had had no knowledge of what she had done?"

"I did."

"What was her response?"

"She said that of course she couldn't let me know what she was doing while she was doing it because I would be too weak to allow it to happen. She also called me a stupid fool for not understanding that Jack Conboy and Vivian had both been the cause of their own undoing. She also charged that I was a stupid fool if I didn't realize that if she hadn't maneuvered Jack Conboy into marrying her, sooner or later Vivian would have used the chloral hydrate to get me out of the way so she, Vivian, could have Conboy."

"How would you describe the demeanor of Margo Conboy the night in your library?"

"A woman scorned. A woman scorned."

"What happened next?"

"Margo stormed out of the library and out of the house. I returned to my guests and to Peggy, shaken, but I made no mention to anyone of what had occurred."

"How long after that was it before the party ended?"

"About an hour."

"Peggy Kendall left at that time?"

"Yes. I had just received a phone call from overseas. I was on the phone and Peggy kissed me goodnight and left, saying she'd call me in the morning."

"That was the last time you saw Peggy Kendall alive?"

"The last time."

"The next morning while you were getting dressed, you became aware of the police activity outside your house?"

"I did. I went out, was told what had happened, saw that it was Peggy's car, and saw her, dead, before they took her body to the morgue. I went directly to the Seventeenth Precinct and made a full statement to Lieutenant Patterson, as I have to you here today."

"Your witness, Mr. Waller."

"No questions."

"Your Honor, the prosecution would like to call Lieutenant Patterson back to the witness stand."

"Proceed, Mr. Stanton."

"—and after Mr. Harrison concluded his statement to you, Lieutenant, did you tell him anything in regard to the manner in which Miss Kendall met her death?"

"I did. I told him she had been strangled and that certain marks had been left embedded in her throat, presumably left by the object used to strangle her."

"Did Mr. Harrison then tell you what he thought the object used might have been?"

"He did. And acting upon the information he provided us with, we obtained a search warrant and went to the apartment of Mrs. Margo Conboy, on Fifth Avenue, and recovered the object, a long gold link necklace which Mrs. Conboy had worn to the party at Mr. Harrison's house the night before."

"I show you this gold link necklace. Can you identify it?"

"Yes. It has my mark on it. It is the necklace recovered from Margo Conboy's apartment. The necklace she wore at Mr. Harrison's party."

"What did you do with the necklace when you'd recovered it?"

"It was turned over to the police forensic unit so that a comparison might be made between the links of the necklace and the impressions left on the throat of the victim."

"Thank you, Lieutenant. That's all."

"Questions, Mr. Waller?"

"No questions, Your Honor."

"Your next witness, Mr. Stanton."

"The People recall Dr. Carl Russell."

"Dr. Russell, as a homicide forensic pathologist, it is your responsibility to consider all the forensic evidence and judge not only the cause of death but what might have caused the death, is that not correct?"

"That is correct."

"With that in mind, I show you this necklace. From an examination of this necklace, was forensic able to identify it as the object used to strangle Peggy Kendall?"

"Positively."

"I show you this photographic overlay showing in close-up the links of the necklace, and I place it upon the close-up photograph of the marks left on the throat of Peggy Kendall. Do the indentations of the links of the necklace match the marks, the impressions, left on the throat of the victim?"

"Perfectly. As anyone can see."

"Yes. Your Honor, I ask that copies of the overlay and photographs of the victim's throat be examined by the jury and entered into evidence. The prosecution rests its case."

"Mr. Waller?"

"Your Honor, my client, Margo Conboy, has advised me she wishes to change her plea from not guilty to guilty as charged."

"Mrs. Conboy, is that your wish?"

"Yes, Your Honor."

"Is there any objection from the prosecution, Mr. Stanton?"

"No objection, Your Honor."

"Very well. The jury is dismissed. Sentencing will be passed May second. This court is adjourned."

When the actress's body was found in their new luxury apartment, it wasn't exactly the kind of payoff that lottery-winner Alvirah Meehan and her husband, Willy, had expected.

Mary Higgins Clark

The Body in the Closet

If on that August evening, Alvirah Meehan had known what was waiting for them at their fancy new apartment on Central Park South, she would never have gotten off the plane. As it was, there was absolutely no hint of foreboding in her usually keen psyche as the plane circled for a landing.

Even though she and Willy had been bitten by the travel bug after they won the forty million dollar lottery, Alvirah was always glad to get back to New York. There was something heartwarming about seeing the skyscrapers silhouetted against the clouds and the lights of the bridges that spanned the East River.

Willy patted her hand and Alvirah turned to him with an affectionate smile. He looked grand, she thought, in his new blue linen jacket which just matched the color of his eyes. With those keen, twinkling eyes and his thick head of white hair, Willy was a double for Tip O'Neill, no mistake about that.

Alvirah smoothed her russet-brown hair that had been tinted and styled by Dale of London. Dale had marvelled to hear Alvirah was sixty. "You're funning me," he'd gasped.

Alvirah was wearing a khaki jumpsuit that did not quite hide the twenty pounds she could never lose. Gleaming on the lapel was her sunburst pin with its hidden microphone. Alvirah only recorded conversations she thought she could use as material for her feature articles in the *New York Globe*. "The trip was wonderful," she observed now to Willy, "but it wasn't an adventure if you know what I mean. The most exciting thing that happened was when the Queen Mother stopped in for tea at the Stafford Hotel and the manager's cat attacked her Corgis."

"I'm glad we just had a nice, calm vacation," Willy said heartily. "I can't take much more of you getting almost killed solving crimes. I still get nightmares thinking of your face in a gas jet at Cape Cod."

The British Airways stewardess was walking down the aisle of the first class cabin checking that seat belts were fastened. "I certainly enjoyed talking with you," she told them. Willy had explained that he'd been a plumber and Alvirah a cleaning woman until they won the forty million dollar lottery. "My goodness," she said now to Alvirah, "I just can't believe you were ever a char."

In a mercifully short time after landing, they were in a cab, their matching Vuitton luggage stacked in the trunk. As usual, New York in August was in the throes of the dog days, hot, sticky, and sultry. The cab was a steam box and Alvirah thought longingly ahead to their new apartment on Central Park South, which of course would be wonderfully cool. They still kept their old three-room flat in Flushing where they'd lived for thirty years before the lottery changed their lives. As Willy pointed out, New York State was in a lot of financial trouble and you never knew if someday it would go broke and tell the lottery winners to take a flying leap for the rest of their checks. To that end, they had kept the old place and a nest egg in the Citizens of Flushing Bank just in case.

When the cab pulled into the driveway, the doorman, who was costumed in red and gold with a massive black fur hat, opened the door for them. "You must be melting," Alvirah said sympathetically. "You'd think they wouldn't bother dolling you up until they finish the renovations."

The building was undergoing a total overhaul. They'd bought the apartment in the spring and the real estate agent had assured them that the refurbishing would be completed in a matter of weeks. It was clear from the scaffolding in the lobby and the signs warning residents not to lean on any terrace walls that the agent's statement had been wildly optimistic.

When they reached the bank of elevators they were joined by another couple, a tall, fiftyish man and a slender woman in a white silk evening suit whose expression reminded Alvirah of someone who has just opened a refrigerator and encountered the odor of eggs gone bad. I know them, Alvirah thought, and before an elevator dropped to the lobby had rifled through her prodigious memory and categorized the newcomers. He was Carleton Rumson, the legendary Broadway producer and she was his wife, Victoria, a sometime actress who had been a Miss America runner-up thirty years ago.

"Mr. Rumson!" With a smile that softened her somewhat jutting jaw, Alvirah reached out her hand. "I'm Alvirah Meehan. We met at the Cypress Point Spa in Pebble Beach. What a nice surprise. This is my husband, Willy. Do you live here?"

Rumson's smile came and went. "We keep an apartment for convenience." He nodded to Willy then grudgingly introduced his wife. The elevator door opened as Victoria Rumson acknowledged them with the flicker of an eyelid. What a cold fish, Alvirah thought, taking in the perfect but haughty profile, the pale blond hair pulled back in a chignon. Long years of reading *People, Us, The National Enquirer*, and gossip columns had resulted in Alvirah's brain becoming the repository of an awesome amount of information about the rich and famous.

They had just stopped at the 34th floor as Alvirah remembered her Rumson tidbits. Rumson was famous for his wandering eye. His wife's ability to overlook his indiscretions had earned her the nickname of "See-no-evil Vicky."

The operator opened the door but Alvirah did not budge. "Mr. Rumson," she said, "Willy's nephew, Brian McCormack, is a wonderful playwright. He's just finishing his second play. I'd love to have you read it."

Rumson looked annoyed. "That's why I have an office," he told her. "It's listed in the phone book."

"Brian's first play is running off-Broadway right now," Alvirah persisted. "One of the critics said he's a young Neil Simon."

"Come on, Honey," Willy urged. "You're holding up these folks."

Unexpectedly the glacier look melted from Victoria Rumson's face. "Darling," she said to her husband. "I've heard about Brian McCormack. Why don't you read the play here? It will only get buried if you have it sent to your office."

"That's real nice of you, Victoria," Alvirah said heartily. "You'll have it tomorrow."

As they walked from the elevator to their apartment,

Willy asked, "Honey, don't you think you were being a little pushy?"

"Absolutely not," Alvirah told him. "Nothing ventured, nothing gained. Anything I can do to help Brian's career is A-okay with me."

Their apartment commanded a sweeping view of Central Park. Alvirah never stepped into it without thinking that not that long ago she had considered her Thursday cleaning job, Mrs. Chester Lollop's house in Little Neck, a miniature palace. Boy, had her eyes opened these last few years!

They'd bought the apartment completely furnished from a stockbroker who'd been indicted for inside trading. The stockbroker had just had it redecorated by an interior designer who, he assured them, was the absolute rage of Manhattan. Secretly Alvirah now had serious doubts about the wisdom of buying the apartment furnished. The living room, dining room, and kitchen were stark white. White low sofas that she had to hoist herself out of, thick white carpeting that showed every speck of dirt, white counters and cabinets and marble and appliances that reminded her of all the tubs and sinks and johns she'd ever tried to scrub free of rust.

There was a large printed notice taped to the sliding glass door leading to the terrace. They hurried over to read it.

A BUILDING INSPECTION HAS REVEALED THAT THIS IS ONE OF A SMALL NUMBER OF APARTMENTS IN WHICH A SERIOUS STRUCTURAL WEAKNESS HAS BEEN FOUND IN THE RAIL AND PLEXIGLAS PANELS OF THE TERRACE.

YOUR TERRACE IS SAFE FOR NORMAL USE, BUT *DO NOT* LEAN ON THE GUARD RAIL OR PERMIT OTHERS TO DO SO.

REPAIRS WILL BE COMPLETED AS RAPIDLY AS POSSIBLE.

Alvirah shrugged. "Well, I certainly have brains enough not to lean on any guard rail, safe or not; as for you . . ."

Willy smiled sheepishly. He was scared silly of heights, and never set foot on the terrace. As he said when they bought the apartment, "You love a terrace. I love terra firma."

Willy went into the kitchen to put the kettle on and Alvirah opened the door to the terrace and stepped outside. The sultry air was a hot wave against her face but she didn't care. There was something about standing out here, looking across the Park, a festive glow from the decorated trees around the Tavern on the Green, the ribbons of headlights from the cars, the glimpses of horsedrawn carriages.

"Oh, it's good to be back," she thought again as she went inside. She pulled the door shut and surveyed the living room, her expert eye observing the degree of activity of the weekly cleaning service. The One-Two-Three cleaners should have been in yesterday and she was surprised to see fingerprints smeared across the glass cocktail table. Automatically she reached for a handkerchief and vigorously rubbed them away. Then she noticed that the tieback on the drapery next to the terrace door was missing. Hope it didn't end up in the vacuum, she thought. At least *I* was a good cleaning woman. She remembered what the British Airways stewardess had said. Or a good char, whatever that is.

"Hey Alvirah," Willy called. "Did Brian leave a note? Looks like he might have been expecting someone."

Brian, Willy's nephew, was the only child of Willy's oldest sister, Madelaine. Six of Willy's seven sisters had gone into the convent. Madelaine had married in her forties and produced a change-of-life baby, Brian, who was now twenty-six years old. Brian had been raised in

Nebraska, wrote plays for a repertory company out there, and came to New York after Madelaine's death two years ago. All of Alvirah's untapped maternal instincts were released by Brian with his thin, intense face, unruly sandy hair, and shy smile. As she often told Willy, "If I'd carried him inside me for nine months, I couldn't love him more."

When they'd left for England in June, Brian was finishing the first draft of his new play and had been glad to accept their offer of a key to the Central Park apartment. "It's a heck of a lot easier to write there than in my place," was his grateful comment. He lived in a brownstone walk-up in Greenwich Village. The other tenant on his floor had four children under the age of five.

Alvirah went into the kitchen. "The only place he leaves a note is on that crazy-looking elephant table in the foyer," she told Willy. "There's nothing there now." She raised her eyes. Two champagne glasses and a bottle of champagne were on a silver tray on the sideboard. The champagne, a gift from the broker who'd handled the apartment sale, was standing in a wine cooler half-filled with water. The broker had several times informed them that it cost five hundred dollars a bottle and was what the Queen of England enjoyed sipping.

Willy looked troubled. "That's that stuff that's so crazy expensive, isn't it? No way Brian would help himself to that. There's something funny going on." Alvirah opened her mouth to reassure him, then closed it. There *was* something funny going on and her antenna told her trouble was brewing.

The chimes rang. Willy hurried to open the door. An apologetic porter was waiting with their bags. "Sorry to be so long, Mr. Meehan. So many residents are helping themselves to the service elevator that the staff has to stand in line for it." At Willy's request, he deposited the bags in the bedroom then departed smiling, his palm closing over a five dollar bill.

Somberly Willy and Alvirah shared a pot of tea in the kitchen. Willy kept staring at the bottle of fit-for-a-queen champagne. "I'm gonna call Brian," he decided.

"He'll still be at the theater," Alvirah said, closed her eyes, concentrated, and gave him the number of the box office.

Willy dialed, listened, then hung up. "There's a recorder on," he said flatly. "Brian's play closed. They talk about how to get refunds."

"The poor kid," Alvirah breathed. "Try his apartment."

"Only the answering machine," Willy told her a moment later. "I'll leave a message for him to call us."

Alvirah suddenly realized how weary she was. As she collected the teacups she reminded herself that it was five in the morning, England time, so she had a right to feel as though all her bones were aching. She put the cups in the dishwasher, hesitated, then rinsed out the unused champagne glasses and put them in the dishwasher too. Her friend, Baroness Min von Schreiber, who owned the Cypress Point Spa where Alvirah had gone to be made over after they won the lottery, had told her that expensive wines should not be left standing. Something about the corks getting dry. With a damp sponge, Alvirah gave a vigorous rub to the unopened bottle and the silver bucket and put them away. Turning the lights out behind her, she went into the bedroom.

Willy had begun to unpack. Alvirah *did* like the bedroom. It had been furnished for the bachelor stockbroker with a kingsized bed, a triple dresser, night tables large enough to hold books, reading glasses, and mineral ice for Alvirah's rheumatic knees, and comfortable easy chairs by the window. However the decor convinced her that the trendy interior designer must have been weaned on Clorox. White spread. White drapes. White carpet.

The porter had left Alvirah's hanging bag spread out across the bed. She unlocked it and began to remove the suits and dresses, critically eyeing her new purchases. Baroness von Schreiber was always pleading with her not to go shopping on her own. "Alvirah," Min would argue, "you are natural prey for saleswomen who have been ordered to unload the buyer's mistakes. They sense your approach even while you are still on the elevator. I'm in New York enough. You come to the Spa several times a year. I will shop with you."

Alvirah wondered if Min would approve of the orange and pink plaid suit that the saleswoman in Harrod's had raved over. She was sure she wouldn't.

Her arms filled with clothing, Alvirah opened the door of her closet. She glanced down and let out a shriek. Lying on the carpeted floor, between the rows of Alvirah's size 10 DDDD designer shoes, green eyes staring up, crinkly blond hair flowing around her face, tongue slightly protruding, the missing drapery cord around her neck, was the body of a slender young woman.

"Blessed Mother," Alvirah moaned, as the clothes fell from her arms.

"What's the matter, Honey?" Willy demanded, rushing to her side. "Oh my God," he breathed, "who the hell is that?"

"It's . . . it's . . . you know. The actress. The one who had the lead in Brian's play. The one who ate a plate of string beans at the opening night party. The one Brian is so crazy about." Alvirah squeezed her eyes shut, glad to free herself from the glazed expression of the body at her feet. "Fiona . . . that's who it is . . . Fiona Winters."

*   *   *

Willy's arm firmly around her, Alvirah walked to the low couch in the living room, the one that made her knees feel as though they were going to stab her chin. As he dialed 911, she forced her head to clear. It doesn't take a lot of brains to know that this could look very bad for Brian, she thought. I've got to get my thinking cap on and remember everything I can about that girl. She was so nasty to Brian. Did they have a fight?

Willy crossed the room, sat beside her and reached for her hand. "It's going to be all right, Honey," he said soothingly. "The cops will be here in a few minutes."

"Call Brian again," Alvirah told him.

"Good idea." Willy dialed quickly. "Just that darn machine. I'll leave another message. Try to rest."

Alvirah nodded, closed her eyes, and immediately turned her thoughts to the night last April when Brian's play opened.

The theater had been crowded. Brian arranged for them to have front row center seats and Alvirah wore her new silver and black sequin dress. The play, *Falling Bridges*, was set in Nebraska and was about a family reunion. Fiona Winters played the socialite who is intensely bored with her unsophisticated in-laws, and Alvirah had to admit she was very believable. Alvirah liked the girl who played the second lead much better. Emmy Laker had bright red hair, blue eyes, and portrayed a funny but wistful character to perfection.

The performances brought a standing ovation, and Alvirah's heart swelled with pride when the cries of "Author! Author!" brought Brian to the stage. She didn't know her palms could make such a racket, and when Brian was handed a bouquet and leaned over the footlights to give it to her, she started to cry.

The opening-night party was in the upstairs room of

Gallagher's Steakhouse. Brian kept the seats on either side of him for Alvirah and Fiona Winters. Willy and Emmy Laker sat opposite them. Up close, Fiona was even more striking than her pictures, but Alvirah immediately sensed there was something hard and calculating about her. It didn't take Alvirah long to get the lay of the land. Brian hovered over Fiona Winters like a lovesick idiot. Winters had a way of putting him down that made Alvirah want to dump the plate of string beans she was gnawing on over her head. Winters let them know about her high-class background, "The family was appalled when after Foxcroft I decided to go into the theatre." She then proceeded to tell Willy and Brian, who were thoroughly enjoying sliced steak sandwiches with Gallagher's special fries, that they were likely candidates for a heart attack. Personally, she never ate meat.

She took potshots at all of us, Alvirah recalled. She asked me if I missed cleaning houses. She told me Brian should learn to dress better and with our income she's surprised we don't help him out. She jumped on that sweet girl, Emmy Laker, when Emmy said Brian had better things to think about than his wardrobe.

On the way home Alvirah and Willy had solemnly agreed that Brian had a lot of growing up to do if he didn't see what a mean type Fiona was. "I'd like to see him get together with Emmy Laker," Willy had announced. "If he had the brains he was born with he'd know that she's crazy about him. And that Fiona has been around a lot. She must have eight years on Brian."

The bell rang vigorously. Alvirah worried, I wish I'd had a chance to talk to Brian before the cops came.

The next hours passed in a blur. As her head cleared a bit, Alvirah realized that she was able to separate the

different kinds of law enforcement people who invaded
the apartment. The first, of course, were the policemen in
uniform. Then detectives, photographers, the medical
examiner. She and Willy sat together silently observing
the goings-on.

Officials from the Central Park South Towers office came
too. Very flustered they were. "We hope there will be no
unfortunate publicity," the resident manager said. "This
is not the Trump organization."

Their original statements had been taken by the first two
cops. At three in the morning, the door from the bedroom
opened. "Don't look, Honey," Willy cautioned Alvirah.
But she could not keep her eyes away from the stretcher
that two somber-faced attendants carried out. At least the
body of Fiona Winters was covered. God rest her, Alvirah
prayed, visualizing the tousled blond hair, the pouty lips,
the sharp teeth that had snapped at the string beans with
righteousness and gusto. She was not a nice person but
she certainly didn't deserve to die.

Someone came to sit opposite them, a long-legged
fortyish man who introduced himself as Detective Rooney.
"I read your articles in the *Globe*, Mrs. Meehan," he told
Alvirah, "and thoroughly enjoyed them. It was terrific the
way you solved that case on Cape Cod last summer."

Willy smiled appreciatively but Alvirah wasn't fooled.
She knew Detective Rooney was buttering her up to make
her confide in him. Her mind was racing trying to figure out
ways to protect Brian. Automatically she reached up and
switched on the microphone in her sunburst pin. Later she
wanted to be able to go over everything that was said.

Detective Rooney consulted his notes. "According to
your earlier statement, you've just returned from a vacation abroad and arrived here around ten p.m. You found
the victim, Fiona Winters, a short time later when you

began to unpack. You recognized Miss Winters because she played the lead in your nephew Brian McCormack's play."

Alvirah nodded. She noticed that Willy was about to speak and laid a warning hand on his arm. "That's right."

"From what I understand, you only met Miss Winters once," Detective Rooney said. "How do you suppose she ended up in your closet?"

"I have no idea," Alvirah said heartily.

"Did she have a key to this apartment?"

Again Willy's lips pursed. This time Alvirah pinched his arm. "Keys to this apartment," she said thoughtfully. "Now let me see. The One-Two-Three Cleaning Service has a key. Well, they don't really *have* a key. They pick one up at the desk and leave it there when they finish, so maybe you can't count them. My friend Maude has a key. She came in on Mother's Day weekend to go out with her son and his wife to Windows on the World. They have a cat and she's allergic to cats so she slept on our couch. Maude can sleep on a picket fence. I told her to hold on to that key. Then Willy's sister, Sister Patricia, who's the principal of a school in Belle Harbor, has a key. Not that she uses it much but she did stay for the annual meeting of the diocesan teachers. Then . . ."

"Does your nephew, Brian McCormack, have a key, Mrs. Meehan?" Detective Rooney interrupted.

Alvirah bit her lip. "Like the others, Maude and Sister Patricia and . . ."

"Brian McCormack has a key." This time Detective Rooney raised his voice slightly. "According to the concierge, he's been using this apartment frequently in your absence. It will be only a matter of time before we learn whether he was here with Miss Winters yesterday. It's impossible to be totally accurate before an autopsy, but the

Medical Examiner estimates the time of death at between eleven a.m. and three p.m. yesterday." Detective Rooney's tone became speculative. "It will be interesting to know where Brian McCormack was during that time frame."

They were told that before they could use the apartment, the investigative team would have to dust it for fingerprints and vacuum it for clues. "The apartment is as you found it?" Detective Rooney asked.

"Except . . ." Willy began.

"Except that we made a pot of tea," Alvirah interrupted. I can always tell them about the wine glasses and the champagne but I can't untell them, she thought. That detective is going to find out that Brian was crazy about Fiona Winters and decide it was a crime of passion. Then he'll make everything fit that theory.

Detective Rooney closed his notebook. "I apologize for having to inconvenience you but I understand the management has a furnished apartment you can use tonight."

Fifteen minutes later, Alvirah, a hairnet covering her Dale of London coiffure, Ponds Vanishing Cream generously smeared on her face, a long-sleeved cotton gown protecting her from the overly cool air-conditioning, was gratefully hunched against an already dozing Willy. Tired as she was, it was hard to relax. She thought this could look very bad for Brian but there had to be an explanation. Brian wouldn't help himself to that five hundred dollar bottle of champagne and he certainly wouldn't kill Fiona Winters. But how did she end up in my closet?

Alvirah began to feel her eyelids grow heavy. She drifted off uttering a prayer for the deceased Fiona and wondering if they grew string beans in heaven.

Despite the late hour they went to bed, Alvirah and Willy were up at seven o'clock. As their mutual shock over the body in the closet wore off, they began to worry about Brian. "No use fretting," Alvirah said with a heartiness she did not feel. "When we talk to him, I'm sure everything will be cleared up. Let's see if we can get back into our place."

They dressed quickly and hurried out. Carleton Rumson was standing at the bank of elevators. Attired in a casual sports shirt, linen jacket and slacks, he still managed to convey to Alvirah the look of a man on his way to the execution chamber. His complexion was sallow. Dark pouches under his eyes added ten years to his appearance. Automatically, Alvirah reached up and switched on the microphone in her sunburst pin.

"Mr. Rumson," she asked, "did you hear the terrible news about the murder in our apartment?"

Rumson pressed vigorously for the elevator. "As a matter of fact, yes. Friends in the building phoned us. Terrible for the young lady, terrible for you."

The elevator arrived. After they got in, Rumson said, "Mrs. Meehan, my wife reminded me about your nephew's play. We're leaving for Mexico tomorrow morning. I'd very much like to read it today."

Alvirah's jaw dropped. "Oh that's wonderful of your wife to keep after you about it. We'll make sure to get it up to you."

When she and Willy got out at their floor, she said, "This could be Brian's big break. Provided . . ." She left the sentence unfinished.

A policeman was on guard at the door of their apartment but admitted them after consulting Detective Rooney. When she stepped into the foyer, Alvirah had two immediate impressions. The all-white decor would never look the same. Every surface was smeared and she realized the investigators must have been dusting for fingerprints. The dark, sooty stuff they'd sprinkled had drifted onto the white carpeting. The second and most important impression was that seated across from Detective Rooney, looking bewildered and forlorn, was Brian. Alvirah's heart skipped a beat as she rushed to embrace him.

Brian jumped up. "Aunt Alvirah, I'm so sorry. This is awful for you."

To Alvirah he looked about ten years old. His tee shirt and khaki slacks were rumpled; the laces on his sneakers were loose; his feet were innocent of socks. If he had dressed to escape a burning building he could not have been more disheveled.

Alvirah brushed back the sandy hair that fell over Brian's forehead as Willy grasped his hand. "You okay?" Willy asked.

Brian managed a troubled smile. "I guess so."

Detective Rooney interrupted. "Mr. McCormack just arrived, and I was about to inform him that he is a suspect in the death of Fiona Winters and has the right to counsel."

"Are you kidding?" Brian asked, his tone incredulous.

"I assure you, I'm not kidding." Detective Rooney pulled a paper from his breast pocket. In a matter-of-fact voice he read the Miranda warning, then handed it to Brian. "Are you able to read? If you are, please read this and let me know if you understand its meaning."

"Is he able to read?" Willy asked indignantly. "My sister, God rest her, used to tell us how he could read the labels on soup cans when he was four. What's more he's a writer. That's one heck of a question."

"It's all right, Willy," Alvirah said quietly. "Detective Rooney is only doing his job."

Rooney looked at Alvirah and Willy. "Our people are through. You can stay in the apartment now. I'll take Mr. McCormack's statement at headquarters."

"Brian, don't you say one word until we get you a lawyer," Willy ordered.

Brian shook his head. "Uncle Willy, I have nothing to hide. I don't need a lawyer."

Alvirah kissed Brian. "Come right back here when you're finished," she told him.

The condition of the apartment gave her something to do. Alvirah put on a pair of comfortable old slacks and an oversized tee shirt, an outfit left over from her cleaning days, and got to work. She dispatched Willy with a long shopping list, warning him to take the service elevator to avoid any reporters who might be in the lobby.

As she vacuumed and scrubbed and mopped and dusted, Alvirah realized with increasing dread that cops don't give a Miranda warning unless they have pretty good reasons for suspecting someone's guilt. Oh Brian, Brian, she worried.

The hardest job was to vacuum the closet where she'd found the body. It was as though she could see again the unfocused eyes of Fiona Winters staring up at her. That thought led to another one. If Fiona had opened the door of the closet and had been strangled by someone who came up behind her she wouldn't have been found lying on her back, facing upward.

Alvirah dropped the handle of the vacuum. She thought, those fingerprints on the cocktail table, the way they'd looked as though a hand had dragged along the surface. Suppose Fiona Winters had been sitting on the couch, maybe leaning forward a little and her killer walked behind the couch, slipped that tie-back around her neck and twisted it, wouldn't her hand have pulled back like that? "Saints and angels," Alvirah whispered, "I bet dollars to donuts I destroyed evidence."

The phone rang just as she had changed into a bright green jumpsuit and was fastening her pin on the lapel. It was Baroness Min von Schreiber calling from the Cypress Point Spa in Pebble Beach. Min had just heard the news. "Whatever was that dreadful girl thinking about getting herself killed in your closet?" Min demanded.

"Buh-lieve me, Min, I don't think she did it on purpose," Alvirah answered. "I met her once in my life when we went to see Brian's play, and the cops are questioning Brian right now. I'm worried sick. They think he killed her."

From three thousand miles away, Min's snort boomed through the telephone. "Brian! What nonsense. He wouldn't hurt a lamb. But you're wrong, Alvirah. You met Fiona Winters out here at the Spa."

"Never," Alvirah said positively. "She was the kind who got on your nerves so much you'd never forget meeting her."

There was a pause. "I am thinking," Min announced. "Give me a minute." Her tone became triumphant. "You're right. She came with someone and they spent the weekend in his cottage. They even had their meals served there."

Something made Alvirah ask the question. "Who was she with?"

"That hotshot producer she was trying to snare. Carleton Rumson. You remember him, Alvirah. You met him another time when you were here alone."

At noon when Carleton Rumson returned, he cursed himself for being a fool. In the morning he had left by the service door and avoided the reporters. Now they swarmed around him in the lobby and besieged him with questions about Fiona Winters's death.

"Yes, Miss Winters appeared in several of my productions. She was a talented actress, a star. No, I had no idea she was visiting in this building. If you'll excuse me."

He managed to shoulder his way to the street. Had he touched anything in that apartment yesterday? he wondered. Had he left fingerprints? The thought sent cold chills through his body.

Alvirah surveyed herself in the mirror. Why can't I look the way I do when they put my makeup on at the Spa, she wondered, then shrugged. As long as Willy keeps thinking I'm gorgeous, what difference? She went into the living room and out onto the terrace.

The humidity was near saturation point. Not a leaf in the park stirred. Even so, Alvirah sighed with pleasure. How can anyone who was born in New York stay away from it for long, she wondered. She heard the front door open. Willy called, "I'm home, Honey."

As they unloaded the grocery bags she told him about Min's call. "Fiona Winters was mighty thick with Carleton Rumson," Alvirah explained. "That doesn't mean that she knew Rumson lived here or that she saw him yesterday, but it certainly opens possibilities."

Willy had brought in the newspapers and somberly they went through them. One headline screeched MURDER ON CENTRAL PARK SOUTH; another LOTTERY WINNER FINDS BODY. Carefully Alvirah read the lurid accounts. "I didn't scream and faint," she scoffed. "Where'd they get that idea?"

"According to the *Post*, you were hanging up the fabulous new wardrobe you bought in London," Willy told her.

"Fabulous new wardrobe! The only expensive thing I bought was that orange and pink plaid suit, and I know Min is going to make me give it away."

There were columns of background material on Fiona Winters: The break with her socialite family when she went into acting. Her uneven career. She'd won a Tony but was notoriously difficult to work with, which had cost her a number of plum roles. Her break with the Meehans' nephew, playwright Brian McCormack, when, to accept a film role, she'd abruptly walked out on his play, forcing it to close.

"Motive," Alvirah said flatly. "By tomorrow they'll be trying this case in the papers and Brian will be found guilty."

At twelve-thirty Brian returned. Alvirah took one look at his ashen face and ordered him to sit at the dining room table. "I'll make a pot of tea and fix you a hamburger," she said. "You look like you're going to keel over."

"I think a shot of scotch would do him a lot more good than tea," Willy observed.

Brian managed a wan smile. "I think you're right, Uncle Willy." Over hamburgers and french fries he told them what had happened. "I swear I didn't think they'd let me go. They're sure I killed her."

"Is it okay if I turn on my microphone?" Alvirah asked.

This time Brian's smile was real. "Aunt Alvirah, you were still on the plane when Fiona died. You can't solve this one. But go ahead."

Alvirah reached up and fiddled with the sunburst pin, her finger touching the microphone switch. Her manner became brisk. "Brian, tell us exactly what you told them."

Brian frowned. "A lot of stuff about my personal relationship with Fiona. They don't believe that I was sick of her lousy disposition and falling in love with Emmy. I told them that when she quit the play it was the last straw."

"But how did she get in my closet?" Alvirah asked. "You must have let her into the apartment. No one else would."

"I did. I've been working here a lot on the new play. You were coming back so I cleared my stuff out day before yesterday. Then yesterday Fiona phoned and said she was back in New York and would be right over to see me. By mistake I'd left the notes for my final draft here with my backup copy. I told her not to waste her time, that I was heading here to get my notes and then was going to be at the typewriter all day and wouldn't answer my door. I found her parked downstairs in the lobby and rather than make a scene let her come up."

"What did she want?" Alvirah and Willy asked simultaneously.

"Nothing much. Just the lead in *Nebraska Nights.*"

"After walking out on the other one!"

"She put on the performance of her life. Realized how much she loved me. Begged me to forgive her. Said she'd been a fool to leave *Falling Bridges.* Her role in the film was ending up on the cutting room floor, and the bad publicity about dumping the play had hurt her. Wanted to know if *Nebraska Nights* was finished yet. I'm human. I bragged about how good it is. Told her it might take time to find the right producer but when I did it was going to be a big hit."

"Had she ever read it?" Alvirah asked.

Brian studied the tea leaves in his cup. "These don't make for much of a fortune," he commented. "She knew the story line and that there's a fantastic lead role for an actress."

"You certainly didn't promise it to her?" Alvirah exclaimed.

Brian shook his head. "Aunt Alvirah, I know she played me for a fool but I couldn't believe she thought I was that much of a fool. She flat out asked me to make a deal. She had access to one of the biggest producers on Broadway.

If she could get it to him and he took it, she wanted to play Diane, I mean Beth."

"Who's that?" Willy asked.

"The name of the leading character. I just changed it on the final draft last night. I told Fiona she had to be kidding but if she could pull that off I might consider it. Then I got my notes and tried to get her out of here. She said she had an audition at Lincoln Center and wanted to stay for an hour or so. She wouldn't budge, and I finally decided there probably wasn't any harm in leaving her and I wanted to get to work. The last time I saw her was just about noon and she was sitting on that couch."

"Did she know you had a copy of your new play here?" Alvirah asked.

"Sure. I took it out of the drawer of the elephant table and was talking to her when I was getting the notes." He pointed in the direction of the foyer. "It's in that drawer now."

Alvirah got up, walked quickly through the living room to the elephant table, and pulled open the drawer. As she had expected, it was empty.

Emmy Laker sat motionless on the oversized club chair in her West Side studio apartment. Ever since she had heard about Fiona's death on the seven o'clock news, she'd been trying to reach Brian. Had he been arrested? Oh God, not Brian, she thought. What should I do? Despairingly she looked at the luggage in the corner of the room. Fiona's luggage.

Yesterday morning the bell had rung at eight-thirty. When she opened the door, Fiona swept in. "How can you stand living in a walk-up?" she'd demanded. "Thank God some kid was making a delivery and carried these up." She'd dropped her suitcases and reached for a cigarette. "I came in on the red-eye. What a mistake to take that job. I told the director off and he fired me. I've been trying to reach Brian, and decided he was probably here." She looked amused. "I'd have thought by now all those adoring glances from you would have gotten to him."

At the memory, rage swelled again in Emmy. "I hated her," she said aloud. As though she were still across the room, she could see Fiona, her blond hair tousled, her body-hugging jumpsuit showing off every inch of that perfect figure, her cat's eyes insolent and confident.

She was so sure that even after the way she treated Brian she could still walk back into his life again, Emmy thought, remembering all the months when she had agonized at the sight of Brian making a fool of himself over Fiona. Would that have happened again? Yesterday she had thought it possible.

Fiona kept phoning Brian until she reached him. When she hung up, she'd said, "Mind if I leave my bags here? Brian's playing hard to get. He's on his way to the cleaning woman's fancy pad. I'll head him off." Then she'd shrugged. "He's so damn provincial but it's amazing how many people on the coast know about him. I must say, from what I read of *Nebraska Nights* it has all the earmarks of a hit. It's good news that he's finished it. I intend to play the lead."

Now Emmy got up. Her body felt stiff and achy. The old window-unit air conditioner was rattling and wheezing, but the room was still hot and humid. A cool shower and a cup of coffee, she thought. Maybe that will clear my head. She wanted to see Brian. She wanted to put her arms around him. I'm not sorry Fiona's dead, she admitted, but oh, Brian, how did you expect to get away with it?

She had just dressed in a tee shirt and cotton skirt and twisted her red-gold hair in a chignon when the buzzer from downstairs rang. Let it be Brian, she prayed. But when she answered, it was to hear Detective Rooney announce that he was on his way up.

This is starting to make sense," Alvirah said briskly. "Brian, is there anything you left out about Fiona Winters' being here? For instance, did you put the bottle of that fit-for-a-queen champagne in the silver bucket yesterday?"

Brian looked bewildered. "Why would I do that? I don't even like the stuff and I certainly wasn't toasting Fiona."

"That's what I figured." Oh boy, what a story that is going to make for the *Globe*, Alvirah thought. Fiona didn't hang around here because she had an audition. It's my bet she phoned Carleton Rumson and invited him down here. That's why the wine glasses and champagne were out. She gave him the script and then, who knows why, they got into a fight. But proving it is something else. "I've got my thinking cap on," she told Brian. "I want you to go home and get your final copy of the play. I talked to Carleton Rumson, the producer, about it, and he wants to see it today."

"Carleton Rumson!" Brian exclaimed. "He's the biggest on Broadway and the hardest to reach. You must be a magician!"

"I'll tell you about it later. He and his wife are going away, so let's strike while the iron is hot."

Brian glanced at the phone. "I should call Emmy. She certainly must have heard about Fiona by now." He dialed the number and waited. His tone disappointed, he said, "I guess she's out."

Emmy was sure it was Brian phoning but made no move to pick up the receiver. The thin, somber-faced man sitting across from her had just asked her to describe in detail what she had done the previous day. Emmy chose her words carefully. "I left here about eleven o'clock and I went jogging. I got back about one-thirty and stayed in the rest of the day."

"Alone?"

"Yes."

"Did you see Fiona Winters yesterday?"

Emmy's eyes slid over to the corner where the luggage was piled. "I . . ." She stopped.

"Miss Laker, I think I should warn you that it will be in your best interest to be completely truthful." Detective Rooney consulted his notes. "Fiona Winters came in on Aerial Airlines flight 2 from Los Angeles, arriving at approximately seven-thirty a.m. She took a cab to this building. A delivery boy who recognized her assisted her with her luggage. She told him that you would not be glad to see her because you're after her boyfriend. When Miss Winters left to meet Brian McCormack, you followed her. The doorman at 205 Central Park South recognized you. You sat on a park bench across the street watching the building for nearly two hours and then entered it by the delivery door which had been propped open by painters." Detective Rooney leaned forward. His tone became confidential. "You went up to the Meehan's apartment, didn't you? Was Miss Winters already dead?"

Emmy stared at her hands. Brian always teased her about how small they were. "But strong," he'd laugh when they'd arm-wrestled. Brian. No matter what she said, she would hurt him. She looked up at Detective Rooney. "I want to talk to a lawyer."

Rooney got up. "That is, of course, your privilege. I would like to remind you that if Brian McCormack murdered his ex-lover, you can become an accessory after the fact by concealing evidence. And I assure you, you won't do him any good. By tomorrow we expect to have an indictment from the Grand Jury."

When Brian reached his Greenwich Village apartment, there was a message on the recorder from Emmy. "Call me, Brian. Please." Her voice was low and strained. Brian's fingers worked with frantic haste as he dialed her number.

She whispered, "Hello."

"Emmy, what's the matter?" He could see her, small and pretty and vulnerable. "I tried you before and you were out."

"I was here. A detective came. Brian, I have to see you."

"Take a cab to my aunt's place on Central Park South. I'm on my way back there."

"I want to talk to you alone. It's about Fiona. She was here yesterday. I followed her over to that apartment."

Brian felt his mouth go dry. "Don't say anything else on the phone."

At four o'clock, the bell rang insistently. Alvirah jumped up. She had been sitting at the dining room table, where at least the chair felt like a chair and not a sleeping bag. "Brian forgot his key," she told Willy. "I noticed it on the foyer table."

But it was the producer, Carleton Rumson, who was standing at the door. "Mrs. Meehan, forgive the intrusion." He stepped inside as he spoke.

Alvirah did not miss the fact that he leaned his palm on the elephant table.

"I mentioned to one of my assistants that I was going to look at your nephew's play. Apparently he saw his first one and thought it was very good. In fact, he had urged me to see it." Rumson walked into the living room and, uninvited, sat down. Nervously he drummed his fingers on the cocktail table.

"Can I get you a drink?" Willy asked. "Or maybe a beer?"

"Oh, Willy," Alvirah said. "I'm just sure that Mr. Rumson only drinks fine champagne. Maybe I read that in *People*."

"As a matter of fact, it's true, but not right now, thank you." Rumson's expression was affable, but Alvirah noticed the pulse jumping in his throat. "Where can I reach your nephew?"

"He'll be here pretty soon. I'll call you the minute he gets in."

"I'm a fast read. If you could send the script up, he and I could get together an hour or so later."

When Rumson left, Alvirah asked Willy, "What are you thinking?"

"That for a hotshot producer, he's some nervous wreck. I hate people to tap their fingers on tabletops. Gives me the jitters."

"It was giving him the jitters not to have the chance to do it here." Alvirah smiled mysteriously.

Less than a minute later the bell rang again, this time a tentative, soft ring. Alvirah hurried to the door. Emmy Laker was there, wisps of red hair slipping from the chignon, dark glasses covering half her face, the tee shirt clinging to her slender body, the cotton skirt a colorful whirl. Alvirah thought that Emmy looked about sixteen.

"That man who just left here," Emmy stammered. "Who was he?"

"Carleton Rumson, the producer," Alvirah said quickly. "Why?"

"Because . . ." Emmy pulled off her glasses revealing swollen eyes.

Alvirah put firm hands on the girl's shoulders. "Emmy, what is it?"

"I don't know what to do," Emmy wailed. "I don't know what to do."

Carleton Rumson returned to his apartment. Beads of perspiration stood on his forehead. Grimly he decided he was a hell of a lot better producer than actor. That Alvirah Meehan was no dope. That crack about the champagne hadn't been social chitchat. How much did she suspect?

Victoria was on the terrace. She was wearing white slacks and a white knit sweater. Sourly Rumson thought it was a damn shame some fashion columnist had once written that with her pale blond beauty Victoria Rumson should never wear anything except white. Victoria had taken that advice to heart.

She turned to him calmly. "I've always noticed that you get ugly to me when you're upset. Did you know Fiona Winters was staying in this building? Perhaps it was at your request."

"Vic, I haven't seen Fiona in nearly two years. If you don't believe me, too bad."

"As long as you didn't see her yesterday, darling. I understand the police are asking lots and lots of questions. It's bound to come out that you and she were, as the columnists say, an item. Have you followed up on Brian McCormack's play? I have one of my famous hunches about that."

Rumson cleared his throat. "That Alvirah Meehan is going to have McCormack send up the play when he gets in. After I've read it I'll go down and meet him."

"Let me read it too. Then I might just tag along. I'd love

to see how a cleaning woman decorates a posh apartment." Victoria Rumson linked her arm in her husband's. "Poor darling. Why are you so nervous?"

When Brian rushed into the apartment, his play under his arm, Emmy was lying on the couch, covered by a light blanket. Alvirah closed the door behind him and watched as he knelt beside Emmy and put his arms around her. "I'm going inside and let you two talk," she announced.

Willy was in the bedroom laying out clothes. "Which jacket, Honey?" He held up two sports coats.

Alvirah's forehead puckered. Absently she tucked back a strand of hair. "My Dale of London set is falling apart," she announced. "You want to look nice for Pete's retirement party but not like you're trying to show off. Wear the blue jacket and the white sports shirt."

"I still don't like to leave you tonight," Willy protested.

"You can't miss Pete's retirement dinner," Alvirah said firmly. "And Willy, if you have too good a time, I want you to promise me not to drive home. Stay at the old apartment. I feel good that it's right across the street from the Shamrock Inn. You know how you get when you're with the boys."

Willy smiled sheepishly. "You mean if I sing 'Danny Boy' more than twice, that's my signal."

"Exactly," Alvirah said firmly.

"Honey, I'm so bushed after the trip and with what happened last night, I'd just as soon have a few beers with Pete and then come back."

"That wouldn't be nice. Pete stayed at our lottery-winning party till the morning rush started on the Expressway. Now we've got to talk turkey to those kids."

In the living room Brian and Emmy were sitting side by side, their hands clasped. Alvirah's heart melted at the sight of the troubled young faces. "Have you two straight-ened things out yet?" she demanded.

"Not exactly," Brian said, his voice low. "Apparently Emmy was given a rough time by Detective Rooney and she refused to answer his questions."

Alvirah fiddled with her sunburst pin, switching on the microphone. "I have to know everything he asked you."

Hesitantly Emmy told her about the encounter with Rooney. Her voice became calmer and her poise returned as she said, "Brian, you're going to be indicted. He's trying to make me say things that will hurt you."

"You mean you've been protecting me." Brian looked astonished. "There's no need. I haven't done anything. I thought . . ."

"You thought that Emmy might be in trouble," Alvirah told them.

With Willy she settled on the opposite couch facing them. She realized that Brian and Emmy were sitting directly in front of the place on the cocktail table where the fingerprints had been smeared. The drapery was slightly to the right. To someone sitting on this couch, the tieback would have been in full view.

"I'm going to tell you two something," she announced. "You each think the other might have had something to do with that woman getting herself killed and you're both wrong. So just say straight out what you know or think you know. Brian, is there anything you've held back about seeing Fiona Winters yesterday?"

"Absolutely nothing," Brian said promptly.

"All right. Emmy, your turn."

Emmy stood up and walked over to look out at the park. "I love this view." She turned to Alvirah and Willy. "I've met Brian here a few times." She shrugged. "Yesterday when Fiona left my apartment to meet Brian, I think I went a little crazy. He had been so involved with her. Fiona is . . . was . . . the kind of woman who can just beckon to men. I was so afraid Brian would take up with her again."

"I'd never . . ." Brian protested.

"Keep quiet, Brian," Alvirah ordered.

"I sat on the park bench a long time," Emmy said. "I saw Brian leave. When Fiona didn't come down I started to think maybe Brian had told her to wait. Finally I decided to have it out with her. I came up the service elevator because I didn't want anyone on the staff to see me and tell Brian I'd been here. I rang the doorbell and waited, and rang it again and then I left."

"That's all?" Brian asked. "Why were you afraid to tell that to Detective Rooney?"

"Because when she heard Fiona was dead she thought that maybe the reason she didn't answer was because you'd already killed her." Alvirah leaned forward. "Emmy, why did you ask about Carleton Rumson when you got here? You saw him yesterday, didn't you?"

"As I came down this corridor he was just ahead of me going toward the passenger elevator. He glanced back over his shoulder. I knew he looked familiar but didn't recognize him until I saw him again just now."

Alvirah stood up. "I think we should call Mr. Rumson and ask him to come down and meet Brian and I think we should call Detective Rooney and ask him to be here too. But first, Brian, give Willy your play. He'll run it up to the Rumsons' apartment. Let's see. It's nearly five o'clock. Willy, ask Mr. Rumson to phone when he's ready to bring it back."

The intercom buzzer sounded from the lobby. Willy answered it. "Detective Rooney's here," he said. "He's looking for you, Brian."

*   *   *

There was no trace of warmth in Rooney's manner. "Mr. McCormack, I'm going to ask you to come down to the station house for further questioning. You have already received the Miranda warning. I would again remind you that anything you say can be used against you."

"He's not going anywhere," Alvirah said firmly. "Detective Rooney, I've got an earful for you."

It was nearly seven o'clock, two hours later, that Carleton Rumson phoned and asked if he might talk with them. In the meantime, Alvirah had made tea and sandwiches and Willy had dressed for Pete's retirement party. They had told Detective Rooney about the champagne and the glasses and the fingerprints on the cocktail table and about Emmy seeing Carleton Rumson near the apartment, but Alvirah could tell none of it cut much ice with Rooney. He's closing his mind to everything that doesn't fit his theory about Brian, she thought.

A few minutes later, Alvirah was astonished to see both Rumsons enter her apartment. Victoria Rumson was smiling warmly. When introduced to Brian, she took both his hands and said, "You *are* a young Neil Simon. I read your play. Congratulations."

When Detective Rooney was introduced, Carleton Rumson's face went ashen. He stammered as he said to Brian, "I'm terribly sorry to interrupt. I'll make this brief. Your play is wonderful. I want to option it. Please have your agent contact my office tomorrow. And now, my dear."

Victoria Rumson was standing at the terrace door. "You were so wise not to cover this view," she told Alvirah. "My decorator put in curtains and blinds and I might as well be facing an alley."

She sure took her gracious pills this morning, Alvirah thought.

"I think we'd all better sit down," Detective Rooney suggested. "Mr. Rumson, I have a few questions for you."

Alvirah pulled up a dining room chair. She could think better when her knees weren't banging into her chin. Min had suggested that maybe she should have a little surgery on her jaw. "No one need have a lantern jaw in this day and age," Min had told her. But Alvirah had gotten used to her jaw. It was only when her knees banged against it that she was aware that it jutted out a little.

"Mr. Rumson, you knew Fiona Winters?" Detective Rooney asked.

Alvirah began to think she had underestimated Rooney. His expression became intense as he leaned forward.

"Miss Winters appeared in several of my productions some years ago," Rumson said.

He was sitting on one of the couches next to his wife. Alvirah noticed that he glanced at her nervously.

"I'm not interested in years ago," Rooney told him. "I'm interested in yesterday. Did you see her?"

"I did not." To Alvirah, Rumson sounded strained and defensive.

"Did she phone you from this apartment?" Alvirah asked.

Detective Rooney stared at her. "Mrs. Meehan, if you don't mind, I'll conduct this questioning."

"Show respect when you talk to my wife," Willy bristled.

"I just meant that if she did phone from here, there'll be a record of it so I hate to see Mr. Rumson get in trouble by lying," Alvirah injected.

Victoria Rumson patted her husband's arm.

"Darling, I think you may be trying to spare my

feelings. If that impossible Winters woman was badgering you again, please don't be afraid to tell exactly what she wanted."

Before their eyes, Rumson seemed to visibly age. His shoulders went slack. His even features became pinched and lifeless. When he spoke, his voice was weary. "As I just told you, Fiona Winters acted in several of my productions. She . . ."

"She also had a private relationship with you," Alvirah interjected. "You used to take her to the Cypress Point Spa." I hate to be a buttinsky, she thought as Detective Rooney glared at her, but this guy is too much of a smoothie. He'll explain himself away if I don't get him rattled.

"I have not had anything to do with Fiona Winters for several years," Rumson said. His glance at Alvirah was cold and angry. "Yes, she phoned yesterday just about noon. She told me she had a play she wanted me to read. Assured me it had the earmarks of a hit and she wanted to play the lead. I was expecting a call from Europe and agreed to come down and see her in about an hour."

"That means she called after Brian left," Alvirah said triumphantly. "That's why the glasses and champagne were out. They were for you."

"Did you come to this apartment, Mr. Rumson?" Rooney asked.

Again Rumson hesitated.

"Darling, it's all right," Victoria Rumson said softly.

Not daring to look at Detective Rooney, Alvirah announced, "Emmy saw you in the corridor right outside my door a few minutes after one."

Rumson sprang to his feet. "Mrs. Meehan, I won't tolerate any more insinuations from you. I was afraid Fiona would keep contacting me if I didn't set her straight.

I came down here and rang the bell. There was no answer. The door wasn't completely shut. I pushed it open and called her. As long as I was this far, I wanted to be finished with it."

"Did you enter the apartment?" Rooney asked.

"Yes. I walked through this room, poked my head in the kitchen and glanced in the bedroom. She wasn't anywhere. I hoped she'd changed her mind about seeing me and I can assure you I was relieved. Then when I heard the news this morning, all I could think of was that maybe she was in that closet when I was here and I'd be in the middle of this." He turned to his wife. "I guess I am in the middle of it, but I swear that's true."

Victoria touched his hand. "I know it is, and there's no way they're going to drag you into this. What a nerve that woman had to think she should have the leading role in *Nebraska Nights*." Victoria turned to Emmy. "Someone your age should play Diane."

"She's going to," Brian said. "I just hadn't told her yet."

Rooney folded his notebook. "Mr. Rumson, I'll ask you to accompany me down to headquarters. Miss Laker, I'd like you to give a complete statement as well. Mr. McCormack, we need to talk to you again, and I do strongly urge you to engage counsel."

"Now just one minute," Alvirah said indignantly. "I can tell you believe Mr. Rumson over Brian." There goes the option on the play, she thought, but this is more important. "You're going to say that Brian maybe started to leave, decided to come back and tell Fiona to clear out, and then ended up killing her. I'll tell you how I think it happened. Rumson came down here and got in an argument with Fiona. He strangled her but was smart enough or curious enough to take the script she was showing him."

"That is absolutely untrue," Rumson snapped.

"I don't want another word discussed here," Rooney ordered. "Miss Laker, Mr. Rumson, Mr. McCormack, I have a car downstairs."

When the door closed behind them Willy put his arms around Alvirah. "Honey, I'm going to skip Pete's retirement party. You look ready to collapse."

Alvirah hugged him back. "No, you're not. I've been recording everything. I need to listen to the playback and put on my thinking cap. I do that better alone. You have a good time and remember . . ."

"I know. If I sing 'Danny Boy' more than twice, sleep at the old place."

Still, the apartment did feel terribly quiet after Willy left. Alvirah decided that a warm soak in the bathtub Jacuzzi might take some of the stiffness out of her body and clear her brain.

The hot, scented, swirling water only made her realize how tired she was and how good it would feel to go to bed. Instead, she dressed comfortably in her favorite nightgown and Willy's striped terry cloth robe. She set the expensive cassette player her editor at *The New York Globe* had given her on the dining room table, then took the tiny cassette out of her sunburst pin, inserted it in the recorder, and pushed the playback button. She put a new cassette in the back of the pin and fastened the pin to her robe just in case she wanted to think out loud.

For several hours she sat listening intently to her conversations with Brian, with Detective Rooney, with Emmy, with the Rumsons.

Outside the night was cloudy and the lights from the Tavern on the Green and the buildings on Fifth Avenue and Central Park West shone hazily in the darkness.

When Alvirah looked at the clock, she was surprised to
see that it was nearly eleven o'clock. She stared at the door
in the foyer, visualizing Fiona Winters opening it for
Carleton Rumson.

What was it about Carleton Rumson that bothered her
so much? Methodically Alvirah reviewed meeting the
Rumsons at the elevator when she and Willy arrived from
the airport. He was pretty cool that night, but when we
bumped into him the next morning he sure had changed
his tune, even reminded me he wanted to read the new
play right away. She remembered how Brian had said that
nobody could get to Carleton Rumson.

That's it, she thought. He wanted to see the play
because he already knew how good it was. It was just he
couldn't admit that he'd already read it. Wait till Detective
Rooney hears this.

The phone rang. Startled, Alvirah hurried over to pick it
up. It was Emmy. "Mrs. Meehan," she whispered,
"they're still questioning Brian and Mr. Rumson, but I
know they think Brian's guilty."

"I just figured everything out," Alvirah said triumphantly. "How good a look did you get at Carleton
Rumson when you saw him in the hall?"

"Pretty good."

"Then you could see he was carrying the script of the
new play, couldn't you? I mean, if he was telling the
truth that he only went down to tell Fiona to leave him
alone, he'd never have picked up that script. But if they
talked about it and he read some of it before he killed
her, he'd take it and figure a way to meet Brian. Emmy,
I think I've solved the case." She waited for Emmy's
response.

When it came, Emmy's voice was barely audible. "Mrs.
Meehan, I swear Carleton Rumson wasn't carrying any-

thing when I saw him. Suppose Detective Rooney thinks to ask me that question? It's going to hurt Brian when I tell him the truth."

"You have to tell the truth," Alvirah said sadly. "Don't worry. I still have my thinking cap on." When she hung up, she turned the cassette player on again and began to replay her tapes. She replayed her conversations with Brian several times. There was something he had told her that she was missing.

Finally she stood up and stretched. Tightening the cord on Willy's robe, she decided that a breath of fresh air wouldn't hurt a bit. Not that New York air is fresh, she thought as she opened the terrace door and stepped out. This time she went to the Plexiglass wall and let her fingers rest on the railing. If Willie were here he'd have a fit, she thought. But I'm not going to lean on it. There's just something so restful about looking out over the park. I think one of the happiest nights of Mom's life was when she had a sleigh ride through the park when she was sixteen. She always talked about it. It was because her girlfriend Beth asked for that for her birthday.

Beth!

Beth!

That's it! Alvirah thought triumphantly. Again she could hear Brian saying that Fiona Winters wanted to play the part of *Diane*. Then Brian corrected himself and said I mean *Beth*. Willy asked who's that and Brian said the name of the lead in his new play, that he'd just changed it in the final draft. Alvirah switched on her microphone and cleared her throat. Better get this all down. It would help to have her immediate impressions when she wrote the story up for the *Globe*.

"It wasn't Rumson who killed Fiona Winters," she said, her voice confident. "It was his wife, See-no-evil Vicky.

She was the one who kept after Rumson to read the play. She was the one who said Emmy should play *Diane.* She didn't know Brian had changed the name. She must have listened in when Fiona phoned him. She came down while he waited for his call from Europe. She didn't want Fiona to get involved with Rumson again, so she killed her, then took the script. That was the copy she read, not the final draft."

"How very clever of you, Mrs. Meehan."

The voice came from directly behind her. Alvirah felt strong hands at the small of her back. She tried to turn and felt her body press against the railing and Plexiglass wall. How did Victoria Rumson get in here, she wondered, then in a flash remembered that Brian's key had been on the elephant table. With all her strength she tried to throw herself against her attacker, but was too late. A blow on the side of her neck stunned her. She spun around and sagged against the railing. Only vaguely was she aware of a creaking, tearing sound and Willy's voice frantically calling her.

Willy hadn't stayed to sing even one chorus of "Danny Boy." After dinner, a few beers, and a chance to congratulate Pete on his retirement, he'd begun to feel rotten. Something was bugging him that told him to go home. He froze when he entered the apartment and saw the struggling figures at the terrace railing. Shouting Alvirah's name, he rushed across the room. "Come in," he pleaded, "come in," then realized what the other woman was doing. He took one step out onto the terrace, saw a section of the wall separate and fall, leaving a yawning space next to Alvirah. Willy took a second step toward that space and fainted.

Beth! Diane! All the way from the police station to Central Park South, Emmy sat on the edge of the seat in the cab. She'd been in the precinct waiting for her statement to be typed up, heartsick with worry about Brian, remembering the way he'd looked at her when he told Victoria Rumson that she, Emmy, was going to have the lead in his new play. I don't care about playing Diane as long as Brian's all right, she'd thought, then corrected herself. Not *Diane*. Brian changed the name to *Beth*. Then in her mind she again heard Victoria Rumson say, "You should play the part of Diane." That was when it all fit. Victoria Rumson, wildly jealous of her husband, Victoria who had almost lost him to Fiona a couple of years ago.

Emmy had jumped up and run from the station house. She had to talk to Alvirah before she said anything to the cops. She heard a policeman call after her but didn't answer him as she hailed the cab.

When she reached the building, she raced to the elevator. She heard Willy shouting as she came down the corridor to the apartment. The door was open. She watched Willy go out on the terrace and fall. She saw the silhouettes of the two women and realized what was happening.

In a burst of speed Emmy rushed out to the terrace. Alvirah was facing her, swaying over the open space. Her right hand was grasping the railing that was still in place. Victoria Rumson was pummeling that hand with her fists.

Emmy grabbed Victoria's arms and twisted them behind her. Victoria's howl of rage and pain rose above the crashing of the terrace wall as it fell to the street. Emmy shoved her aside and managed to grasp the cord of Alvirah's robe. Alvirah was teetering. Her bedroom slippers were sliding backwards off the terrace. Her body swayed as she hovered thirty-four stories over the sidewalk below. With superhuman strength Emmy pulled her forward and they fell together over the collapsed but comfortable form of the unconscious Willy.

*   *   *

Alvirah and Willy slept until noon. When they finally awakened, Willy insisted Alvirah stay put. He went out to the kitchen, returning fifteen minutes later with a pitcher of orange juice, a pot of tea, and a plate of toast. After her second cup of tea, Alvirah regained her customary optimism. "Boy, was it good that Detective Rooney came barging in here after Emmy and caught Victoria Rumson trying to escape. And you know what I think, Willy?"

"I never know what you think, Honey," Willy sighed.

"One of the reasons Carleton Rumson never wanted a divorce is because he didn't want to split his money. With See-no-evil Vicky in jail, he won't have to worry about that. I bet anything he still produces Brian's play.

"And Willy," Alvirah concluded, "I want you to have a talk with Brian to tell him he'd better marry that darling Emmy before somebody else snaps her up." She beamed. "I have the perfect wedding present for them, a load of white furniture."

The doorbell rang. Willy struggled into his robe and hurried out. When he opened the door, Brian and Emmy came in. Willy took one look at their radiant faces and entwined hands and said, "I hope your favorite color is white."

Sometimes a body is found enrobed in a work of primitive art. . . .

Stanley Cohen

Hello! My Name Is
Irving Wasserman

Morty Kaplan was definitely excited about something as he arrived home from his office on a perfect summer day. When he entered the co-op building on East 67th at Third, even Tony the doorman noticed it while pulling the door open for him.

"You just swallow the canary, or what?" Tony quipped.

"Mostly what, Tony. I gave up on canaries years ago. Nothing but feathers and bones."

"Yeah? What about that feather on your necktie?"

Morty grinned. "You're quick, kid. I'll give you that. See you later."

Morty took the elevator to the seventeenth floor, unlocked the door, and went inside. He threw his jacket across a chair and walked into the kitchen where Evelyn was at the sink, rinsing lettuce for the salad.

"And how's the world's most lovable endodontist?" she asked, not looking up from her work. "You root a few hot canals, today?"

Morty walked over to her and gave her fanny a little caress, his usual way of letting her know he was home. Then he gave her a pleasing little kiss behind her ear, an action that was maybe a little less routine, but not out of character. "I just might have a pleasant little surprise for you, today."

She whirled around to face him, a bright expectant smile on her face. "What?" She was into pleasant little surprises.

"You know the rug you've been wishing we could find for the den?"

"What about it?"

"You know, something authentically Navajo, or even quasi-Hopi, something that looks like it had been made by real, honest-to-goodness American Indians?"

"Oh, cut the crap and get to the point, Morty."

"I may, and listen closely, I'm saying, I may, I may have found you the rug you want."

Evelyn was all smiles. "Where? I've been shopping for months and I'm convinced there's not one in this city that's even close. At any price."

"Well, I may have found one. In fact, when you see this rug, you're not going to believe what you're looking at."

"Is it going to cost a fortune? You're always saying that you're not willing to spend a fortune for it. . . . Wait a minute. Where would you be seeing any rugs today?"

Morty's eyes gleamed. "I saw one. And we could have it for nothing."

"What are you talking about?"

"Are you ready for this? As I was walking home from the office just now, I saw this rug that somebody had thrown out on top of a pile of stuff left for pickup, and I took a look at the corner of it, and it really does look like just what we want."

"All you saw was a corner of it?"

"It was tightly rolled up and taped with heavy tape."

"Well, if somebody threw it out, it's probably a mess."

"Not necessarily. Not in that neighborhood. East Sixty-second between Second and Third? That block is all million-dollar town houses. Latching onto a discarded anything in that block can be very promising. Very promising. Nothing about throwaways in that block would surprise me."

"Well, why didn't you just pick it up and bring it then?"

Morty smiled at her and then shifted into a poor excuse for a body builder's stance. He was slight in build, with a paunch, a receding hairline, glasses, and delicate hands. "I know you think I can lift the world," he said, "but that thing was heavy. I could tell just from pushing at it. And it was bulky and lumpy. Whoever threw it out must have gotten rid of a lot of other junk, heavy junk, by rolling it up inside before they taped it up. Admittedly, after we get it up here and get a look at it, we may decide we don't want it, but considering how long we've been shopping for this thing, I certainly think it's worth a look."

"It'll probably be gone before you can get back. This is New York, you know."

Morty smiled. "I thought of that when I looked at it. So, I sort of rearranged the pile a little. I put some other stuff on top of it."

"Get our neighbor down the hall to help you. The big Swede. Lars. He'd be more than glad to, and he could probably carry you *and* the rug. And go *now*. Before somebody else gets it."

"Why don't you give him a call?" Morty said. "He likes you."

The rolled-up rug was definitely heavy. Very heavy. But Lars, their big Swedish neighbor from down the hall was up to the task. And they were something to look at as they moved along, carrying it. Lars, a giant of a man, had the bulk of the load on his shoulder. Morty walked with his considerably less powerful shoulder under the front end of the thing, where he provided little more than balance. If that.

When they reached the building, Tony the doorman pulled the door open for them. "A new rug, huh? What? D'you find that somewhere?"

"Does it surprise you?" Morty asked.

"Surprise me? Nothing surprises me in this city." Then he grinned at Morty. "What? You couldn't carry it yourself? You had to get Mr. Swenson to help you?"

"You want to try carrying it, Tony? Go ahead. Take it upstairs for us. Lars and I will watch the door for you."

Tony grinned. "I gotta stay here."

It took some negotiating for Morty and Lars to get their burden into the elevator, but they managed. When they reached the door to the apartment, Evelyn opened the door for them. She took one look at the rolled-up rug and had trouble containing her excitement. Since it was a hand-woven Indian rug, its design was the same on both sides.

"Blacks and grays and whites," she said in a controlled manner. "Morty? Do you happen to know what this might be?"

He smiled and nodded. "I think so," he said with certainty, sensing that she didn't want to discuss too much in front of Lars. He and Lars continued struggling with the rug, placing it finally in the den, in position to be unrolled.

"Well," she said, looking at Lars and then at Morty, "I've got to get the fish out of the oven or it'll be spoiled. So I guess we'll have to leave this till after we eat. Lars, would you like to stay and have a bite with us?"

"Oh, thanks, no," he answered, "but you call me if you need any more help. Any time. Okay?" And he meant it. A gentle giant. And a friend among friends.

"Another time," Evelyn said warmly, trying not to let her sense of relief be too obvious. She wanted to get him the hell out of there so she could look at the rug.

After she'd seen him to the door and closed it, she turned to Morty. "Are you thinking what I'm thinking?"

"I sure am." He loved when she got really excited about something.

"That rug looks like an authentic 'Two Gray Hills.' And an early one, at that. If it's in any kind of good condition, do you have any idea what it's worth? That size rug?"

"A lot of money, I'm sure."

"I saw a tiny throw rug that was supposedly a 'Two Gray Hills' at that Indian Museum on upper Broadway, and it cost nearly a thousand dollars. I don't think you can even order them in room size any more. Morty, this rug could be a real collector's item."

"Believe me. I've been thinking about it."

"Let's go look at it," she said.

"I thought you wanted to eat first."

"The fish's not going anywhere. I've got to look at that rug."

They went into the den to examine their prize, or confirm that it was in fact a prize. Morty very meticulously cut the duct tape wrapped around the rug in four places, and they began unrolling it.

Evelyn liked what she saw as they unrolled it slowly along the floor. The colors! The design! Based on all her research and endless shopping, it was just what she'd pictured in her mind's eye. And it wasn't stained, or even soiled. It was in beautiful condition. Almost like new. Why would anyone throw it away? A piece of art, no less. . . . Only in New York. And especially an area like that block of East Sixty-second. Someone was redecorating? Out it went. . . . But why was the rolled-up rug so bulky and misshapen? What bunch of junk was inside it?

When they reached the end of the rug, she found out. And she fainted dead away. Inside the rug was the body of a middle-aged man, dressed in a fine dark suit with an expensive silk tie. And affixed to the lapel of his jacket was one of those familiar sticky labels which read:

Hello! My Name Is
Irving Wasserman

Morty revived her with a cold, wet towel.

She sat bolt upright and looked around. "Where is he? Or was I dreaming?"

"I dragged him into the bedroom."

"Not our bedroom!"

"The *other* bedroom."

She reached for the towel that was soaking wet at one end and patted her face with the dry end. Then she began to examine the rug with a decorator's eye. She got to her feet and walked around it. "I like this rug. I LIKE this rug. I'll bet the Museum of the American Indian would like to have this baby. And it's in perfect condition. Perfect."

"Well, almost perfect."

"What about it is not perfect?"

"It's missing one of the corner fringes. See, down there at the other end? at the corner?"

"I'd hardly have noticed it. Even *I'm* not that fussy."

"Well, don't get too excited about it. What makes you so sure the police'll let us keep it?"

Evelyn looked at him with alarm. "Have you called the police?"

"No, but I'm getting ready to, right now."

"No!"

"What do you mean, no?"

"I mean, no, don't call the police. I want this rug. If you call the police, you know as well as I do that they'll take it. It's evidence. Morty, I want this rug. Do you know how long I've been looking for exactly this rug? Exactly this rug?"

Morty threw up his hands and looked skyward, his usual gesture when faced with one of Evelyn's absolutely immovable sudden positions. Maybe *this* time he could get some help from above. "Evelyn, listen to me."

"Forget it," she snapped. "I want this rug."

"Will you listen a minute?"

"No. I don't want to hear it."

"Okay, you don't want to hear it. But what are we going to do with Irving in there?"

"I don't know. We'll have to think of something."

"Evelyn, if we call the police now and tell them exactly what happened, and with Lars Swenson as our witness, everything'll be fine. And after the smoke clears, and the excitement is over, I'm sure they'll let us have the rug."

"You're sure? How sure? Can you call them and ask them? No. And I want this rug. Morty, I want this rug. I don't want it leaving this room."

"Then what do we do with Irving? Shall we put him in the bathtub and start buying ice?"

"We'll have to think of something. All we need is some way to get him out of here. I don't have any guilty conscience, Morty. We didn't kill him. We're not responsible for his being dead."

"Well, whoever was sure knew what he . . . or she, but presumably he, was doing." He smiled a little smile of respect. "A real professional, whoever did that. A really neat job."

"What are you talking about?"

"I've read about cases like this one," he said, reflectively. "They take a small calibre gun like a twenty-two short that shoots with a fairly low muzzle velocity and they stick it under the chin, pointed sort of up and toward the back of the head, and they fire. It's instant and painless. And neat. Because with the low muzzle velocity, the bullet doesn't come out. It just enters the cranial cavity and ricochets around, making scrambled eggs out of the brain. But from the outside, neat. The victim looks normal. Just a tiny clean hole where the bullet enters."

"How do you know so much about muzzle velocity? You've never touched a gun in your life."

"I've read about it. I think it was an article in the *Times* magazine about professional hit men and their techniques. . . . Evelyn, what do you propose doing with Mr. Wasserman?"

"I'll think of something."

Morty took the garbage out to the disposal chute, which was located in a utility closet off the corridor. The closet was completely at the other end of the corridor from their door. And there were eleven other co-op apartments on the floor. What were the odds, say, in the middle of the night . . .? And if somebody did see them? What then?

He opened the port to the chute and dropped in the bag, and as he listened to its descent, he studied the opening. It was a close fit for the small garbage bag. For a man the size of Irving? Who was also a mite paunchy? He thought about Irving getting stuck between floors. But that presumed getting Irving into the chute at all, which wasn't possible. Forget it. The garbage chute was definitely not a viable solution.

When he reentered the apartment, he found Evelyn

tugging at a window. "Evelyn. You don't just throw bodies out of windows."

She turned to face him. "Then we'll have to think of something else. Right?"

"Listen to me. We've got to call the police, and quick. Lars is our alibi for having him here, and the longer we wait, the more questionable our story's going to be. Lars won't lie about *anything*. Am I right?"

"We're *not* calling the police."

"Well, if we wanted to call one, we wouldn't have to go far. There's one on duty right across the street from this building at all times . . . God, I'm sure glad it's Friday, at least. I don't expect to get much sleep while Irving is with us."

"We'll have to come up with a plan for getting him out of here. That's all. Because we're keeping the rug."

"Evelyn, listen to me. Number one, we live next door to our temple. Next door. But that's nothing. Forget that. As long as we don't try to carry him out while services are letting out, we're okay there. Now for number two. Number two, we live across the street from the Russian Embassy. The Russian Embassy! And directly across from our front door is a guard shack which just happens to be occupied twenty-four hours a day by two of New York's Finest, because the Embassy is there. That's number two. And it's not bad enough that they're *there*, they even come across to *this* building to use that bathroom down in the basement. And if that wasn't enough, now for number three. Number three, we have our own doormen on duty, also twenty-four hours a day."

"Morty, we didn't kill this man. Someone else killed him. Someone murdered this poor man and left him out there on the street. We brought him in here by mistake, and all we have to do is figure out some way to get him back outside without anybody noticing. And without calling the police. Because we're keeping the rug.''

"Evelyn, you're repeating yourself." Then he stopped, and started wondering if he would ever be able to make himself believable when he began explaining what he was doing with the corpse of Irving Wasserman. Surely some of the prisoners in Attica, or wherever, would need root canal work.

And with that notion, and unable to think rationally because of the feverish state of his mind, he went into the living room and dropped himself into his big chair and flipped on the tube. The Mets were two behind going into the sixth. Couldn't they have been winning big this one time?

During the bottom of the ninth, with the Mets still two behind, but with two on and nobody out, Evelyn came and stood between Morty and the television. "I have a plan, '' she said. "It's not a wonderful, grandiose plan, but it's a plan, and I think it'll work. And I frankly can't think of any other way to do it.''

Behind her, on the tube, there was a lot of excitement and a lot of cheering, but he wasn't quite sure what had happened. He'd set the volume low. And it was always her practice, when he was watching and she wanted to talk to him, to stand between him and the screen to be sure she had his attention. So, under the circumstances, about the best response he could manage was a rather annoyed, "Tell me about it.''

Saturday. Morty entered the surgical supply store and looked around. He made a point of going to a store other than the one he used for his own office needs because, as he ruminated about the situation, when you've got a house guest like Irving, it tends to make you a little self-conscious. He certainly didn't want to have to discuss with people who knew him what a dentist needed with a wheelchair.

The night before had been bad, but perhaps not quite as bad as he'd anticipated. The Mets had managed to tie the score in the ninth and then win it in the fourteenth, and staying with this had helped him fall asleep, for a couple of hours, anyway, before he woke up, starkly awake, thinking about Irving in the next room.

He paid for the chair in cash, of course, reflecting on the fact as he did that he was thinking like a criminal, leaving no written records or receipts. Then he asked the clerk if the rather large carton could be wrapped.

"Wrapped? You want this wrapped?"

"It's . . . it's going to be a gift." And as he said it, he flushed with guilt, realizing that although he might have paid with cash, he was certainly leaving an indelible impression on the clerk's mind.

"You want it gift-wrapped? A wheelchair?"

"It doesn't have to be exactly gift-wrapped. Just wrapped. In plain paper is okay. With a rope around it so I can handle it." Things were going from bad to worse. That clerk would never forget him. But he wanted to get the carton past Tony, and into his building without its contents being obvious. Problems. Nothing but problems. At least the store wasn't close to home. It was a ten-dollar cab ride there. And it would be another ten-dollar cab ride back. But worth it.

He helped the clerk, and another clerk, finally get the carton covered with plain brown paper and a few dozen yards of tape, then a rope for carrying. Before walking out, he rather sheepishly asked, "Uh, if this is not exactly right, it can be returned, can't it?"

The two clerks looked at him in disbelief. After a

moment, one of them said, "In the carton. And keep the cash receipt." And the other said with a grin, "Don't let it get messed up."

Morty lugged the carton to the street and hailed a cab.

Tony pulled the door open for him when he arrived, and he dragged the carton inside.

"You need a hand with that?"

"Thanks, Tony, but I can handle it okay."

"Hey, we won last night. In the fourteenth."

"I stayed up and watched it. Till the end."

"It's about time Strawberry did something, huh?"

"Yeah."

He carried it into the elevator and pressed seventeen. Another hurdle passed. Tony did as he was supposed to do for a change. Just open the door and not ask a lot of questions. When he reached the seventeenth floor, he started to lift the carton and the rope came loose. He pushed the carton along the carpeted hallway to their door, unlocked it, and then shoved the carton inside.

"You're awfully quiet, tonight, Morty. You, too, Evelyn. Everything okay?" Arnie Perlman, a dentist and close friend, and one of Morty's best sources of referrals, kept looking, first at Morty, then at Evelyn."

"We're fine, Arnie. I stayed up a little late is all. I got hooked on the Mets game."

"The Straw-man really hit that thing," Arnie said. "When he connects, he can give it a ride."

"You watched it, too."

"What else?" Arnie said.

And in a separate conversation between the women, Phyllis asked Evelyn, "What'd you do, today?"

"I spent most of the day shopping. I felt like getting out today."

"Speaking of shopping, did you ever find that rug you were looking for? You know, for your den?"

Evelyn flushed and looked at Morty, who'd heard the question. Then she looked back at Phyllis.

"Did I say something wrong?" Phyllis asked. Then she smiled. "Oh, God, don't tell me I brought up a sore subject or something."

"No, of course not." Evelyn answered. She glanced at Morty again, and then, "As a matter of fact, we may have spotted one that we're going to consider."

"Really? Where'd you find it? I figured you'd probably have to go to New Mexico or somewhere."

"Oh, at a little shop over on . . ." Evelyn looked at Morty. "Morty, where was that little shop we found?"

"I don't remember, exactly. Somewhere down in the Village. I have it written down at home."

They finished dinner and walked outside.

"Why don't you guys come back to our place for a nightcap?" Arnie asked.

Morty and Evelyn quickly begged off. And Morty looked nervously at his watch. They didn't have a lot of time left to get back home, according to their plan. Service in the restaurant had been slower than usual. The doormen at their building changed shifts at eleven, and they had to be back before Tony left. They hoped the old man, Manolo, who worked nights, wouldn't show up early and see them come in alone. If that happened, they'd have to postpone their plan another night, and that could be disastrous. Would Irving keep that long? Morty pictured himself going into the Food Emporium and trying to look casual when he checked out with thirty or forty five-pound bags of ice.

But they'd elected not to cancel their date with the Perlmans. It might provoke some questions. Besides, they could use the evening out. And Irving certainly wasn't going anywhere.

They made it back in time. Tony greeted them, and the old man was nowhere in sight. There was a bit of activity, however, around the guard shack across the street. The cops changed shifts at eleven, as well. They watched for a moment as the blue and white police van drove away, and then went inside. They entered the elevator and both exhaled.

Waiting time. One, one-thirty, two. They sat and stared numbly at the tube.

"I think we should start getting him into the chair and ready to go," Evelyn said.

Morty nodded. "I think you're right."

"You know what I was thinking," Evelyn said. "I was thinking that he really needs to be wearing a turtleneck so that the hole won't show. You know. Just in case."

"You're probably right."

"I think a white one, to be dressy enough to go with that dark suit he's wearing"

"My new white turtleneck. Right?"

"I'll buy you another one. Besides, you'll get to keep his tie. You said you liked his tie . . . And maybe we should stick a Band-Aid over the hole."

Morty, with his most resigned sigh, breathed, "Okay, why don't we go do it? Come on."

"We? You'll have to do it. I'm not touching him. Oh, and another thing. Why don't you put some of my makeup on him so he doesn't look so pasty-faced? A little rouge, maybe."

"What do I know about applying makeup? Can't you do that one thing?"

"I told you, I'm not touching him. You'll do it fine. Just

a little rouge so he has some color . . ." She smiled. "My husband, the undertaker."

Not at all amused, Morty got slowly out of his big chair and moved toward the bedroom.

Four-thirty A.M. That moment of darkest night and deepest sleep. That moment when, even in New York, the pace of life slows to a crawl. A crawl, maybe. But in New York, one can never count on the pace of life grinding to a complete halt. Not at any hour. There is always a reasonable likelihood of activity on the streets of Manhattan.

Irving was in the chair, ready to go. And getting him there had been no easy task for Morty. He'd struggled with the clothes while Irving was still on the floor. First the jacket, then the shirt and tie, the Band-Aid, and then Morty's new white turtleneck. And a struggle it had been. Especially the turtleneck. Finally, the jacket, once again. The sticky tag was still on the lapel. Morty was beginning to get into the macabre humor of the whole business as he smoothed out the tag, making sure it was on there securely.

HELLO! MY NAME IS

Irving Wasserman

After he'd finished dressing Irving, he'd dealt with the makeup. Like a real pro, he'd covered the crisp white turtleneck with a towel. The more he fussed with the stuff, the worse things seemed to get. But by this time, he was really amused by what they were doing. Almost giddy. To the point of giggling as he put on too much rouge, then tried to wipe some off, then tried a little powder, then more wiping and rubbing and smearing. He thought about using a little mascara, or adding a touch of lipstick, and this made him whisper aloud, "I am from Transylvania." The final effect was one of Irving looking not just healthy, but ruddy, in fact, even more than ruddy. Flushed. And that was perfect.

Then came the job of getting Irving into the chair. And Morty was almost not up to it. With his physique, he was not used to lifting people. Having his hands in their mouths, yes, but not lifting them. In the process of straining and struggling, he was face-to-face, no, cheek-to-cheek with Irving, and as he puffed and sweated, the lyric strains of "Dancing Cheek to Cheek" tripped lightly through his head. Once Irving was into the chair, he went into the bathroom and wiped the makeup off his cheek, deciding finally that nothing less than a shower would do. And with time to burn, he'd taken a nice long one.

They rolled Irving to the door, and Evelyn opened it and peered out. No one in sight. As it should be. She could think of no one on their floor that she'd expect to be up and around at that hour. They moved soundlessly to the elevator, pressed the button, and waited. It arrived, they pushed Irving into it, and pressed LOBBY. As the car began its less than reckless descent, Morty held Irving's collar with one hand to keep him from pitching forward.

The car stopped at the ninth floor, and they looked at each other, panic-stricken. The door opened and a rather nice looking young man, perhaps in his late twenties, entered the car. He looked at Irving curiously and then at the two of them. Then he looked away, not wanting to appear intrusive or judgmental. Morty sized him up as probably leaving some young woman's apartment. At four-thirty in the A.M.? Morty felt a twinge of jealousy.

When the young man glanced again at Irving, Morty, feeling obliged to comment, said, "Demon rum."

And the young man, feeling obliged to respond, said, "It can do it."

"We're taking him back to his place," Morty said. "It's not the first time."

"But it's going to be the last," Evelyn said, suddenly. "He's disgusting," she added. "He does this every time he comes over, and the next time, I'm not giving him anything to drink. I'm sick and tired of his passing out like this."

The young man nodded and looked relieved when the car stopped. The door moved slowly open and the young man hurried across the lobby.

They rolled Irving out of the car, and as they had hoped, Manolo, the old night man, was dozing on a sofa in the lobby. Manolo woke up when he heard the young man press the inside release and exit to the street. Manolo glanced around and saw them coming toward the door, pushing Irving.

As Manolo started to get to his feet, Morty said quickly, "It's okay, Manolo, we can let ourselves out. Thanks."

Manolo nodded, smiled, and made a thank you gesture with a nod and a wave of his hand. Then he dropped back on the couch and got comfortable again.

When they reached the sidewalk, certainly the tensest moment in the plan, Morty said, "Get back with the car as quick as you can."

And Evelyn promptly responded, "Would you expect me to drive around for a while, first?"

"Just be as quick as you can. Okay?"

Evelyn headed across Third and east on Sixty-seventh to the all-night garage a block away where they kept their car. Morty pushed the chair into what he hoped was the least illuminated spot in front of the building. He looked across the street at the little police shack, but could not tell if the cops inside were watching him. Realizing Evelyn would not be able to bring the car right to the door of their building because of a couple of POLICE LINE sawhorses, he moved a short distance toward the corner of Third Avenue, gripping Irving's collar tightly, and trying to appear as relaxed and casual as possible.

Suddenly a cop emerged from the shack and started across the street toward the building. Morty watched in horror, his heart pounding so furiously he could hear it. Was the cop coming toward him? The cop glanced in his direction and went to the door of the building, where he tapped on the glass. Manolo scrambled to his feet and opened the door, and the cop disappeared down the stairs, heading for the lavatory in the basement.

After what seemed an interminable few minutes, he finally saw Evelyn coming. She pulled the car up, and he quickly opened the back door. He began struggling with Irving and was near collapse from fright. What if the cop returned and happened to be one of the "good-guys"? He'd probably stroll over and offer to lend a hand. And the cop would surely know a stiff when he saw one. How would he explain Irving? . . . Uh, well, you see, Officer, we found him on East Sixty-second Street, rolled up in a rug . . . And you didn't call the police? . . . Uh, my wife was afraid you'd take the rug.

Somehow he managed to get Irving into the back seat of the car and into an upright position. He collapsed the wheelchair and placed it in the trunk. Then he ran around to the driver's seat and climbed in as Evelyn moved over. As they drove by the guard shack, Morty looked but could see no activity in the little structure. Had they been watching him? Maybe it was only the one cop. Or maybe, if there was another one, and if God was with them, the other cop was cooping, taking a little snooze for himself.

Morty drove to the corner of Lexington Avenue and stopped a bit abruptly for the light, and as he did, Irving heaved forward, slipping down, out of sight.

"Where are we taking him?" Evelyn asked. "You said you had a place all picked out."

"It's a fitting place for so special an occasion. A high and significant place." Morty was gradually calming down as he drove, and his sense of macabre amusement with the whole business was returning. "It's a place with a marvelous view," he added.

"A view? Morty, where are we taking him?"

"Wait and see."

A light rain began to fall as they cut back to the East Side, headed north on FDR Drive, onto the Harlem River Drive, and up to the George Washington Bridge. They crossed the bridge into Jersey, went immediately north on the virtually deserted Palisades Parkway, then pulled off at the first overlook, the Rockefeller Overlook, which provided an inspiring view of the Hudson, the opposite shore, the bridge, and beyond it, the skyline of Manhattan. He knew the spot well from having grown up in Jersey, and as he expected, there were no cars in sight. Who comes to an overlook at five in the morning? Especially when it has started raining.

"Is this perfect?" Morty breathed, feeling pleased with himself. "We'll leave him here to be the master of all he surveys." To which he added, "He can watch the dawn come up like thunder over Yonkers 'cross the way."

He pulled the car over parallel to the row of large rocks that provided a barrier to the bluff overlooking the river, and then, out of nowhere, lights flashing, a highway patrol car pulled quickly over next to him. Morty let out a tiny moan of dismay. His life, as he knew it, was over. All because of a lousy rug. He was ready to collapse into tears.

But Evelyn prodded him. "Morty! For God's sake, be cool. He fell down, in back. He's out of sight."

The trooper rolled down his window and shined a flashlight in Morty's face, signaling to Morty to roll his window down. Morty slowly did as he was told. The trooper studied Morty and Evelyn for a moment, and his expression changed. It softened, as if he couldn't possibly suspect this innocuous-looking couple of anything illegal. "Are you two all right?" he asked.

"We're fine, Officer, fine," Morty managed to get out.

"It seemed an odd time for anyone, like yourselves, that is, to be coming in here."

"It's our anniversary, Officer," Evelyn said. Morty turned and looked at her.

"Anniversary?" the officer asked. An amused smile.

"Fifteen years ago we got engaged on this spot. And at just about this time, believe it or not."

The officer looked as if, with that bit of information, he'd finally heard it all. "Well, congratulations. You two take care, hear? I wouldn't hang around this spot too long at this hour."

"Thank you, Officer," Morty said. And they watched as the patrol car roared away toward the exit and disappeared.

"Did he check our license plate?" Morty asked.

"He didn't check anything," she answered. "He didn't look at anything but our innocent faces."

"Good. You know something? You've got the makings of a great criminal mind."

Morty got out of the car and hurried around to the other side. He opened the back door and dragged Irving out, pulling him between two of the large rocks that formed the barrier to the high, steep bluff. Then he propped Irving up against one of the rocks, facing the river, in position to enjoy the view. "Stay loose, old friend," he muttered to Irving. He hurried back into the car and headed for the exit, and home.

The rain grew heavier, and it pelted Irving's face, but Irving did not flinch. The ink on the sticky tag on his lapel was not waterproof, and the rain caused his name to streak, and finally to wash completely away.

Monday morning. In an elegantly appointed town house in Boston's Back Bay area, Mrs. Ira Waterman answered the phone. ". . . no, I don't know where Mr. Waterman is . . . no, I don't know how to get in touch with him . . . no, I, please let me explain. Mr. Waterman and I are separated. We are not in touch and have not been for quite some time, and I frankly have no idea as to his whereabouts, nor do I wish to have . . . yes, he could be in New York, I suppose. We did live there at one time when we were still together, and I think he still has business there. But he could also be most anywhere, and I assure you, I haven't the faintest notion where . . . you're very welcome."

Monday afternoon. Jack Sandifer entered the plane for his flight back to Chicago, went to his seat, and got comfortable. He was a tall man, lean, blond, athletic, striking in appearance.

After completing the project for which he'd flown east, he'd enjoyed a pleasant weekend in the Big Apple. A stay at the Pierre, a meal at Le Cirque, a couple of tough-ticket shows, *Les Miz* and *Phantom*. And this was in addition to the satisfaction of having been paid for a job properly done. The fifty thousand in bearer bonds was in his luggage. He always specified bearer bonds. Asking for cash always seemed a little lacking in class.

As the plane-loading process continued, he riffled through the *Post* he'd bought in the terminal. He studied the article about an unidentified man being found at an overlook off some parkway in New Jersey. A parkway in Jersey? And wearing a white turtleneck? "How in hell?" he said to himself. He glanced at the young woman who had taken the seat next to him. She was beautiful. She could easily be a model.

He reached into his shirt pocket and took out the little tuft of carpet fringe, examining it briefly and then putting it back. This business of keeping mementos of each of his projects was definitely a dangerous one, but it gave his work a quality, an edge of excitement, actually, that pleased him.

He'd liked his client. A very feisty lady for being so educated and polished. He smiled as he thought about her emphatic instructions. "I want you to remove all identification from him, and then label him in some way with his name before he changed it twenty years ago. And then deliver him back to our old address. That should do it for me."

And then she'd added the part about the rug. "Oh. And could you get that horrid Navajo rug of his out of the library? I've hated it since the day he bought it. Maybe you can think of some way to use it on this assignment. That would indeed be a nice touch."

The flight attendant came around to take drink orders. He asked for a couple of Scotches and then asked the woman next to him if she'd like a drink.

"Sure," she said with a disarming smile. "Thanks." And as their continuing conversation established that they were both returning to Chicago, where they both lived, she asked, "What sort of work do you do?"

"I'm a paid assassin."

"Gimme a break. Seriously, what do you do?"

"Actually, I deal in unusual antiques, specifically in primitive art. For example, I just delivered an authentic hand-woven, one-of-a-kind, antique Navajo rug to the City for a client. For which I was extremely well paid, I might add."

"Extremely? May I ask how extremely?"

"How's fifty-thousand? And to help me celebrate, have dinner with me when we get to Chicago."

Again that marvelous smile. "I'd love it,"she said.

A body is found near the stage door of the Goodkind Theater on West 45th Street . . . which only proves that life is not a very long run.

Dorothy Salisbury Davis

A Silver Thimble

Julie Hayes was not overjoyed to see Ralph Abel. They had first crossed paths years before during a somewhat turbulent period in her life. She had thought him very young for his years, naive, and this at a time when she herself was being urged by therapist, husband and a would-be employer to grow up. She had bought a painting of Abel's called *Scarlet Night,* the only canvas in his disastrous exhibit that he had not afterwards destroyed. She paid him a hundred dollars for it and more or less agreed to pay him another hundred if ever he returned to New York and needed it. How Julie parted with *Scarlet Night* is no more relevant now than, say, how she parted from her husband or her therapist. They are much of the past, as indeed she thought Ralph Abel until the morning he showed up in the rotunda of *The New York Daily* building. It was one of the rare days she'd gone into the office. Ordinarily she faxed her copy for the column "Our Beat."

They came around the turning world—a great globe sunk in the rotunda—one on either side of it. She thought she recognized him.

He knew he recognized her. "Mrs. Hayes—Julie— remember me?"

It was the tassel of hair she remembered him by first, dangling almost into his eye, but it had gone from the color of golden straw to a dusty pewter. "The kid from Iowa," she said, "and Paris, France!"

"And Naples, Italy. That was my best place. I should never've come home."

"Ralph Abel." She held out her hand.

"I've changed a little, haven't I?" The squint lines had deepened around the no longer so blue eyes, and the smile was slower. All that youthfulness had gone somewhere else.

"If you're not in a hurry," and she was sure he wasn't, that he had found what he had come for, her, "let me buy us a cup of coffee." It was the least of hospitality she could offer.

In the coffee shop Abel took off his pea jacket and hung it over the back of the chair. It looked to have been to sea many times.

"Merchant Marine?" Julie asked.

"St. James-on-Hudson Thrift Shop."

"That's one I've missed."

He cocked a skeptical eyebrow. She did not look thrift shop. "I've been back for a while," he said. "It's like my grandfather used to say, How you gonna keep 'em down on the farm after they've seen Paree? I tried, but Keokuk didn't seem like home anymore." While he talked he took a silver thimble from his pocket and fingered it as he might a talisman, which indeed it was. "I don't know if you met the Goldman brothers. Their father was a tailor. Mine was too. So they gave me their old man's thimble to kind of speed me home. It's my good-luck thing." He wrapped his long fingers around the thimble, clutching it. "Julie, remember you said you'd give me another hundred for *Scarlet Night* if I ever showed up and asked for it?''

She nodded. She'd been waiting.

"I'm not asking for it. I know you must've got rid of *Scarlet Night* by this time. I would myself if I was you. Did I tell you, when I was painting it I had in mind the red light district, Place Pigalle, in Paris?"

Julie grinned. Either he had told her or she had guessed it.

"It's the only place in Paris, France, where I got any loving, ma'am."

She laughed. "You're right. I didn't keep the painting, but I'm good for the hundred dollars."

"Now you wait a minute . . ." Abel himself paused while the waitress brought their coffee and he emptied four sugars into his. "There was something else you said: you allowed as you'd like to see my proletarian sketches."

The word sounded so old-fashioned. "I did say that," Julie said, whether or not she had said it then.

"I'd like to show them to you now if you'd be willing. I don't mean the same old ones I had then. They're dead and gone, but I've been doing New York things. Sort of like the Ashcan School, if you know what I mean. If I'd lived back then, that's where I'd belong. What I'm doing now— they're kind of like what you do with words in 'Our Beat.' "

That, of course, got to her.

It took him less than ten minutes to get his portfolio where he had left it with a book-shop friend on 43rd Street. Julie signed him in and took him up with her to the city room of *The New York Daily*. The double desk she shared with her partner, Tim Noble, was alongside the glass and composition wall that partitioned the vast city room from the corridor running alongside it. Tim greeted her, "Hello, stranger," and gave Abel a quick appraisal when she introduced him. She'd been known in her day to collect some pretty exotic types.

Abel laid out several of his sketches on her desk. He was wearing the good-luck thimble. No wedding band, she noted. His affinity with the so-called Ashcan School of painters was evident. He might call his work sketches, but they were tinted, mostly pastel colors that enhanced the bold, dark strokes. She picked up one, a woman standing outside a bar window, her forlorn face reflected in the glass, and stood it on the ledge behind her desk to see it from a greater distance. Deft as a conjurer, Abel lined up several other of the sketches along the ledge. Julie stayed with the bar scene: indoors, a man and a woman had turned, heads almost touching, to see the woman staring in at them. Their faces were grey, distraught.

"Hey," Julie said. She liked it.

The color rushed to Abel's face. "Do you know them?"

"Well, no. But I feel as though I do." She moved on to the other sketches. She felt a relationship with the subject in almost all of them. You might call the subjects banal, too many street people with their sordid burdens, street entertainers, a street fight, a basketball player, a dog-walker, the leering image of his slobbery hound. "From life," she said.

"Sometimes from memory. I'm pretty good that way."

"I wouldn't want you for an enemy."

"Julie, I'm a pussycat. It's for fun."

A phrase ran through her mind: you could die laughing. She was thinking of the two on the barstools. It was easy to imagine the woman outside the window with a gun in her hand.

Tim and a few colleagues with nearby desks came up to see the pictures. Julie introduced Ralph Abel. "You wouldn't think he was from Iowa, would you?"

Someone who had gone to journalism school in Missouri

wanted to know where in Iowa he'd come from, and hearing, volunteered that he once went with a girl from Keokuk. Small world.

When Abel had gathered his sketches back into the portfolio, Julie said, "How about that hundred dollars . . . "

He started to take the sketches out again.

She stopped him. "Do you have a gallery?"

He nodded. "I'll be having a show soon."

Julie wrote out the check. "I hope the gallery's a good one."

Again he blushed, possibly remembering the fiasco of his last New York sojourn. She wondered if the Maude Sloan Gallery was still in business, but she had no intention of bringing up the name. "Will you send me an invitation?"

"Absolutely."

She walked him to the elevator, where they shook hands. He brushed back the thatch of hair and said, "May I?" He bent and kissed her cheek.

In the next few days Julie found herself looking at people as though through Ralph Abel's eyes. He had given her a gift, a sharpened awareness, and she regretted not having got his address or phone number. As though to have asked him for it would have committed her. She even thought of doing a bit of detective work to try to find him. But there never seemed to be enough time.

It was Tuesday morning, October 23rd, when Tim called her, a week to the day from when she'd brought Ralph Abel and his portfolio to their desk. "I may have some rough news for you," he started. "That Iowa fellow with the paintings? Let me read you a Manhattan dateline and see what you think: 'The body of a man about thirty years old was discovered at eleven-thirty last night in the

Goodkind Theater Arcade on West 45th Street. He had
been shot in the back at close range. A number of people,
including the company of *Remembering Amy*, passed him
by as they left the theater. The doorman himself had
assumed the figure was that of a street person huddled in
the shelter of the arcade. It is an area frequented by the
homeless. Police suspect robbery to have been the motive
since no identification was found on the body. The police
did find a silver thimble in the victim's pocket . . . ' Didn't
your friend have a thimble he kept putting on and taking
off that day in the office?"

"He did," Julie said. "Is there a phone line for information?"

Tim read her the number. "I'm sorry about your friend.
If you want some extra time, Julie, the column's in good
shape."

Now there was time, she thought.

Julie hadn't wanted to call the police. She had been to the
morgue too often, but at the request of Detective Herrick,
Midtown Homicide, she viewed the body. It was that of
Ralph Abel, and after the identification she rode back to
Herrick's headquarters with him and taped her statement
about where and when she had last seen the victim. She
was even able to tell the story of the thimble, except that she
had forgotten the name of the brothers who had given it to
him. "It was a long time ago," she concluded.

"And in another country," a strong, familiar voice said
from behind her.

She looked round to see Lieutenant David Marks smiling at her somewhat sardonically. "Homicide—theater—
Manhattan: it had to be Julie Hayes I was listening to.
Come see me when you're through here. I'll send for
coffee."

Julie promised to call Herrick when the name of the brothers came to mind, and she used his phone to call her bank. If Ralph Abel had cashed her check, he might have put an address under the endorsement.

Marks, too, had lost some of his lean handsomeness since she had last seen him. The under-eye puffiness reminded her of her ex-husband. The photographs on the detective's desk were of an elderly man and woman. He was still a bachelor, she assumed. He had occasionally taken her to dinner, but it always coincided with a homicide investigation, and more than once they had reached swords' points over an association she was trying her best to escape: Sweets Romano, the art-collecting gangster who had somehow appointed himself her patron. She dreaded the possibility that Marks would make some remark about it now.

He didn't. "Have you seen *Remembering Amy?*" he wanted to know.

"I haven't. My partner covered it for the column."

"I have," Marks said. "It's interesting that about twenty minutes into the second act there's a shoot-out onstage. Very noisy. Almost as loud as the music. That makes a good cover for a premeditated blast on the other side of the wall, wouldn't you say? . . . Did he have any enemies that you know of, Julie?"

She had given her statement, and for several reasons she did not want to go into her earlier acquaintanceship with Abel, not without knowing more of his life since than she did now. "The truth is, Lieutenant, I scarcely knew him at all."

"Just doing your civic duty this morning?"

"I thought it the decent thing to do, yes."

A young officer brought two mugs of coffee from the squad room, trying without success not to spill. The floor was polka-dotted from previous failures.

"Don't you find it hard to believe a whole parade of people passed him by?" Marks asked. "He was there close onto two hours."

"I could have passed him by, I guess," Julie said. "It's happening to all of us."

Marks made a noise of agreement. "What was the French film a few years ago? *We Are All Murderers*. So, what we have here is a street crime till we find out differently."

"You mean it's on the back burner already?"

Marks grunted. "Not when you're around."

He had to take a phone call very shortly. Julie took one gulp of coffee for appearances. Then Detective Herrick came to the doorway and said her Chemical Bank call was on another line. She and the lieutenant waved to each other.

Her check made out to Ralph Abel had been cashed by Jacobs Books and Art Supplies on East 43rd Street and was deposited with their bank on October 16. That was the date Abel had brought his portfolio to her. He would seem to have gone back to the Jacobs store after he left the *Daily* office. She gave the information to Herrick, and as a sort of *quid pro quo* he told her that an empty wallet that might have belonged to the victim had been found in a dumpster on Ninth Avenue and 44th Street. Herrick went out with her and commandeered a departing squad car to drive her home.

The wind was cold and the sky grey when she started out from "the shop," as she called her combined home and local office on West 44th Street. She was getting to know the neighborhood homeless. What a contradiction when you thought about it, the neighborhood homeless. She stuck a dollar in the sleeve of a woman who never seemed to stray far from the OKAY Pizza Shop. If you could live on fragrance, that was the place to be. What she hadn't been aware of until this morning was the number of dumpsters in the theater district: down with the old, up with the new. Building everywhere. What colossal luck if Ralph's wallet was found and turned in so soon. Then she saw how it could happen: a lot of wood scraps, molding and such, was to be salvaged out of a dumpster for a drum fire along the waterfront.

The arcade between the Goodkind Theater, where the musical *Remembering Amy* was playing, and the Markham, which was dark, was cordoned off, posted *Crime Scene*. The police technical truck was parked just inside the barricade, several technicians working under floodlights a few feet this side of the stage door. Uniformed cops were urging the gawkers, including Julie, to move on. As Marks had said, it was almost incredible that at the very least, a hundred people had walked around the huddled figure—actors, of notoriously kind hearts, stage crew, musicians, not to mention the fans of Betty Mercer, who played Amy. Couldn't they tell the color of blood? They didn't look, they didn't see. They hardly knew he was there. It was only afterwards, reading or hearing about it, they might recall, as from their subconscious, that they had seen him. Except for the doorman, the last man out. She thought she'd make him the focus of her paragraph in "Our Beat."

Julie stepped into the lobby, where a bevy of cops were warming themselves, and where there was a pretty good line at the box office. Homicide was good for business. When she saw Michael Dorfman in the cage she remembered that he was the company manager. It surprised her when he came out and took her hand. Dorfman was a theater man who hated actors unless they were stars. He generally tried to ignore Julie, who had been an actor briefly, never a star.

"What a bloody mess this is," Dorfman said, "and the very week we go into the black. We paid off our investment Saturday night."

"Congratulations," Julie said. "On the payoff, not the mess."

"Isn't it worth an item?"

"A whole paragraph, especially if you can tell me what the victim was doing here."

"He was here because I did a good deed." Dorfman squinted at her to see how she took to that idea.

She didn't quiver an eyebrow.

"Got time for a cup of coffee?"

"Orange juice, since you paid off the national debt."

Dorfman had his own booth in Joey Fay's restaurant. He ordered without losing stride.

"Here's what happened: It was last Thursday. I was in the office, going over the prop expenses—Jesus, how those guys can spend money—anyway, I was up there with the books when Tony, the press agent, brings in this bedraggled-looking character with a hank of hair falling over his eye and a drawing case under his arm. 'This guy's looking for you, Mike.' Tony shoved him in the door and took off. I'll make a long story short: I thought he was trying to sell something, but it turned out he was putting together a book of New York sketches and he wanted to know if he could do some of *Remembering Amy*. He was personable enough when you got to talk with him, and he showed me a couple of things that looked good. Some other time I might've checked his credentials, you know, publisher, etc., but he seemed legit, *was* legit as far as I know, and it being Thursday, we were having a run-through on the set for June Pryor, who's going in for Betty on matinees. That's another item, by the way." He chortled and lit a cigarette while the coffee and orange juice were served.

Dorfman was one of the last great chain smokers. "Anyway, I took him down and settled him in the fifth or sixth row, made him shade his flashlight. Believe it or not, he had a thimble on his finger. That's how I knew for sure it was the same guy this morning. When they ran up the rag, I cleared it with the stage manager and June. . . . she's star material, by the way. You watch that gal. She's a baby Merman." Dorfman took a long slurp of coffee. Burnproof lips. "That's pretty much what I told to Homicide a couple of hours ago. Now I've given you the jump on your tribe. How about that?"

Why the jump? Julie wondered. "When he arrived with his sketchbook, Mr. Dorfman, did he ask for you by name?"

Dorfman squeezed out a tight little smile, not pleasant. "I understand he asked for the boss. Julie, you'd make a hell of a detective. You should've been a cop."

"Maybe it's not too late yet," she said.

"That was a joke, sweetheart. Any more questions?"

"What was he doing in the arcade last night?"

"I suppose he was heading for the stage door. There's a lot of girls go out that way every night."

"Did he mingle after Thursday's rehearsal—say, to show off his sketches?"

Dorfman shrugged. "Ask the police. If he did, they're going to find it out, don't you think?"

She nodded and finished her orange juice. "Thanks, Mike."

"I wondered how long it was going to take you to call me Mike. Try and catch the matinee Saturday. Give Tony a ring early."

Traffic was jammed when she went out. She looked down the street to see what was holding it up. Her eyes glanced off the marquee of the Golden Theater. The Goldman brothers!

She stopped at the Goodkind and picked up a program. There had to be somebody in the cast she knew. The question she hadn't asked Dorfman because she knew she wouldn't get an answer: out of all the shows on Broadway, why did Ralph Abel choose *Remembering Amy?* Or were there others who had turned him down? Ask the police, Julie.

She bypassed the *Daily* office and went directly to Jacobs Books and Art Supplies. It was Jacobs the younger who had been friends with Ralph Abel. "Not real chums, you know, but we worked with the same model in life classes last spring. My dad gave him a discount here." The young Jacobs ran his hand through already scattered hair. "Why can't I believe it? A bullet in the back. So what else is new, right? Would you believe a schlock place like this and we've been broken into three times in a year?"

"I believe," Julie said. It was getting to be an article of faith.

"Whoever's going to do his obit," Jacobs said, "ought to know he got a major prize in the Midwest a year ago, the Ryerson Award. It was for a watercolor somebody bought and gave to the Art Institute in Chicago. That doesn't mean they're going to hang it, you understand, but they didn't turn it down. Some places like that would, you know."

Julie made a note of the prize. "Funny he didn't mention it when he was showing his pictures at my office."

"Well, maybe I know why and maybe I don't. The reason he came back to New York—he was here ten years ago and went home trashed. The reason he came back, the same gallery owner got in touch with him after the award and said she'd like to represent him again. . . ."

"Maude Sloan?" Julie cried, hardly able to believe it.

"That's the one. He came running. When I met him last winter he was skipping over the top of the world. He's done some great things, Mrs. Hayes, really good. You saw that collection. I asked him when he parked it here, what was he doing? Did his gallery know? They wouldn't like him peddling things. He was supposed to have a show this fall. Why muck it up? Because I need money now. When he came back and cashed your check, he bought a lot of basic stuff. I kept telling him, you've already got this, you've got that. Then it came through to me, he was so broke he'd been kicked out of where he was living and the crummy landlord must've kept his things on account."

"Could be," Julie said. There was no point to questioning Jacobs' version.

"And the bastard who shot him, what did he get?"

Julie laid her hand on that of Abel's friend and thanked him. In the rear of the shop, the elder Jacobs was framing pictures. Julie experienced an association that fled on the instant, leaving her with the infuriating certainty that whatever she'd lost was important. It wouldn't come back, so walking to the office, she thought about Maude Sloan.

By now Maude Sloan must be an even older older woman. Ralph had not mentioned her, and Julie had all but asked him the name of his gallery. A reasonable question: so why hadn't she asked it? For the simple reason she had already suspected it was Maude Sloan. She remembered having sat in a SoHo restaurant with Ralph the day she'd bought *Scarlet Night*. Over bowls of barley soup she had tried to bolster his self-esteem. It was floor-level. Maude and the art establishment had flattened him the day before. Yet, he had started over. And had he swum right into the same net? Lover again, discarded again? He had called himself a pussycat. And he was, person to person. But there was a rage and terror in those pictures as well as exuberance and mockery. She would give a lot, she thought, to see them again.

The current exhibit at the Sloan Gallery was flamboyant. It made Julie think of exotic birds flying all over the place. She wondered if the artist was a new flame of Mrs. Sloan's. Mrs. Sloan was at her desk behind the center partition. She started up when Julie appeared, seeming not to have heard her enter the gallery. The lines in the woman's face had diminished since last Julie had seen her, but instead of looking younger, she looked restored, elegant but not very healthy.

"I didn't mean to scare you, Mrs. Sloan. I don't know if you remember me, Julie Hayes."

"I know you, Julie Hayes. I've thought of you more than once in the last few days. I suspected Ralph might look you up again. Am I right?"

"He brought his portfolio to show me at the office."

"And did you buy something?"

"No. I paid him the hundred dollars I owed him on my last purchase. But I like the work he was doing this time around."

"That portfolio belongs to the gallery, you know."

A crazy conversation under the circumstances. "Mrs. Sloan," Julie said quietly, "you do know that Ralph Abel is dead?"

The woman slumped back in her chair. What color there had been in her face drained away, leaving a sorry mask of makeup. "Where? . . . When? Could no one have called me?"

"There was no identification on him, only the silver thimble." Julie had to believe she was shocked. She told her what she knew of the circumstances.

"Shot? Are you sure?"

An odd reaction. "In the back at very close range."

Mrs. Sloan moistened her lips, a need Julie associated with fear. The woman finally made a limp gesture of hospitality, motioning Julie into the chair at the side of her desk. "I've been waiting for him to come back."

"You were living together?" Julie suggested.

"He lived with me until . . . when? Saturday, a week ago Saturday. Then history repeated itself."

Julie waited through a heavy silence.

Sloan suddenly went on the offensive. "What are you doing here? You didn't come just to tell me my lover was dead."

"I came because he is dead. A good artist is dead and I want to know why."

"And do you think the reason may lie with me?"

"That hadn't occurred to me," Julie said.

"I would have died for him." That sounded more like melodrama than truth.

"The police are going to ask you if he had any enemies," Julie said.

"Let them ask."

If she was going to be shut off, she might as well ask the question outright: "What happened that Saturday?"

"Didn't he tell you?"

"Your name wasn't even mentioned."

"Thank you both. What happened, we went through his watercolors on the table there behind me. I set aside those I thought a good basis for an exhibit. He was mad to exhibit. We quarreled. He called me a philistine, grabbed the ones I had selected and bolted out of the gallery with them. That was the last I saw of him. Now are you satisfied, Mrs. Hayes?"

"I won't be until I know what happened to him."

"Were you in love with him?"

Julie shook her head. "In the paintings he left behind, are there scenes from theater? Not just street entertainers, I mean stage interiors, live shows."

"No. He didn't think his technique was up to that."

"Would you mind letting me look through them?"

Maude Sloan was a long time answering. Then: "Yes. I would mind."

"He wasn't working on a book of Broadway sketches?" Julie persisted.

"Not unless he took it up after he left me. Now will you have some compassion and take yourself out of here?" Julie was rounding the partition when Maude Sloan called after her, "Will I be able to claim his remains?"

"Ask the police," Julie said. For the life of her, she could not summon compassion on demand.

The nineteenth-century cobblestones were still the foundation over which today's traffic bumped and groaned. The buildings on Greene Street had in large number gone up in the early 1900s to house manufactory and commerce. Now they were a mix of galleries, boutiques and clubs. Julie stood a moment remembering the morning ten years before when she had come and found the Maude Sloan Gallery locked. A young girl in shaggy shorts had come up and pushed the buzzer that brought Ralph Abel to the door. That was the morning after his failed show.

Now she went along and made several tries before she got access to a phone book, where she looked up the name Goldman. In time she found two Goldmans, Ben and Sam, at the same address on Church Street. She could walk it.

Julie chose the carpentry shop ahead of the deli, two businesses these Goldmans ran side by side. They lived upstairs over the carpentry shop. She thought she remembered the rugged face of the man who came from the back of the shop. "I don't see him, but I'm a friend of his," he responded to her question about Ralph Abel.

"It's a long time," Julie said, "but I remember your waiting with your truck outside the Maude Sloan Gallery to help him move his paintings."

"Oh, my God. He's done it again!"

"Yes, but something worse, Mr. Goldman. He was killed last night."

Sam Goldman sat down on a barrel head and quietly rocked himself. Then he said, "Let's go next door and tell my brother."

In the late afternoon the deli custom was light. Julie told them what she knew of Abel's death.

"You see, Sam," his brother said, "we don't read the papers. So much violence, but you don't read about it, you don't escape it anyway."

The Goldman brothers wanted to be helpful, but they had seen very little of Ralph Abel since his return to New York. "It was like he was ashamed he'd gone back to that woman," Sam explained. "All the galleries in New York, uptown, downtown, what did he need her for? But did he listen to us?" He shook his head.

"You know who she should talk to," Ben said. "Sylvia Bellows."

"The kid with the nickname Silly?" Julie remembered. She was the one who had pushed the buzzer for her that ten years ago.

"That's the girl, but she's not a kid anymore. She's . . ."

"Something else," his brother put in. Their eyes and hands were eloquent. "She will take Ralphie's death very hard. You know, Ben, that boy was possessed . . . doomed."

Julie forestalled the melancholy ramble. She might come back for it later. "Does Sylvia live around here, Mr. Goldman?"

Ben nodded. "But where? I have a phone number for her. Sometimes she works here during the lunch hour. Without the luncheon business, we'd starve. Without us, she'd starve. An artist: in this neighborhood it's contagious."

"In this neighborhood it's the plague," Sam added.

Julie's memory of Sylvia had a lot in common with the little match girl in the illustrated *Hans Christian Andersen* of her childhood. In other words, she saw her as a street urchin. But the young woman who told her of her frustrated love for Ralph Abel was something quite different. She was the well-rounded personification of an artist's model. Renoir would have loved her. You could bet Maude Sloan would take a sour view of Ralph's having her for a student.

"She's a bitch and a bully, and if the police give her that goddamned thimble, I hope she sticks it in her mouth and chokes on it." Sylvia started to cry again. "Let me get a Kleenex or something." It gave Julie a chance to look around. A warehouse basement with a lot of street furniture: "Hippydom" was still alive. Without windows, she did her painting under two klieg lights that might have been picked up from a movie shoot.

She gave her nose a good blow and sat down again at the porcelain-topped table alongside Julie. She stretched and cocked her head to see what Julie had written. "You can't say I was a student of Ralph's. I mean he gave me some good points on space and color, but he gave me confidence, and that's even more important. I entered one of my things in a scholarship contest he told me about, and I might've won it—one of the judges told me I got to the finals. But Maude Sloan said no, and she was on the committee. She'd also put up a chunk of the money. That's where the power is, Julie, the money. When Ralph heard what she'd done—she really savaged me, I could've been killed a lot easier—but when he found out, that's when he split. He walked out on her.

"He came here that night, a week last Saturday. He didn't even have a razor or a toothbrush, just an armful of watercolors he grabbed from where they'd been sorting them out when he blew up at her. You know what she shouted after him? 'I own you, Ralph Abel, body and soul.' She's a devil, right? He sold his soul to the devil."

Julie diverted her. "Do you have those paintings, Sylvia?"

"No, but I think I know where they might be. Do you want a drink or anything? Ever hear of Thunderbird?"

"Yes," Julie said, "and no thanks."

"I don't even have a joint." She *was* a hippy, a throwback.

"Just talk," Julie said.

"We didn't either one of us have much money, just seventeen dollars between us. That was when we talked about you and how you'd promised him a hundred dollars, and how you'd wanted to see his sketches and never did."

"I know that part," Julie said.

"But you don't know: he said he was free of the bitch Maude, free at last, and what made him free was hate, not love. He said he hated her. You want to know? My heart sang, it danced to its own drumbeat. Here was the father, the brother, the teacher, the lover (I hoped) I'd never had. My mother was a hippy, she raised me on East 9th Street on marijuana and flowers, bean curd and meditation, and never a man who stayed longer than two weeks. Then we moved to Greene Street and I learned to sit yoga fashion on a garbage can and beg quarters from the beautiful

people. I'm sorry. What I'm trying to say is that Saturday
was the happiest day in my whole goddamn life."

"I got it," Julie said. The woman's eyes were aglow with
the recollection and tears.

"We decided to blow the seventeen bucks on the best
meal we could get for the money. Ralph knew of this
restaurant, the Piccolo Paradiso, in Little Italy. He had a
friend who hung out there. Ralph thought he might be
part owner. And he was there at his own table. As soon as
we sat down, he came over and put his arm around Ralph.
His name was Al. 'My mother calls me Alfredo. I'm Al.' "
Sylvia mimicked the speech. "He kissed my hand. 'Sylvia.
Who is Sylvia?' he says as though he'd made it up himself.
We were his guests. We were to take whatever the waiter
brought us, and he told the waiter I don't know what, but
there was a lot of *amore* in there. Julie, we ate like pigs. I
ate like a pig. Ralph sat there, tugging at that lock of hair
and grinning at me. I think he fell in love with me.
Almost, anyway. His friend, Al, pulled up a chair at our
table when we got to dessert and ordered it for us—that
creamy ice cream in a chocolate crust? Oh, God, it's a good
thing I'm below poverty level."

Julie grinned. "And you were such a skinny kid."

"Anyway, while we ate that gorgeous melt, Al wanted to
know all about the painting business. Ralph told him about
how I'd almost won a scholarship and what happened and
how he'd moved out on Maude, the whole mix. Could've
been he was a little drunk. But Al got so emotional about
it—'Honor, what does a man have if she takes away his
honor? You don't go near that woman ever again. You
cannot tame a shrew.' Honest to God, Julie, he said that.
Then he wanted to know where Ralph was going to stay.

" 'With me!' I said it before I even knew I was going to.
Ralph just winked at me."

" 'I got a room over the gym,' Al says. 'You're welcome to it. There you will see all kinds of human nature. You want to draw pictures, in the baths, in the gym, it's waiting for you.' Ralph thanked him and said first he wanted to get his things away from Maude's, and then they'd talk. See, he didn't want anybody to pay his way for him ever again.

"But this Al says, 'You want me to take care of things with Maude? No problem.' At that point I began to wonder. Is Alfredo gay or what? But that night Ralph told me how he'd met him. He was sketching over on Mulberry Street. He could do it—swish—so fast, almost like a camera, then afterwards he worked on it from memory . . . Julie, could it be a mistake and not him that's dead?"

Julie shook her head. "He was sketching on Mulberry Street," she prompted.

"Al was sitting outdoors having cappuccino with another guy. Both of them were leaning back, their faces in the sun. It was San Genarro week, with the pennants and flowers . . . All of a sudden they realized Ralph was sketching them. The one guy got up and went inside, but Al invited Ralph to have a cappuccino with him. Then he told him he wanted the drawing. Ralph didn't want to give it to him. It was rough, it wasn't finished. 'You make a friend for life . . . give it to me just like it is. It's very good. It's beautiful. How much you want for it?' Ralph just tore the page out of his sketchbook and gave it to him. Then he wanted Ralph to sign it. He wanted the name of the artist on it. So he did.

"I didn't meet Al till the restaurant. And that night Ralph did stay with me. It was . . ." Sylvia's eyes misted again. "It was good. We'd've been great together, but that was the last time I saw him. The next day he put his paintings in one of those cellophane bags you get from a dry cleaner. I can still see him standing there before he took off, twisting the thimble round on his finger. Are the police going to give that thimble to her?"

Julie shrugged. "Probably. It was on his person and she intends to claim his body."

"I want it." Miss Lonely Girl, Julie thought, wanting to live with a ghost. "What he said was, 'When I'm rich and famous, Silly, I'll come and get you and we'll go to Paris, France.' "

"And meanwhile?"

"I'm pretty sure he took Al up on the offer of the room over the gym. He always wanted to draw athletes from life."

"How about theater?"

"You mean right onstage? I don't think so. He liked the outdoors things, mimes, street musicians, etc."

Julie looked at her watch. It was almost seven. She hesitated and then plunged ahead with the invitation: "What do you say we walk over to the Piccolo Paradiso if you'll let me buy you dinner?"

"I don't know whether I hope Al is here or not," Sylvia said as they approached the restaurant. "I can't stand to see a man cry."

Piccolo Paradiso was a family restaurant with front and side door entrances, white tableclothes and napkins, wine served in pitchers, a lot of kids, a lot of noise, imitation Tiffany light fixtures.

"The trouble with kids," Sylvia said, "they don't sit still. Ralph told me if you want to sketch them, you've got to freeze them in your mind." She leaned toward Julie. "That's Al going into the kitchen. His table is the one near the kitchen door."

Julie felt relieved somehow not to meet Al just then. All she saw of him was a small head, a V-shaped back, and piled-up shoulders. "I think you'd have to freeze a chorus line, too," she said, "if you were going to sketch it. You do know, don't you, where Ralph was killed? Near the stage door of the Goodkind Theater."

"What was he doing there?"

"The number one question," Julie said. "He did some sketches there during rehearsal last Thursday—with the permission of the management. There has to be a connection."

"He couldn't ever afford to go to theater except when Bitch Sloan took him. Hey! What if Al introduced him to somebody who set it up?"

Out of the mouths of babes, Julie thought: it was an idea she'd been skirting since Al came into the scene. Who is Sylvia? and You can't tame a shrew. It sounded as though Al was working on a theatrical education.

The waiter came with the menus. He looked to have been around as long as the restaurant itself. He didn't have many smiles left. Sylvia asked him what he would recommend. "Anything I wouldn't recommend, lady, it wouldn't be on the menu."

When he'd taken their orders and headed for the kitchen, Sylvia said, "He didn't even recognize me, and it's the same waiter."

"A lot of people in and out," Julie said. Nevertheless, she felt he ought to have remembered. Sylvia was memorable. Julie's gut feeling was that the restaurant was well connected with the Mafia. How about Al? "Do you know Al's last name?"

"I don't. I don't think I ever heard it even. Should I ask the waiter?"

"No. Let's not do that. Let's just make out like we're a couple of tourists."

"From Keokuk, Iowa," Sylvia said.

Al did not appear again. The disappointment did not affect Sylvia's appetite, and when Julie went to pick up the check, she had to borrow five dollars from her. She decided against using a credit card, by which anyone in the house who wanted to could identify her.

She and Sylvia walked from the restaurant to the same Chemical bank where she had gone ten years ago to get the hundred dollars to pay Abel for *Scarlet Night*. Talk about déjà vu. A *New York Daily* truck went by and dropped a bundle of the early edition at a shop on Broadway. They bought a copy and went inside to the light to read it. The headline answered that number one question:

SLAIN ARTIST HAD DATE WITH ACTRESS

Ralph Abel had made a date the previous Thursday with Doreen Grey, a member of the *Remembering Amy* cast, to sketch her in costume in her dressing room after the Tuesday night performance. When Abel failed to show up, she thought he had been "putting her on" and went along with others of the company to Joey Fay's for supper. Like everybody else, she thought the huddled figure in the arcade was a drunk or "on something."

Comparatively little external bleeding had occurred, according to the medical examiner, because the bullet had not exited from the victim's body. It was removed during autopsy and turned over to ballistic experts.

Meanwhile, the artist's pen and paint box had been recovered from a trash bin at a 44th Street building site. His paint box, Julie noted, but not the sketchbook.

"Everything's so goddamned tidy," Sylvia said. "You'd think they were talking about a clock or a word processor. He was a human being!" She was about to cry again.

Julie gave her a hug and offered to drop her home in a cab. Sylvia declined and strode out on her own, calling thanks for the meal over her shoulder. Julie hailed a cab. She knew what Sylvia meant, but instead of feeling primed for tears herself, she felt drained of them, and she had not wept a drop.

It was after ten when she got home. Somewhere during the long day, her own caring anger over Ralph Abel's murder had been muted by the collecting of information that might or might not fit into a deadly collage. She was almost an hour sorting out the phone calls picked up by the answering service since morning. The usual hype materials that went into the care and feeding of a gossip columnist. Nothing pertained to Abel's death. She experienced an almost overpowering urge to let the whole thing go. What were the police for anyway? And by what colossal arrogance did she pit herself against them? Come on, Julie, the truth: You're scared. Never mind who is Sylvia. Who is Al?

She dug out the playbill of *Remembering Amy* from her carryall. There were almost as many producers listed in the credits as there were players. A lot of money had come together for the production, and if some of it was unwashed, most of the clean contributors wouldn't know it. The *Who's Who in the Production* revealed that Michael Dorfman, company manager of *Remembering Amy*, was also president of Investors Alert, one of the coproducers. How to get at the information as to whether a guy named "Al" was among Investors Alert was more than she could cope with at that hour.

She was finishing her *items* for the column, a pretty humdrum lot, she felt, when Lieutenant Marks phoned her in the morning and asked what she could tell him about Michael Dorfman. "I suppose what I'm asking is whether he's the sort of man who would take in a scruffy-looking character off the street who happened to have a sketchbook under his arm, and let him doodle his way through a rehearsal of one of the hottest shows on Broadway."

"Ralph Abel was not a doodler," Julie said, "but I see your point. I've been asking myself the same question, and the answer is no. I don't think Ralph went in cold to see him. He'd be too shy, for one thing. I think somebody set it up ahead of time."

"And thereby set the death trap for your artist friend," Marks said. "Let's talk. Your place or my place? Julie, I'm kidding! Tell me when and I'll send a car."

In his office, the phone cut off, Julie consulted her notes and put on record her interviews with Dorfman, Jacobs, Maude Sloan, the Goldman brothers and Sylvia.

"She's the gold mine, isn't she?" Marks said. Then, "Herrick's men got to Maude Sloan last night. They'll catch up with you yet."

Very playful, Julie thought.

Marks sat a moment thinking. "Let's do another take on Sylvia, if you don't mind, and see if anything more comes up."

Something more did come up. She remembered when Abel was showing her his paintings, her particular feeling about the couple in the bar frozen by the gaze of the woman looking in at them, the intensity of it. She connected it now with Al when he discovered Abel was sketching him and another man.

Marks agreed that she might have something. "Let's see who's on duty that knows the mob." He went out to the desk. When he returned he took the possibility further. "Let's say the bird in flight didn't want to have his picture drawn. Or maybe Al Whoever didn't want to be partnered in a sketch with him. You ought to know that mobsters are camera-shy. Have you ever seen a picture or painting of Sweets Romano?''

The name had to come up, Julie thought. But she had not ever seen a likeness of him, and what art collector on Romano's scale would not have his own portrait in his collection?

Detective Herrick and another man, Detective John Reilly, came in, Reilly carrying a huge hasp of *Wanted* flyers. Marks pointed to the hasp, grinning. "See what I mean about camera-shy?''

He set aside the hasp and reconstructed from Julie's statement: "Name is Al: he frequents a restaurant on Mulberry Street called Piccolo Paradiso. He owns or runs an athletic club . . . Julie?''

"He probably fancies himself a benefactor of the arts,'' she carried forward. "A hunch says he may be a hidden investor in the musical *Remembering Amy* . . .''

"We could get a court order and see their books for investors,'' Marks said, "but we're on pretty thin grounds at this point.''

Reilly, who looked like Julie's notion of a boxer, a face Abel might have loved to sketch, rubbed a bumpy chin with the back of his hand. "I think I've got him for you, sir,'' he said quietly. "Gentleman Al Savoldi. But I've got to tell you, the only thing he ever did time for was contempt: he refused to testify against his friends. Big deal: honor. But without him the case went down the drain. I'd call him a low-level mafioso. He runs errands for the big boys and probably does a lot of laundry.''

"Is he a killer?'' Marks wanted to know.

"I wouldn't say so, but he sure as hell has friends in the business. Nominally he runs the Bowery Boys Athletic

Club, but we're pretty sure he's a front for Big Red
Marielo, who's one of our top 'wanted.' " He tapped the
hasp. "He *is* a killer."

"Could he be the second man in the sketch?" Julie
addressed her question to Marks.

Marks asked Reilly, "Do you have a mug shot of him?"

"How many do you want?"

When Reilly left them, Marks said to Herrick: "Why
don't you go back to the company manager and try to
break down his story of how Abel got to him?"

"Can I use the name Al Savoldi on him?"

"That's what we got it for," Marks snapped. Afterwards
he said to Julie: "If we break Dorfman, then we can move
on Savoldi. You have to believe if he *is* guilty, he has an
alibi as tight as a bear trap."

"I'd give a lot to see those sketches again Ralph brought
to my office, and if Ralph was staying in that athletic club,
that's where they are unless they've been destroyed."

Marks stared at her, anger flaring up in his eyes. "If
you're thinking of going after them, don't. You have
contributed greatly, but enough, Mrs. Hayes."

Julie was on her way, her own temper building. "It was
nice working with you, Lieutenant."

"Julie—hold it!" And when she looked back: "Don't you
realize what the name Julie Hayes could mean to him?
Sweets Romano. And let me tell you, Gentleman Al would
be a hell of a lot more scared of him right now than of the
New York Police Department. Don't screw us up, Julie."

Julie saluted him and walked out. If she had used her
credit card at the restaurant the night before, the Romano
jinx would already have done its work.

When Maude Sloan opened the gallery at one P.M., Julie
was waiting for her. Maude looked as though she hadn't

had much sleep, and as soon as she put her purse down, she got out a cigarette. A large NO SMOKING sign hung on the back wall.

"You don't give up easily, do you?" She lit the cigarette. "What now?"

"The same old thing: please let me see the paintings or sketches Ralph didn't run away with. I feel sure the answer to his death is in the painting . . . if I could just ask the right question. Did he ever paint the same scene twice?"

"Most artists do—some many times."

"But from memory?"

"He did often work from memory," Maude said slowly. Her whole body seemed to go taut.

"Please," Julie said, for she felt she was close. "I do believe you loved him. So you have to care what happened to him. Yes?"

Maude nodded and seemed unable to stop nodding. She squashed out the cigarette.

"During the San Genarro festival," Julie said, "he did a sketch of two men outside a coffee shop. Did you ever see it?"

"Yes."

"Could I see it now?"

"I don't have it. A man claiming to be a friend of Ralph's came looking for him Saturday night—a week after Ralph left. I thought when he came in the door he looked like Mafia. My first thought was that now they were moving in on the art galleries, a protection racket. He kept saying what a nice place I had, expensive fixtures, some of the pictures must be valuable. When I said that Ralph wasn't with the gallery anymore, he said he thought he might have stopped back. 'I am supposed to pick up the paintings for him he left with you, Mrs. Sloan.' It was late, there was no one in the gallery. I was frightened. And then I remembered where I'd seen him before and why I thought he was a gangster. I got out the remaining pictures. When I said they were all I had, it was a foolish thing to say because it made him suspicious. Something in the way he moved in behind me, I thought he was going to attack me." She paused and lit another cigarette. "I moved away to where I could see him. He might have had a gun. I didn't see it. 'I know you,' I said. 'No, you don't. I'm not famous,' he said. I turned the pictures one by one until we came to the men outside the coffee shop. He looked at it and then at me as though he could not believe it. All he said was, 'I'll take it.' And I said, 'Take them all,' which is just what he did."

Al would have seen the duplicate sketch as betrayal, Julie thought. "Things begin to make sense," she said.

"I didn't know there was an earlier version," Maude said. "So you asked the right question after all."

The police would have a lot more of them. Julie had just one: "Was it just a sketch or was it a watercolor?"

"A watercolor. Too garish. The other man's face was fire truck red."

Barley soup: the second bowl in ten years. But what a sentimental journey! Julie tried to work out from her notebook a timetable for Ralph's last days. A sticking point with the police was why the killer would choose so public a place as the arcade if the murder was premeditated: the locale was the big argument for random violence. But if Al was looking for him when he went to the Sloan Gallery on Saturday, he might still have been looking for him Tuesday night, and this time with deadly intent. Of course: they were still friends when Dorfman, on Al's request(?), allowed Ralph to sketch *Remembering Amy*.

Ralph might well have told his mentor he had a date with Doreen Grey to add a dressing room scene. The theater could have been the only place Al knew to look for him by then. Julie noted in the margin: the pen and paint box turned up in the refuse bin, but not the sketchbook.

So, assuming Ralph kept in touch with Al for most of the week after he'd left Maude Sloan, when did he break away, why, and where did he go? Another question: Where did he get the case, the portfolio, a big, old-fashioned envelopelike carrier with ties like shoestrings? When he'd left Sylvia he was carrying the paintings in a cellophane garment bag.

A thrift shop? St. James-on-Hudson? Where he had bought the seaman's pea jacket.

She was a very tall woman, her grey hair stacked loosely on the top of her head. If Julie had guessed a profession for her, it would have been poet, or, on hearing her voice, an Irish radical, the likes of whom she knew achingly well. She was the keeper of the day at the thrift shop run for the benefit of St. James-on-Hudson.

"I didn't know his name, I hadn't heard it before, but I loved his pictures. There used to be fellas like him in Dublin. They'd be wanting to sell you a poem or a song, and as often as not it'd turn out you were buying Thomas More, or worse, Robbie Burns.

"You'll know he was as poor as a church mouse, and with all that talent. I gave him the case for his things. It was around here for years. What I took out of it were some cuttings of Greek sculpture from the year 1907. He showed me the paintings, one by one, and some sketches he'd done freehand . . ."

"When was this?" Julie asked.

"Would it be Monday week, the first time? It would, for

I'd washed my hair on Sunday and it's always wild the next day. He even did a quick drawing of me, a few strokes, and there I was more like me than myself. Then he put a three-cornered hat on my head and I looked like Marianne Moore. Do you know who she was?"

"The poet," Julie said, and grinned.

"He was going to do something that week he had never done before. He had permission to sketch a live show on Broadway. It was my suggestion to him that what he should be doing was a book. He could call it *Manhattan, Morning, Noon, and Night,* something catchy. I told him to find somebody to collaborate with, someone to write the lyrics. He asked me if I knew a columnist on *The New York Daily* by the name of Julie Hayes. I did, and of course, that's how I recognized your name when you came in."

"He came to see me the next day," Julie said. "But he didn't mention a book at all."

"He might have been waiting to get the theater sketches in there, don't you think?"

Julie nodded.

"He came back on Saturday last in the morning. We put a suit of clothes on him from the rack in the other room. I think he'd been out in the cold all night. The notion came to me he was on the run—that's something an Irish person knows in their bones. I suppose anyone who comes from an occupied country does. He was carrying the portfolio with him, but it was all askew. One of the strings had broken. I told him he could leave it here. I'd take good care of it for him. And very gently, not to hurt his pride, I told him about the men's shelter run by St. James if ever he needed a place to stay. Nothing fancy, but safe and clean. 'Safe!' he almost laughed. Or cried. Before he went out he told me he wanted to give me something for all my kindness. It was the silver thimble, and I wish now I'd taken it, but I knew it was his bit of luck to carry with him, and wasn't it there to identify him when nothing else was left, poor man!"

"Do you still have the portfolio?" Julie wanted to know.

"I do. I'm sure he'd want you to have it . . ."

Julie stopped her. "That's for the police or somebody else to decide. Just keep it safe for now."

Her urgency to see it was quite spent.

On November 3rd the police of three different agencies raided the Bowery Boys Athletic Club. They confiscated a large sum of money, presumably the collections on illegal gambling. But their real catch was "Big Red" Marielo, one of the FBI's most wanted persons. He'd been hiding out in a luxury suite at the back of the club. Also taken into custody was Al Savoldi, known as Gentleman Al, now being held under suspicion of murder in the death of the artist Ralph Abel.

A body is found . . . a beautiful reporter for The New York Times, *discovered lying on the floor of her East Side apartment, a bullet in her heart. And to solve the crime means looking into the hearts of others.*

Lucy Freeman

The Case on Cloud Nine

In his office high above Central Park South, Dr. William Ames, prominent New York psychoanalyst, turned on the radio to listen to the news on Channel 4 as he waited for his next patient.

Suddenly he heard the name "Kate Locke." Then the words: "Her body was discovered fully dressed in the living room of her penthouse by the elevator man last night at nine P.M. He saw the front door was open, walked in and found her lying on the floor. The coroner said she had been murdered about two hours before. The burglar shot her once in the heart."

"Oh, my God!" Dr. Ames said the words aloud. His next thought was of Thomas Duncan, Kate's fiancé, whom he expected any moment for his regular nine A.M. appointment. He wondered if Duncan would show up. He would certainly need the session to speak of his deep loss, his equally deep rage, his horror.

He walked to the window and looked out at the bare trees of early December. He thought of how Duncan had become a patient in a most unusual way. One evening Dr. Ames received a telephone call from a former patient, Judge Philip Winters, who asked if he would take into therapy a man who owned the well-known Sierra restaurant in mid-Manhattan. The man had been brought before him for failure to declare $200,000 in profits from an illegal gambling den in his restaurant. When Duncan agreed to pay what he owed, the judge also ruled he had the choice of going to prison for five years or visiting a psychoanalyst. The judge suggested he see Dr. Ames, and so far Duncan had not missed a session, five times a week, for eight months.

Dr. Ames liked Duncan, a tall, slim man of thirty-nine. His face had a rangy quality, a Manhattan version of Gary Cooper. Duncan at first seemed startled to find his psychoanalyst had no beard, no foreign accent, spoke perfect English. Soon Duncan was lying on the green leather couch, slowly starting to talk of his inner and outer life.

Within two months he revealed he had fallen in love with Kate Locke, who had covered his trial. She had called him for a special interview focusing on a man who chose psychoanalysis over prison. He had taken her to dinner, to Broadway plays, to baseball games at Shea Stadium, they fell in love, planned to marry the first of the new year. He had given her an emerald engagement ring bought at Tiffany's, a ring she said she would never remove. It would be the first marriage for both, though Kate had confessed to a year's relationship with James Marshall, the newspaper's city political reporter.

Duncan had also told Dr. Ames that Jess Tracy, his partner at the Sierra, had risked his own life to save Duncan's in Vietnam when he was shot in the stomach. They decided then, if they got home alive, to start a supper club in Manhattan. Duncan had studied architecture in college, Tracy was a certified public accountant, and they believed they would make a good team. Duncan had told Dr. Ames, "When the government caught up with us, the least I could do was to take the rap. Repay the man who saved my life."

Dr. Ames walked back to his desk, looked at his watch; it was nine-fifteen. Undoubtedly Duncan would not show up. But suddenly his patient walked in the door. There were deep circles under his earnest brown eyes, his face was unshaven, paler than usual. He looked at Dr. Ames, asked grimly, "You know about it?"

"I'm so sorry, Mr. Duncan. It's a tragic time for you." Dr. Ames' voice held deep sympathy.

Duncan took out a handkerchief, blew his nose. Then he said, "I've shed enough tears to float the Empire State Building."

"You can sit in the chair today if it's easier to talk," Dr. Ames suggested.

But Duncan headed for the couch, saying , "I'm used to this by now," and threw himself on it. He lay silent several moments, then said, his voice breaking, "The only thing the burglar, or whoever killed Kate, took was the emerald ring I gave her. She only wore it two weeks. It was her engagement present."

"Do you have any idea who might have killed her?" Dr. Ames asked. "Did she have enemies?"

"Just the Mafia. She was writing a series about them that was to appear the first of the year." He added, "She told me the Mafia bosses were furious because she delved so deeply into their shady ways. But the police, according to this morning's paper, say it was a burglar. They said there were three murders in that neighborhood in the last few months."

Knowing he was not being professional but wanting Duncan to consider all possibilities, Dr. Ames said, "That reporter, James Marshall, was also furious at Kate for ditching him for you, wasn't he?"

"I suppose he might have killed her and made it look like a burglary," Duncan said.

"It *is* suspicious that only her engagement ring was stolen," Dr. Ames agreed. "He might have seized it out of revenge."

"I want to help catch the killer, not just sit quietly on the sidelines," Duncan said.

Dr. Ames suggested, "May I ask you to sit quietly just for now?"

"Why?" Torment in his voice.

Dr. Ames explained, "Not long ago I became friends with a detective who is probably handling this murder because Kate's apartment lies in his precinct. I helped him solve a case by interpreting the last dream of a patient of mine who was murdered. The dream held clues that expressed his fear of a certain person."

Then thoughtfully, "I'd like to ask Detective Jack Lonegan his thoughts about Kate's death. He's a sensitive man who respects psychoanalysis."

Duncan said gratefully, "Thanks, Dr. Ames. I never expected help from you on the murder of the first woman I loved with all my heart. I'll wait and do nothing."

He fell into a long silence. Dr. Ames said gently, "Cry all you want. That's why we have tears. Get the feelings out."

Before lunch Dr. Ames called the Nineteenth Precinct on East Sixty-seventh Street. He even remembered the number; he had dialed it several times on the "dream" case. Lonegan had since asked him to team up on other murders, but Dr. Ames firmly declined, though he liked and respected Lonegan and even derived a certain satisfaction from "sleuthing."

A masculine voice announced, "Nineteenth Precinct." Dr. Ames asked, "May I speak to detective Jack Lonegan?"

The voice replied, "I'll connect you with the Squad." The detective squad.

Then Dr. Ames heard the deep, casual voice he knew well say, "Lieutenant Lonegan."

"Jack, this is Bill Ames. How are you?"

"Well! What a pleasant surprise, Doc." He sounded delighted. "I'm usually the one to call you out of the blue."

"It's a reversal, Jack. This time I need your help."

"Another patient murdered?" Excitedly.

"No. That's rare. It's the murder last night of a well-known young woman reporter in your precinct, Kate Locke. She was about to marry a patient of mine."

"I'm working on the case, Doc." Lonegan sounded almost exuberant as he asked, "Will you help me like before?"

"I might try, Jack. You know I prefer not to, but once in a while I give in. What can you tell me?"

"What can *you* tell me? We don't know a thing yet. Does your patient have any clues?"

"He thinks it might be a member of the Mafia. She was getting inside information for an important series."

"Hey, Doc, that's a good tip!" Gratitude in his voice. "I don't buy the burglar story. I rarely do. More often it's someone in the family who has nursed a grudge." Silence, then, "Any other suspects?"

"There's a reporter at the paper who was furious at her for jilting him. They had been lovers for almost a year."

"Will you give me his name, Doc?"

"James Marshall. He works in the city room of *The New York Times*."

Lonegan asked, "What about the guy she was planning to marry? Your patient?"

Dr. Ames was silent; he had not thought of Duncan as a killer. He said, "Jack, I don't believe he could harm a hair of Kate's beautiful blond head. He was deeply in love with her."

Lonegan said, "Hey, Doc, I have an idea. Will you do what you did for us last time we worked together? Interview these two guys you suspect?"

"The *Times* reporter would be easy. But what about the Mafia? Where would I start finding a killer in that mob?"

"We'll give you a name," Lonegan said. "We know the top hit men. There's one in particular we've been trailing in the area where Miss Locke was murdered. I'll call back after I talk to the chief and get the okay."

"Any time after four, Jack. I take a half-hour break then."

"To drink coffee, I'll bet. I know you love good coffee." He added quickly, "Besides scotch."

"You guessed it. I'll wait for your call."

As Dr. Ames hung up, he thought of Lonegan's suggestion that Duncan might have murdered Kate. But if he, as a psychoanalyst, was any judge of character, Duncan would never murder anyone, unless you called killing a Vietnamese in wartime murder.

Promptly at four, just as his patient walked out of the office, Dr. Ames heard the phone ring. He settled at his desk, took up pen and pad to note Lonegan's suggestions, raised the phone to his ear.

"Ready, Doc?" Lonegan's voice.

"Pen poised and waiting, Jack."

"Anthony Lulla is the chief hit man for the Mafia. One of our undercover agents said Lulla had been given orders to stalk Kate. Lulla tells us over the phone he's got an alibi. We told him we'd book him unless he saw you."

"You really want me to interview a hit man?" Dr. Ames was not sure how he felt about this.

"Something new for you, eh, Doc?" A laugh.

"I never particularly wanted to meet one." Sarcastically.

"They look and act just like you and me. It's only inside they're more vicious." Lonegan chuckled again. "You've led a sheltered life."

Until Thomas Duncan walked into my office, Dr. Ames thought, and now I'm mixed up with gamblers, crooks, lady reporters who get shot and hit men.

Lonegan was saying, "Number two is James Marshall, the political reporter. He has no alibi. Says he was walking home to his apartment in Greenwich Village at the time Miss Locke was shot. But he can't produce a witness."

Dr. Ames sighed. Once again he was caught in another unusual exploration for a murderer. "I could cancel patients for the afternoon the day after tomorrow." This would be enough notice for his patients.

"That would be great, Doc," Lonegan said. "We're way ahead now, knowing you'll help. Your first interview day after tomorrow will be with Anthony Lulla. I'll make it near your office. Right in front of the bears at the zoo."

"My favorite spot in the city!" Sarcasm again.

"Probably Lulla's too," Lonegan chortled. "Nothing like a big, furry bear to get the fear muscles going. We'll tell Lulla you'll be there at three. When you're finished, go to the third floor of the *Times* building at Forty-third Street just west of Seventh Avenue and ask for James Marshall. We'll tell him to reserve time for you then."

Dr. Ames sighed. "Yes, sir, General Lonegan. I'll report

back to you at once. As soon as I've finished both interviews."

"I'll wait even if it's midnight," Lonegan said. "Waiting eagerly. Like last time. Come up with another winner, Doc."

"I can't promise a thing," Dr. Ames said, "but I will try to find some clues."

Wednesday was warm for December; the sun felt invigorating as Dr. Ames, wearing his black wool coat, gray leather gloves, no hat, walked toward the zoo. He rounded the small lake in which floated a large red modernistic wooden sculpture, anchored to the bottom. The lake served as home for the swans and ducks that swam nonchalantly amidst pop bottles, soggy newspapers, chewing gum wrappers.

He wondered what kind of man could brutally mark for murder, and coldly carry out the execution of, another human being purely for profit. It had to be a man without a conscience, who had never developed a sense of right and wrong. From Adam and Eve on, man struggled to control murderous impulses dangerous to himself and others. The Ten Commandments expressed man's first great attempt to become civilized, followed by the teachings of Christianity.

The zoo was deserted. Dr. Ames walked past the sea lions splashing in the circular pool, toward the cage that held two white polar bears. In front of it stood a short, stolid man in a gray woolen coat, gray cap, no gloves. He jerked his head nervously first to the right, then left, as though expecting someone from either direction.

Dr. Ames walked up to the man, asked, "Are you Anthony Lulla?"

The man stared at him without expression, then mut-

tered, "You the shrink?" His florid face gave no sign of
emotion. A walking zombie, Dr. Ames thought, and why
not? He needed to keep intense murderous impulses
repressed, yet ready for unleashing on demand—the
going price of a hit.

"Shall we find a quiet bench?" Dr. Ames suggested. "I
don't think it's too cold to sit for a few minutes."

"Yeah," Lulla grunted. "Let's go hunt a bench."

Even the search for a bench, Dr. Ames realized, was
graphically stated in terms of stalking a victim.

With Lulla scuffling silently by his side, Dr. Ames
retraced his route past the sea lions, back to the small lake.
Lulla seemed anxious, as if he wanted to get a painful
moment over as quickly as possible. He could without a
qualm kill an utter stranger who had done him no harm,
but his anxiety was aroused at the thought of being asked
about a hit.

They found an empty bench facing the lake and sat side
by side in the comfort of the late afternoon sun. Lulla took
out a pack of cigarettes, offered it to Dr. Ames. He said,
"No thank you." He could not bring himself to accept a
cigarette from a hit man.

"Let's get something straight," Lulla announced
hoarsely. "I didn't go into that murdered dame's apartment. Nobody gave me an order to shoot anybody. First I
hear of her is when the pigs come to my house and accuse
me."

Gangsters were selfish, greedy, murderous children,
Dr. Ames thought. Give me what I want or I will kill you.
They were sadistic, temper-tantrum-ridden infants who
refused to grow up and sooner or later paid for it, either in
prison or violent death from rival mobsters. You could sell
your soul to childhood only so long.

Feeling that it was futile, but determined to pursue the

interview for Lonegan's sake, Dr. Ames asked, "You're sure you never saw Kate Locke?"

The hoarse voice said, "I couldn't tell you if the broad was tall or short, blond or brunette, flat-chested or with big boobs." Then, in anger, "The pigs can't hold me, they got no proof. They're always trying to pin killings on me."

"I'm not interested in pinning any killings on you, Mr. Lulla. I only want to know the truth. Whether you shot Kate Locke in the heart." Dr. Ames fastened his blue eyes, as steely as he could make them, on the hit man's small hazel orbs. Dr. Ames recognized the meaning of "beady eyes" as he outstared Lulla. He hoped his own eyes held a piercing, bold look that demanded truth.

Lulla said gruffly, "I swear on my wife's Bible I didn't shoot that broad. I'm a very religious man."

Dr. Ames was quick to give up. Even the world's first family had its hit man, he thought. There was simply no way he could tell whether Anthony Lulla killed Kate Locke. He could only report to Lonegan that he thought Lulla capable of the murder, a psychopath, a man without conscience, who probably could kill strangers on command.

Dr. Ames started to feel cold, stood up, said, "I guess that's it."

Lulla jumped to his feet, sighed in relief, flung his cigarette to the ground.

Tongue in cheek, Dr. Ames said, "It's been a pleasure to meet you."

Lulla tossed him a look of sheer disbelief, said, "Likewise," and nervously shot away in the direction of the polar bears.

Dr. Ames walked swiftly to Fifth Avenue, caught a taxi downtown, got off at Forty-third Street and Broadway and made his way the half block westward to the solid structure that was *The New York Times*. The guard at the entrance told him to take the elevator to the third floor; there another guard asked courteously, "May I help you?"

"James Marshall expects me. The name is Dr. William Ames."

The guard spoke into a telephone. Two minutes later a man in his late thirties, with blond hair, brown eyes and an intense look on his rather cherubic face, strode through a door into the reception room. The guard nodded at Dr. Ames. The man walked over to him, held out his hand, said warmly, "Welcome to *The New York Times*, Dr. Ames. Lieutenant Lonegan told me all about you. It's a pleasure to meet a psychoanalyst for a change instead of a politician."

Marshall's engaging manner, Dr. Ames had to admit, was a welcome contrast to Lulla's catatonia. Marshall led him into an adjacent small room whose walls were lined with photographs of New York in the late nineteenth century. Dr. Ames sat in one corner of a green vinyl couch, Marshall in the other.

Dr. Ames thought Marshall looked like an alert, lively man who would be relentless in the pursuit of news. He seemed a bit nervous, but not in the same way as Lulla. Marshall cloaked his nervousness with charm, a charm he thrust at you as though hoping to trap you into revealing yourself without exposing anything of himself. A necessary quality for a reporter.

"Lieutenant Lonegan asked me to tell you everything I know," Marshall said. "I still can't get over the horror of Kate's death. I can't believe anyone on earth would want to kill her. She was a warm, lovely, brilliant woman and a close friend of mine."

He bit his lips, went on, "I don't think it was the Mafia. They have the reputation of never harming a reporter.

Only squealers or traitors within. But I suppose there's always the exception. Kate *was* hitting a lot of Mafia nerve centers."

Dr. Ames asked, "When did you first meet Miss Locke?"

"The day she walked into the city room about three years ago. We started seeing each other regularly last year. My marriage was one of those hot college affairs that soon fizzled. I stayed with Eve because of our ten-year-old son." A pause, then, "I tried to fall out of love with Kate but found myself more and more entrenched. I liked her as a human being, especially her sense of humor."

"Did you plan to marry her?"

"Yes. But Eve kept stalling on the divorce." He added thoughtfully, "I don't want to mislead you, Dr. Ames. Kate believed I never would leave my wife. She told me that over and over."

He again bit his lips, said, "Then about half a year ago she said she was in love with a man who was single and wanted to marry her. From then on she wouldn't even see me for a drink. She insisted our affair was over. She said we couldn't build happiness on the ashes of my marriage."

"Did you accept her decision?"

"I don't accept defeat." Contemptuously. "Who does? Especially in love."

Dr. Ames said quietly, "The person who realizes the situation is untenable or unrealistic."

"I thought Kate and I had something special going. We shared the excitement of the newspaper game. We were great sexual partners, without even trying."

"How determined were you to hold on to her?"

For the first time Marshall glared at his questioner. "I wouldn't try to kill her, if that's what you mean. I loved her very much, but I wouldn't take her life if she left me for another man." He added, "Once I asked how she could fall in love with a gangster. She insisted he was not a gangster, that he once ran a small gambling casino with his partner but that was all."

Dr. Ames waited, and Marshall went on: "I didn't buy that. I told her he probably had to pay off the cops and the Mafia. And that he openly cheated the government. Kate said, 'Don't we all on April fifteenth?' "

Dr. Ames stood up. He thought Marshall might be a possible suspect, though, as with Lulla, he did not have one iota of proof. He shook hands, said, "Thank you, Mr. Marshall. You've been generous with your time. I know you have deadlines to meet."

As the elevator carried him downward, Dr. Ames wondered if Marshall was capable of a murderous fury, if he could destroy the woman he loved rather than let anyone else possess her, in spite of his denial.

Dr. Ames decided to walk the sixteen blocks to his apartment. He needed time to think. Whoever Kate's killer, whether Lulla, Marshall, a burglar or someone else, he carried murderous feelings from childhood, where the intense wish to kill originates. Feelings so intense that eventually he had to spew them on others. There was obviously nobody so prone to murder as a hit man who killed on assignment.

As he walked slowly northward, Dr. Ames thought of the third possible killer, one Lonegan had mentioned—his patient. Dr. Ames wondered if Kate's murderer and Duncan were somehow intertwined. Duncan was not a man you would suspect of killing anyone. But in dealing with the mysteries of the mind, there was no fantasy whose power you could rule out. The wildest, weirdest, most savage wishes exist in complete abandon within the depths of everyone's mind, yoked only by that fragile, intangible thing called conscience.

Dr. Ames had almost reached the front door of the twenty-five-floor building that held his office. He wondered what he could tell Lonegan after the two interviews. He could only say Lulla and Marshall were possible suspects, though he had not a word of proof. Then a sudden thought struck him: there *was* another person who might be able to tell him more about Duncan. Jess Tracy, Duncan's partner, knew him in war, in friendship, in business. Tracy had also met Kate several times, as Duncan had told him.

He looked at his watch; it was five-thirty, a good time to catch Tracy at his restaurant only five blocks east. Duncan had often invited him to stop in, with or without notice. Dr. Ames knew Tracy would be there. It was before the evening rush and Tracy could spare a few minutes to chat. Dr. Ames wanted Tracy's full attention and spontaneous reactions. He turned from the door of his office building, walked east.

In ten minutes Dr. Ames arrived at the dark blue canopy whose silver letters spelled "Sierra." He nodded to the doorman, walked into the wide, empty lobby, then faced a gigantic dining room with walls of a subtle purple. He looked up, saw glittering chandeliers over every fifth table. The two owners had chosen this site carefully, torn apart the first floor of an old private house that Duncan, as architect, had selected.

Dr. Ames walked through a door to the left, into a large room marked "office." A stocky man was seated at a white desk, speaking into the telephone. He looked up, saw Dr. Ames, motioned him to enter. He put his hand over the receiver, called out, "I'll be finished in a minute."

Dr. Ames lowered himself into a white leather chair opposite the white desk. One paneled wall held a print, three feet square, of a Spanish galleon. Brown file cabinets hid a second paneled wall.

Tracy said "Good-bye" into the telephone, hung up, rose to his feet, put out his hand, asked, "What can I do for you?"

"I'm Dr. William Ames, Mr. Duncan's psychoanalyst," he said. "I've wanted to meet you for a long time. I know you saved Mr. Duncan's life in a very brave manner in Vietnam."

Tracy said, "Tom has told me all about you, of course, Dr. Ames. Welcome to the Sierra's inner sanctum." His deep voice was warm. "How can I help you?"

"I'd like to ask a few questions that relate to Mr. Duncan, if you don't mind."

Tracy sat down in his chair, said, "Fire away."

Dr. Ames thought Tracy's rather stalwart face held a mixture of arrogance, sadness and a certain vulnerability. He showed that overeffusiveness that masks enmity. He also looked as if he could be a war hero, and if a movie were made about his heroic rescuing of Duncan, no Cliff Robertson would be needed, Tracy could play himself. Dr. Ames guessed Tracy was about an inch shorter than Duncan's six feet and about ten pounds overweight.

Dr. Ames asked the question he had long wondered about. "Since you and Mr. Duncan were equally to blame for breaking the law on gambling, why didn't you share the sentence?"

"Tom wouldn't let me. He insisted that since I risked my life to save his, he owed me." His brown eyes had a bland look.

"Did you object?"

He shrugged his shoulders. "I sure did, but Tom convinced me it was only fair he take the blame. He said I had a wife and two daughters and shouldn't be tainted. Luckily he didn't land in prison, which made me feel better."

Dr. Ames asked, "Where did you grow up?"

Tracy looked uncomfortable for the first time, shifted around in his chair. Then he said reluctantly, "In a charity dump called The Allerton Orphanage just outside of Philly. I wasn't always an orphan; I had a father until I was nine. My mother died when I was born, and my father took care of me until he lost his job at the post office. Then he began to drink heavily. He got very sick and the welfare people took me away from him. I didn't want to go. I put up a good fight."

Dr. Ames pictured Tracy as a small boy standing defiantly by his father's side, waging a desperate battle against being taken away from the one person in the world left for him to love. No matter how excellent the care at the orphanage, it could never take the place of the love of a parent, no matter how ambivalent that love, how tinged with anger. He thought of William James's line, "The greatest terror of a child's life is solitude."

Dr. Ames asked, "What did you think of Kate Locke's brutal death?"

There was silence; Tracy's geniality seemed to slip for a moment as his face distorted into a grimace that was a mixture of anger and pain, as though he recalled being taken from his father forever. Then he said bitterly, "Just like war. Alive one minute. Snuffed out the next."

Dr. Ames stood up, said, "Thank you very much, Mr. Tracy. I wanted to meet you and get a sense of the relationship between you and Mr. Duncan."

"Stop in for dinner any time." The voice sounded genuine, friendly.

"One of these days I'll make a reservation for my wife and myself. I enjoyed meeting you, Mr. Tracy."

As Dr. Ames walked back to his office, he thought how well Duncan and Tracy fit neatly into each other's needs. Duncan was the intellectual, the man whose heart had not been in waging war, killing other humans. Tracy was more the avenger. He might easily destroy a life, as well as save it, Dr. Ames thought, since his own life meant little to him because of his hurtful, lonely childhood—no mother ever, then his father taken from him too.

Back in his office, Dr. Ames dialed Lonegan. It was nearly seven o'clock, and he apologized, "Forgive me for being late, Jack. I interviewed a third man."

"Oh? Who was he?" Interest in the warm voice.

"Duncan's partner at the Sierra and partner-in-crime because of the gambling. Jess Tracy. He saved Duncan's life in Vietnam."

"How did you make out with the first two, Doc?"

"Score zero, Jack." Dr. Ames sighed. "Nothing concrete to incriminate either. Lulla could have shot Kate on orders from a Mafia boss. Marshall might want to kill her because she dumped him for Duncan. It's totally a guess as to which one might be the killer. Perhaps neither. It may be that mystical burglar. Or someone who hates beautiful, successful young women."

Lonegan asked pleadingly, "Didn't you find out anything?"

Exasperated at himself, Dr. Ames felt even surer he would never make it as a detective. He said, "Not a clue. Sorry I failed you this time."

Lonegan coughed nervously, then said, "I have to ask you this. It's about your patient. Has Duncan said anything on the couch that might implicate him in the shooting? Statistics show most murders are committed by those supposedly nearest and dearest to the victim."

"I thought about that too, Jack. But I'm convinced Duncan loved Kate. He's not the type to kill her or anyone else."

"Okay, Doc. I believe you. I had to ask. Call me if you have second thoughts on any of the suspects, will you?"

"Of course. I'm sorry I haven't had a first thought. I feel a complete failure."

"You get used to failures if you're a detective," Lonegan assured him. "You fail and fail and fail. Then suddenly you come up a winner."

Just like psychoanalysts, Dr. Ames thought after he hung up. Over and over you think you fail to get something vital through to a patient. Then suddenly he surprises you by showing he understands.

Tired from the afternoon's unusual kind of work, he lay down on the patient's couch. He mused, Let's see. Lulla in the park, a frightening specimen of a sadistic man. Marshall in the newspaper office, outwardly charming, inwardly angry.

Suddenly he realized he had not conveyed to Lonegan, nor had Lonegan asked, any description of the third man, Jess Tracy. He now thought of Tracy's face when asked about Kate's death. It held mixed anger and pain, but something else too. The expression of a shamefaced child trapped in a lie or found stealing. Tracy looked as if he were afraid of being caught with his hand in the cookie jar. Or maybe—even—committing murder?

It was just a hunch; only one person could find out for sure. Not Lonegan, not himself. Somehow he had to diplomatically enlist the aid of this third man.

Before he started Duncan's next session, Dr. Ames asked, "Will you sit in the chair for a few minutes? I'd like to talk about something that has nothing to do with your analysis, but it's very important to you."

Duncan eased himself into the patient's chair, faced Dr. Ames, who explained, "At the request of Lieutenant

Lonegan, who is in charge of Miss Locke's case, I've been interviewing some suspects. And though he did not ask me to, I talked to Jess Tracy yesterday."

Duncan said, his voice even, "Jess told me you visited the club. I was pleased you wanted to meet him. And to see the Sierra."

Dr. Ames decided to jump right into the danger zone. He said, "I'd like to ask something I hope doesn't alarm you. Do you think Jess Tracy is capable of murder?"

Duncan fell silent, as though considering this charge, then said slowly, "I don't think Jess would murder anyone except during war. Much less Kate. He knew I loved her."

"That might be the very reason." Dr. Ames' voice was low.

"Jess isn't a homosexual, if that's what you mean." Duncan ran his hands abstractly through his blond hair.

"Homosexuality isn't the only reason for the maniacal jealousy of a man by a man," Dr. Ames said. "There is a deeper, more primitive cause of such jealousy. Tracy saved your life and might have the fantasy you now belong to him. To do with as he wishes. His allowing you to take the blame for the crime of gambling shows this. He used you as part of himself to bear the shame and serve the sentence."

He went on, knowing this might be difficult for Duncan to accept, "If Tracy believed a rival was going to take you from him—you standing for the mother of childhood he never knew and desperately craved—he would once again feel the murderous rage of a rejected, deserted child. As a child he could do nothing about it. As an adult who killed in wartime, he could express his feelings of fury. He might want to destroy any woman with whom you fell in love. Believing if he lost you, he would once again be in a world where no one loved him or cared about him."

"*He* killed Kate?" Duncan gasped in shock.

"We don't know. I'm taking a wild guess."

Duncan looked stricken. "I never thought of Jess as a murderer but a savior. My savior."

"He may not be a murderer. But someone shot Kate, wanted her dead. Took the emerald engagement ring you gave her but left everything else untouched. Does that sound like a burglar?"

Duncan's lips suddenly became set grimly. He asked, "How do we find out if it's Jess?"

"I don't know. But I wanted to tell you I talked to him even though I knew it might interrupt your analysis. It's one thing to go on with analysis, dealing with the trauma of the past, if your life is fairly placid. But it's difficult to try to conduct an analysis when there's so much trauma in the present."

"I realize that, Dr. Ames. You asked me earlier not to intervene. But now what can I do to help?" A plea.

Dr. Ames said what he had planned the night before, since Duncan had led up to it. "For the moment, this is not analysis since a large part of you is seeking vengeance. Do you think you might act as detective, as you originally offered?"

For the first time since Kate's death, Duncan smiled. He said, "I'll do whatever you ask me to do."

"Without letting Mr. Tracy know you suspect him, can you try to sense whether he could have shot Kate? Every fleeting impression is important. I respect your judgment; you can be of great help if you will trust your feelings. You see Tracy almost daily. If he is guilty, you should be able to pick up some clue. A criminal often unconsciously gives himself away because of his deep guilt."

Duncan was silent, as though already planning what to do. Dr. Ames suggested, "And now you can lie down. It's time to get back to the analysis."

Duncan slowly stretched his long legs out on the couch, then seemed to retreat into a stupor. Dr. Ames waited for him to speak, but he remained mute.

"Is something troubling you?" Dr. Ames asked.

He said slowly, "I've had a lot of time to think, these past few days, without Kate. Because of the eight months with you, I realize most of my life I haven't known ninety percent of what I feel. Much less what people around me were doing to themselves and me. It's as if I've been wearing psychological blinders."

He went on reflectively, "When Kate was killed, the so-called burglar stole only the emerald engagement ring I gave her, although there were many other valuable objects staring him in the face in her living room. I don't think Jess, if he was the one to take the ring, would dare sell it. It could be easily traced. And it's valuable. It cost me twelve thousand dollars."

Then he added, "Jess wouldn't dare give it to his wife, Marie, because she might wear it in front of me. But he might hide it in his safe-deposit box at his bank in Great Neck."

And, Dr. Ames thought, if, in Tracy's warped mind, he believed Duncan belonged to him alone because he had saved his life, he might keep the engagement ring for another reason: symbolically, through the dead Kate, the ring would tie him to Duncan.

As Duncan stood up, his session at an end, he said to Dr. Ames, "I want a look at that safe-deposit box. Marie has a key. I'm driving to Great Neck the minute I leave this office. Jess goes to work about noon, and I'll persuade Marie to go to the bank with me and open that box."

Left alone, Dr. Ames thought Duncan seemed more alive than he had been since learning of Kate's death. If the ring was not in the safe-deposit box, at least Duncan

would feel he was trying to find Kate's killer, as he had
offered in the first place.

When Duncan arrived for his session the following
morning, he hurriedly threw himself into the chair, as
though he could not wait to talk. His dark eyes gleamed
with excitement. He started, "Yesterday afternoon Marie
and I drove to the bank. The guard escorted us into the
vault and took out the safe-deposit box. Marie opened it
with her key, and I carried it to a table in the corner of the
room where there was privacy."

He stopped for a moment, then went on, "We found the
box filled with stock certificates in neat stacks, held by
rubber bands. I lifted them out, placed them on the table.
It seemed this was all the box contained."

His eyes fastened on Dr. Ames' face as he said slowly,
"I took a second look. Suddenly, in a corner of the box, I
saw a tiny package wrapped in tissue paper sealed by
Scotch tape. I took it out, slowly peeled off the tape and
tissue paper. A square-cut emerald ring, the one I picked
out for Kate, sparkled up at me. I saw the words I had
composed, 'To dearest Kate, with my complete love,'
written inside."

He stopped, choked up, unable to go on. Dr. Ames
asked, "How do you feel now?"

Duncan said in quiet fury, "I want to kill Jess! If he had
been in that room, I think I would have strangled him. But
I didn't say a word; I didn't want Marie to know the truth.
She asked, 'Who does that ring belong to?' I lied, 'I don't
know. Maybe Jess' father left it to him.' I rewrapped the
ring in the tissue paper, placed it back in the box. I drove
Marie home, asked her not to tell Jess what we did or I'd
be in deep trouble. She promised she wouldn't. I thanked
her sadly, knowing how much tragedy her life would now

hold, and drove home, still feeling the gut wish to kill Jess."

He then cried out, "How could Jess murder the woman I loved?"

Dr. Ames said quietly, "That's why he committed murder. *Because* you loved her. You've never known Jess Tracy. You've had too strong a fantasy about him as the savior of your life."

Duncan said, guilt in his voice, "I did tell him I wanted to go back to being an architect and earn money in that profession. I think he felt a bit rejected."

Dr. Ames suggested, "I believe you have to tell the police what you found, Mr. Duncan."

Duncan's face hardened; he said, "Not yet. I want Jess caught my way. Face to face. Not turning him in behind his back."

Then he asked pleadingly, "Would you meet me at the Sierra at six o'clock tonight? I need you there when I confront him."

With any other patient Dr. Ames would have refused, but he had become so deeply involved in the case, he felt he had to see it through. He said, "I'll be there, Mr. Duncan."

At six o'clock sharp Dr. Ames walked into the Sierra. The maître d' led him to a table where Duncan sat alone. On seeing his psychoanalyst walk toward him, Duncan stood up, said, "Thank you for coming, Dr. Ames. Will you follow me?"

He led the way down the corridor to the door of Tracy's office, which was closed. Duncan's face looked ready for battle as he slowly opened the door.

"Come in, Tom." The pleased voice of his partner.

Tracy looked puzzled as he saw Dr. Ames follow

Duncan into the room. Tracy stood up and asked Duncan irritably, "Why the parade?"

"Sit down, Jess." A quiet but firm request.

Duncan motioned Dr. Ames to one of the white leather chairs, lowered himself into a second. Tracy sat down reluctantly in the desk chair.

"I want to ask you a few questions, Jess," Duncan said.

"Anything, Tom. Haven't I always been open with you?"

"I came to put a few cards on the table, Jess. I loved Kate with all my heart and don't intend to see her murderer go free."

"So?" Challengingly. "What's that got to do with me?"

"I'm afraid it has a lot to do with you."

"What do you mean?" The bulging brown eyes looked innocent.

"There's no time to waste words." Duncan stared at Tracy with the rage of a man ruthlessly betrayed by someone he trusted one hundred percent.

Then he charged, "I know you killed Kate."

"You're crazy!" Contemptuously.

"I have proof. Damning proof."

"Yeah, what?" Scornfully.

"The emerald ring I gave Kate lies in your safe-deposit box in Great Neck. I saw it there." Pure hatred on Duncan's face.

"You what?" Tracy's face flashed equal hatred, as if he wished he had left Duncan to die on that far-off battlefield.

"I drove out to Great Neck yesterday, forced Marie to open the box."

Face even heavier with rage, Jess burst out, "That damned bitch! Letting you see my personal things. Wait until I get *her*."

Duncan looked disgusted. "You've just told me more

about yourself, Jess, than I ever dared know. So that's how little you think of Marie."

"That's what I'd call any bitch who fouls me up." A sneer.

Dr. Ames could not help thinking, That is how he feels about the "bitch" who left him deserted at childbirth, who fouled up his life.

Duncan's voice was deadly calm as he asked, "You killed Kate, didn't you, Jess?"

"I killed the cunt!" Venomously.

"Why, Jess? Why?" As if Duncan could not understand the reason for such overwhelming hatred.

"I warned her to let you alone, stick to her newspaper friends. She wouldn't listen. She set a wedding date, thought I was kidding. That night, after I made sure you had left her apartment, I rang the bell and said I wanted to talk to her. She asked me in. I told her she was the reason you wanted to leave me, go back to being an architect, live a more respectable life. I felt more and more furious. Then I pulled out my gun. One shot did it."

He stopped. "An eye for an eye, so to speak." Then pleadingly, "I saved your life, didn't I? I don't deserve to be left alone now. Thrown to the wolves."

Dr. Ames thought, This is how Tracy felt as a child and all his adult life, thrown to the wolves.

Duncan said, his voice low, "I loved Kate. She had become an essential part of my life. I am grateful you once pulled me out of battle fire, but I once pulled you out of the clutches of the law by being the fall guy."

He added, "A law to which I'm now turning you over."

For the first time Tracy looked frightened, Dr. Ames thought. Tracy begged, "You can't, Tom. Don't squeal on me."

Dr. Ames felt he was not in the room, there were only

the two former close friends, now enemies until death.

"You're going to face a murder charge, Jess." Duncan's voice was clear and loud.

Tracy reeled back in his chair, suddenly pulled a gun from a drawer of the white desk, pointed it at Duncan. They were all now in the same room with death, Dr. Ames thought.

Suddenly Duncan's attitude changed, all hatred on his face ebbed away, as though he understood Tracy's tortured mind. He said, his voice calm, reassured, "Jess, don't make things worse."

"Why not?" Angrily. "I can't burn any more for two murders than one."

"Don't destroy what's been good between us." A plea.

"I don't get it." The gun quivered.

"It wasn't because you saved my life that I teamed up with you. I felt deep affection for you, Jess. I thought you were a man of great courage and imagination." Duncan's voice was low, earnest. "Don't turn coward now. Be brave, like when you raced back into that hell and pulled me out." He added softly, "Let me keep the image of you as a hero, Jess."

There was not a sound in the room; it was as though the three men had stopped breathing. Dr. Ames looked at Tracy, could hardly believe what he saw. Tears rolled down Tracy's cheeks.

He slowly lowered the gun, handed it to Duncan.

Duncan turned to Dr. Ames, asked, "What do we do now?"

"Call 555–9711," said Dr. Ames. "Ask for Lieutenant Lonegan."

The two men sat in the bar on Lexington Avenue, not far from the Nineteenth Precinct; each held a glass of scotch. Lonegan's smile was wide as he said, "Here's to you, Doc, once again. I really owe you this time."

"I couldn't let you down, could I?" Dr. Ames smiled back.

Lonegan looked embarrassed. "I think I let you down at one time by suspecting your patient. And he turned out the hero."

"Don't give it a thought. You didn't know Duncan as well as I did."

Lonegan said, "He told me you helped him realize his partner was the murderer. How did you know?"

"I didn't know. Duncan made the first connection. He came up with the evidence when he obtained proof of his partner's guilt from the safe-deposit box."

"Duncan told me you helped him acquire the inner strength to face Jess Tracy."

"Duncan was very impressive, Jack, a gun pointed at his head, alone in that room except for me."

"Were you scared, Doc?"

"I guess somewhat. But I also had confidence in Duncan. I had the feeling he had taken the lead, finally stood up to the partner who had unconsciously intimidated him. Or maybe his love for Kate was so strong he was determined to make Tracy pay, even if his own life was at stake. There are usually many reasons for both a brave act and a murder. Maybe Duncan didn't want to live with Kate destroyed."

Lonegan asked cynically, "Say, Doc, do you think marriage is ever easy? The wife and I thought of splitting a couple of times."

"What kept you together?"

"Habit. When you've lived with someone almost twenty years, you figure, why change?" Lonegan added reflectively, "There are times I do feel very close to her."

"Isn't that really the most we can ask? Times of pleasure that help us bear the times of pain?"

"You sound like a poet, Doc." Then, "Can a detective be a poet?"

"Why not? And part psychoanalyst too, if he wishes."

"If I stuck around you, I'd be part shrink." Lonegan's voice was wistful. "Won't you change your mind about working with me more often?"

Dr. Ames laughed, sipped away at the scotch. "I'm honored at your proposal, Jack. But I wasn't trained to find murderers, except murderers of the soul."

Lonegan pursed his lips, said, "I guess I have to settle for us as a sometimes-team."

"Let's drink to that."

As they hoisted their glasses, Dr. Ames added, "And here's to Cloud Nine."

"What's that, Doc?"

"It's a metaphor of Duncan's. He compared psychoanalysis to coming down to earth from Cloud Nine, cloud by cloud."

"Poetry again." Admiringly, "I wish I could write poetry."

"You live it, Jack. You deal in justice, poetic and otherwise. You make it possible for poets and all others to live without fear. You help keep us free from the dangers of the madmen in our twentieth-century jungle."

"You mean it, Doc?" Lonegan sounded grateful.

"With all my heart." Dr. Ames looked at Lonegan with affection and respect. "If each of us had to worry about sheer physical protection without the help of heroes like you, there'd be no leisure to work with the psyche. Man does not live by bread alone. Before all else we must feel safe enough to earn that bread."

Lonegan said thoughtfully, sipping his scotch, "Doc,

keep trying to figure out why men have to commit murder, will you? Maybe that way, someday we'll know how to really prevent it." He held up his glass. "Let's drink to that, too."

They raised their glasses high.

A body is found. Bodies are where you find them, but they don't necessarily stay there. And you can't always believe what they tell you.

Mickey Friedman

Night in the Lonesome October

The skies they were ashen and sober;
  The leaves they were crispèd and sere——
The leaves they were withering and sere;
It was night in the lonesome October
  Of my most immemorial year.
      —Edgar Allan Poe, "Ulalume"

One

It had been a windy night. Shortly after dawn I unlocked my iron-barred back door and went out with a cup of birdseed in one hand and a bowl of nuts in the other. I put the seed down on the flagstones under the feeder but held on to the nuts, pressing the bowl against my midsection. Dry leaves crackled under my feet.

I once met a young woman, a graduate student from the Midwest, who had lived in a New York high-rise for two years and honestly didn't believe back yards existed on the island of Manhattan. I described mine: fifty feet to the back fence; ivy; rhododendrons; a chestnut tree; flagstones; a wide flower bed at the back. She looked suspicious. She had heard many tales since she moved here, and some were true and some weren't. If I'd told her how much rent I pay, she might have believed me, since in this city the most credible figures are the astronomical ones.

I don't pay the rent, actually. I should be clear about that. Tony still pays the rent.

Mr. Ulrich's body lay more than halfway to the back fence, and was blanketed with late October leaves. Under his leafy covering he had on a business suit and socks, but no shoes. Mr. Ulrich's first name was Amos, but I didn't know that at the time. Our brownstone doesn't go in for coffee klatches, progressive dinners, or first names. Even if we had, Mr. Ulrich wouldn't have participated because he wasn't here much. Tony never even met him.

I knew him only as Mr. Ulrich, the asthmatic, or perhaps emphysemic, tenant on the fourth (which is the top) floor. On the rare occasions I had encountered him, he was wheezing laboriously up the staircase, gray-faced, leaning hard on the railing. He must have been in his seventies, a frail and mournful man with bristly gray hair and a pencil mustache. His keeping a walk-up apartment so obviously hazardous to his health could be explained in two words: rent control. He paid about a tenth of what the rest of us did. Mr. Ulrich might have his mourners, but since his rent-controlled status expired with him, I doubted the landlord would be one of them.

The side of Mr. Ulrich's head had a lopsided, caved-in look and was matted with dried blood. He lay on his face, his arms outstretched. His navy blue suit had a faint chalk stripe, very conservative, and his socks were black. As I looked down on his body, I heard something scrabbling through the leaves behind me. I started convulsively and dropped the nut bowl, scattering peanuts, filberts, pecans and walnuts everywhere. Two squirrels, the source of the racket, scampered off toward the chestnut tree. In a second or two, though, the greedy buggers came back for their breakfast.

My part of Greenwich Village is as proper and staid as any neighborhood in New York. The transvestite prostitutes patrol closer to the waterfront, ten or twelve blocks away. Although both children and homeless people frequent the Bleecker Street Playground, children are still in the majority. Many of them (accompanied, of course, by parent or live-in babysitter) actually walk to and from school at P.S. 41. On recycling day, neatly bundled stacks of the *Times* (never the *Daily News* or the *Post*) appear at the curb. We're so cute that movie crews regularly disrupt traffic and parking, and our quaint streets lined with row houses are often the background for fashion shoots and music videos. Having a dead body in the back yard may be a common rite of passage in other parts of town, but not here. I went inside to call the police.

While they investigated the garden, I made coffee and called the *patisserie* around the corner to send over scones, croissants, Danish. Bran muffins for those still concerned about bran, *pains au chocolat* for those who weren't. I've never been much of a hostess, but I try to do the right thing. When the pastries arrived I piled them on a tray on the dining table, accessible to those trooping back and forth. Then I went out and hovered next to the house, watching.

Predictably, the children next door—William, Portia, and tiny blond Titania—were goggling through the wooden lattice separating their first-floor deck from my yard. William, who is ten and a natural for Bronx Science when he's old enough, called to me, "Rebecca! Is he *dead?*"

"Becka! *Dead?*" echoed Titania, with his exact inflection. Both she and William seemed delighted. Only Portia looked queasy.

"Yes, I guess he is."

"What happened?"

"Don't you have school today?"

"Teacher's meeting. Was he murdered?"

The children's father was a bond trader and their mother was a lawyer. They couldn't be expected to be here, but where on earth was the *au pair*? "Where's Ingrid?"

"Lars called from Stockholm. She started crying and went to her room."

The romance between Ingrid and Lars was constantly stormy. *"Dead?"* Titania cried again.

A policeman kneeling near Mr. Ulrich's outstretched arm called to another, "Come here and look at this."

I craned my neck. He was indicating something, a bright red something, on the ground. It was, I knew immediately, a plastic Lego block. Titania had been throwing them over the fence lately. It must have been covered, as Mr. Ulrich was, by dead leaves.

The two policemen straightened. The first one called to William, "Hey, kid. This your block?"

William was insulted. "I'm too old to play with Legos."

Portia's eyes widened. "It's mine," she said. She started to gag and ran across the deck and into her house.

"Jeez," the policeman said. He was black-haired and burly, wearing Ray Bans although the sky was dull.

I said, "Officer, Titania probably threw it over the fence. She has a habit of doing that."

"Yeah? Who's Titania?"

I pointed.

"*Dead?*" Titania said.

The policeman and I sat at my dining table next to the mountain of pastries. Nobody was eating. I pressed him to have one, but he said he was on a diet. I told him my name, Rebecca Wisden, and he wrote it in his notebook. He said, "Is it Miss, or—"

"Ms."

He gave me a tired look.

"My husband and I are separated."

We aren't, really. Not legally. I admit Tony doesn't live here anymore, but he comes around sometimes. He had come around only a few days before to pick up his childhood collection of Bozo the Clown 78's. I still have custody of his squash raquet, his executive barbells, and a lifetime supply of red plastic ballpoint pens emblazoned "WNYB Is Great TV," souvenir of his job before last. Ferociously loyal to an employer only until the next one comes along, Tony told me to toss out the pens, but I keep them lying around handy in case I get inspired to write something. Although inspiration doesn't strike as often as it used to.

"What's your husband's name?"

"Tony Trotter."

The policeman didn't recognize it. Tony would have been devastated.

If you live in the New York City viewing area, you've probably seen Tony. He's constantly being wooed from one channel to another with ever-burgeoning salaries and benefits packages. He's the one with floppy blond bangs, horn-rimmed glasses, and loud bow ties. He plays music— "Raindrops Keep Fallin' on My Head," "Cloudy," "Good Day Sunshine," "Misty," "Heat Wave"—to accompany the satellite picture while he delivers his weather spiel. When we married twenty-some years ago, Tony's dearest ambition was to give an invited paper at the American Meteorological Society's annual convention. Now he trades quips with shellac-haired nonentities on the local news five nights a week, capering like a pup despite his forty-eight (don't say I told you) years.

". . . do you do, Ms. Wisden?"

"I'm a poet."

I am. I actually had a book published. One I didn't subsidize.

The policeman's lips twitched. "No kidding," he said, and made a notation. He studied his notebook for a moment and said, "Now, Ms. Wisden, what can you tell me about—"

There's something I haven't made clear. I may have given the impression that Mr. Ulrich had jumped from his fourth-floor window to my ground-floor flagstones and killed himself. He hadn't. Anyone could see he had traveled too far from the building for that.

Clear enough? He didn't fall or jump from his window, or anybody else's. My garden is surrounded by a fence of pointed stakes about eight feet high, and it borders other gardens, not a street or alley.

How does a person, dead or alive, enter my back yard? One possibility, assuming you've gotten through one lock on the front door of the building and two locks on the door of the common entry hall, is to descend the hall stairs to the basement. In the basement, you can unbolt the inside back door, slide the two iron bars out of the locks on the outer back door, and come up the outside stairs beside my windows.

But the easiest way to get out there is through my apartment.

Except to go into the garden, I don't leave the building. Ever. In New York, you can have everything you want delivered—food, medicine, dry cleaning—so the inconvenience is minimal. My growing disinclination to leave home became a bone of contention between Tony and me, since, as a rising star, he got many invitations. For a long time I participated, pulled on my panty hose and made myself amiable to a succession of people whose faces fell upon discovering I was only somebody's wife. Even though, let's not forget, a wife whose poetry had seen publication in an unsubsidized volume.

When I started refusing to accompany him, Tony got petulant. Then he began telling everybody I had agoraphobia, the fear of open spaces. I countered that I didn't have agoraphobia, but a-*bore*-aphobia, which I defined as the fear of being bored to death. Eventually, Tony realized that his world was full of researchers, assistant producers and advertising flunkies who were glad to take up my slack. So the relationship deteriorated.

Funnily enough, the more Tony spread his agoraphobia story, the less inclined I was to go out. By the time he moved to swinging bachelor digs in the Olympic Tower, I was down to quick trips to the corner deli. After his departure I gave up those outings as well. Because I was always around, I became the obvious person to accept the other tenants' UPS packages, let the meter reader in, sign for deliveries. From my street-level front windows I saw which dog owners didn't clean up after which dogs, and which street people didn't replace the lids after rooting in our garbage cans. Still in my forties, I had become the nosy old lady behind the twitching curtain.

I told the policeman I didn't know how Mr. Ulrich came to rest in my garden. I hadn't heard anything, I said. He seemed dubious and asked if he could look around my apartment, which he did while I ate a *pain au chocolat* so they wouldn't all go to waste. By this time, a squad of investigators was in the basement, too, and I could hear others tramping up and down from Mr. Ulrich's apartment, their steps much more vigorous than his wavering tread had been.

The other tenants, as I had told the police, were not at home. Miss Worthington, upstairs from me on the parlor floor, was spending a few days at her boyfriend's farm upstate while she worked on a screenplay. Mr. Stern, on the third floor, had a visiting lectureship in contemporary social issues at some college in the Northwest.

Eventually, the police left. I went out into the garden. The cup of birdseed had been kicked over and scattered, so I got another cupful and filled the feeder. As soon as I went inside again, the sparrows, house finches, mourning doves and pigeons began to flutter down. If you're good to them, they won't desert you.

Oh, Tony. Tony.

The following afternoon, I invited the children next door to have chamomile tea and cucumber sandwiches with me. The invitation was not unusual, as I had them over every couple of months. Naturally, we talked about Mr. Ulrich. By this time the police had discovered that he was Amos Ulrich, a wealthy retired banker who had lived on a Long Island estate. Mr. Ulrich had kept the apartment in our building, the *Times* quoted his widow as saying, for the rare occasions when he came into Manhattan to look after his remaining business interests.

"What a cheapskate." William took another sandwich. "He didn't need a rent-controlled place."

"I guess he didn't get rich throwing money away when he didn't have to." I said. "Stop that, Titania!"

William wrested the sugar bowl from Titania's clutches. Above her loud protests he said, "It's illegal to keep a rent-controlled apartment when you don't live there."

I gave him a who-are-you-kidding look. "It happens all the time." Not wanting to undermine whatever ethics the child had managed to pick up, I added, "That doesn't make it right, of course."

Portia wasn't talking or eating. She slumped in her chair, a pallid, discontented-looking girl, her brown hair held at the nape by an elastic band decorated with two white plastic balls.

"Cat got your tongue, Portia?" I asked.

She swung her head negative.

"A policeman came to talk to us," William offered. "Portia puked."

" 'Puke' is a disgusting word. No, No, Titania! I'd better put the sugar bowl in the kitchen."

Returning to the table, I said, "What did you tell the policeman, Portia?"

Portia looked at me with inexpressive, mud-colored eyes. "Nothing," she answered at last.

I doubted the police would settle for that. "You must have said something."

"She didn't," said William. "She just cried and pu— threw up."

They'd be back, certainly. "What did he ask you?"

I was looking at Portia, but William answered. "Whether she saw anything. How the Lego got there."

"And *did* you see anything?"

William started to speak up, but I shushed him with my hand. "No," Portia whispered.

"You're sure?"

She nodded, eyes on her lap.

Titania upset the milk pitcher, and they left soon after.

*   *   *

Have I mentioned Angelo, my lover? Yes, my lover. As you can imagine, finding a lover isn't easy when you never leave the building. In fact, Angelo found me. He rang the front door buzzer and asked to come in and check out the electricity meter for Consolidated Edison.

It was a September afternoon of gutter-sluicing rain. We gave up buzzing people into the building after Miss Worthington upstairs was ambushed and robbed in her own apartment, so I went to let him in. I noticed at once that this was an extraordinarily handsome new meter reader who had come, he told me, to look into some anomaly in the meter readings. He was solidly built, muscular but not muscle-bound. Damp black hair curled softly around his ears. He had olive skin, wide cheek-bones, slightly tilted dark blue eyes set off by the blue shirt with "Con Ed" stitched on the pocket. He carried a clipboard, and a heavy-duty flashlight dangled from his belt. He smelled like bracing, healthy, completely organic soap.

I pointed out the stairs to the basement, where the meters are, and returned to my apartment. Before long, someone knocked on my door. I yelled to ask who it was and he said, "Con Ed again. Sorry to disturb you."

He looked even better on second sight, standing on my threshold with his bottom lip poked out in an expression of concern. "We got a problem," he said. "Can I use your phone?"

I ushered him to the phone in the kitchen, then hung around in the living room, half-listening. I heard him identify himself as Angelo Fiore. He described the meter problem at some length. My thoughts turned to Tony, as they always do. I pictured Tony walking in sometime and finding me in bed with this scrumptious Angelo Fiore. The thought gave me more pleasure than I'd had in a long time.

After a while, Angelo became less voluble. His side of the conversation was reduced to a string of "Yeahs," followed by, "For Pete's sake, Benny, it's raining cats and—"

More silence, more "Yeahs," and finally Angelo said, in a tone of warning, "OK, but I'm off in half an hour whether he's here or not." I heard him replace the receiver.

He reentered the living room shaking his head. "Tells me to wait till the guy gets here with a truck." He waved and started for the door. "Hey, thanks."

I held up a hand, as if I could send a force field across the room to stop him. "You have to wait here?"

"Yeah. And even then he may not show before my shift is over."

"Well—where will you wait?"

"Outside. No problem." His hand was on the doorknob.

"But it's raining out there."

He shrugged. "In the hall, then. If you don't mind."

He really was a remarkable-looking man. Thirty-two or -three years old, maybe. Dimples. "Wouldn't you like to wait here? Have some coffee? A glass of wine?"

The man with the truck never showed up. Neither of us thought of him again until long after Angelo's shift was over.

I know how shabby this sounds. Self-castigation set in about five minutes after Angelo had freed himself from my clinging arms with a ritual "Call you tomorrow." I was filled with savage regret, but I must confess the regret was less that I had fallen into bed with a Con Ed meter reader (whose gentlemanly attributes extended to producing a condom from his wallet and gallantly wearing it) than it was that Tony hadn't walked in and caught us, guilty and sweaty in the act. "Call you tomorrow" is a promise begging to be broken. I wasn't sure Angelo knew my name, much less my phone number. I would surely never have another opportunity to show Tony I could be a sport, too.

Yet, tomorrow came and, believe it or not, Angelo called. "Hey, doll. When can I come over?" he said. Opportunity had knocked twice. It continued to knock three or four times a week for the next month. Angelo's socks and Jockey shorts turned up in my laundry. He stocked my refrigerator with St. Pauli Girl and pepperoni sticks. When my television set went on the blink, he diagnosed the trouble and fixed it. To seal our intimacy, he took my keys to the hardware store and had a set made for himself.

At six and eleven weeknights, we tuned Tony in on the tube so Angelo could make rude remarks about Tony's manhood. I laughed hysterically, so hard sometimes that I had to blot tears from my eyes and blow my nose afterward.

One day, Tony called and asked if he could stop by to pick up his Bozo the Clown albums. "Tomorrow afternoon," he said. "Can you get them out for me? 'Bozo and the Circus,' 'Bozo under the Sea,' and 'Bozo and the Birds.' "

Angelo wasn't due to come over tomorrow afternoon. "Couldn't we make it the day after?"

Tony drew a long breath. "Why not tomorrow? You aren't going *out,* are you?"

"Ha, ha," I said, and agreed that he could stop by tomorrow. I found the Bozo albums and put them on a chair in the bedroom under a stack of Angelo's Jockey shorts, just delivered clean and folded from the laundry. Since Tony wore boxers, there would be no room for confusion. It wasn't as good as being caught in *flagrante*, but it was the best I could do.

Tony arrived looking nervous and pinched. He needs multivitamins, but forgets to take them. His signature floppy bangs hung lifeless and lank along the top of his horn-rims, and he was chewing his nails again despite his manicure. He walked in and said, "Did you find them?"

"I'm very well, Tony. How are you?"

"Sorry, Rebecca. I'm in a rush here."

"Obviously."

He shoved his hands in his pockets and studied the floor. "Sorry. Really."

Neither of us spoke. Pigeons cooed outside the window where a flock was feeding, their bodies a bobbing mass of purplish-gray. After a moment I said, "I got the albums out yesterday. Now, where did I put them?"

We scanned the available surfaces. Tony riffled through the records. I pressed my lips with my forefinger. "Did I take them into the bedroom? Why would I have done that?"

Tony disappeared down the hall, with me in his wake. He spotted the corner of "Bozo and the Birds" beneath Angelo's shorts. "Here they are," he said. He moved the stack of underwear to the bed and took possession of his precious albums.

"Gosh, I'm sorry," I said. "They were nearly hidden there under Angelo's shorts."

Yes, he asked: "Who's Angelo?"

It was a sweet moment. I bit my lip to make it last. "Angelo's the man I've been—seeing."

I was watching closely. I'm sure he paled. "You're seeing somebody? No kidding."

"Yes. We've been spending a lot of time together lately."

"That's great, Rebecca." I know Tony. The sincerity was forced.

"Yes. Angelo *is* great." I shouldn't have added, but I did, "He's the greatest I've ever experienced, actually."

Tony settled the albums under his arm and checked his watch. "I'd better get along."

Avoidance. I gave him a sweet smile, and a peck on his clammy cheek, and let him go.

And that's why, when I found Mr. Ulrich dead on my bed, I knew exactly what had happened and what I had to do.

Two

The night Mr. Ulrich died, I was eating microwave popcorn and moodily reading some dirges of love and loss by Edgar Allan Poe. The wind was high. The raven's "Nevermore!" resounded in my brain. About ten o'clock I heard a gentle rapping at my apartment door and opened it to find a wheezing, choking Mr. Ulrich leaning there pulling feebly at his collar.

I took his arm and led him inside. His lips were moving, breath rasping in his throat, but I couldn't understand what he was trying to say. "You'd better lie down," I said. Why I took him to the bedroom instead of settling him on the couch, I don't know. Maybe I had the notion he'd be more comfortable if he could stretch out. He sank down on the edge of the bed and sat struggling for breath. Then, to my surprise, he leaned, almost toppled, over, untied his shoelaces, and took off his shoes. He said his first intelligible word: "Bedspread."

He didn't want to put his shoes on the bedspread, for

God's sake. "The bedspread doesn't matter, Mr. Ulrich."
I helped him out of his overcoat, loosened his tie, unbuttoned his top shirt button, and lay him back against the pillows.

He closed his eyes. His breathing became a little easier. As I was pulling down the shades on the front windows he gasped, "*Inhaler*."

"I'll get it for you. Where is it?"

He pointed upward with a quivering forefinger. "Cabinet."

I found his keys in the pocket of his overcoat, rushed out of my apartment and up four flights of stairs. By the time I reached his door I was trembling, but I managed to get the key into the lock. The apartment had the bare, spartan look of the rarely-used *pied-à-terre* it was. I careened into the bathroom, flung open the medicine cabinet— And didn't see an inhaler.

I searched twice through the sparse collection of outdated prescription bottles, over-the-counter stomach remedies and rusting safety razors. Then I went through the bedside table, turning up a box of tissues, cough drops, and a dog-eared paperback of *I'm OK—You're OK*. Cabinet, he had said. I pushed around the canned goods and cooking utensils in the kitchen cabinets, the mismatched china in the glass-fronted built-in sideboard in the dining room. I had given up, and was about to return downstairs, when I noticed a spindly-legged rosewood table by the front door. The damned thing had curving doors in its front. I pulled them open, and located the inhaler at last.

Quite honestly, I was not surprised to find Mr. Ulrich dead when I returned. He had been in a bad way. I was surprised, though, that the side of his head was caved in. It looked as if he'd been struck a solid blow with a blunt instrument, although no blunt instrument was lying around. A little blood, not very much, had seeped from the wound and was gleaming stickily in his hair. His half-open eyes reflected the glow of my bedside lamp.

As I looked at Mr. Ulrich, lacing and unlacing my fingers, I thought: Tony.

My fantasy had, in one sense, come true. Crazed with jealousy by my revelation about Angelo, Tony had been lurking, watching. He saw Mr. Ulrich come in, saw me settle him on the bed and pull down the shades. Enraged, Tony rushed in and finished off poor, speechless Mr. Ulrich.

I was quite sure. All the circumstances fit. It was my fault, for taunting Tony with Angelo's underwear.

Tony cared. Of course I had to protect him.

Most of my garden is flagstones, but along the back fence there is a flower bed perhaps five feet wide. Every spring I plant impatiens there, white and red ones usually, sometimes the salmon for a change. Now the flowers were dead, the earth leaf-covered. A serviceable shovel was leaning against the wall of the house right outside the back door.

I donned my gloves. I took Mr. Ulrich's overcoat and shoes upstairs and put them in his closet. I wiped off the inhaler and replaced it in the rosewood cabinet, and went over everything I could remember touching with a cloth. I took my time. Tony's life depended on it.

About two in the morning, I took Mr. Ulrich under the armpits and pulled him off the bed. I didn't like looking at his face, so I turned him over. He was so wasted, I could drag him easily. What a contrast with my real lover, strapping Angelo!

I had opened the back door in preparation. The kitchen light was off, so it wouldn't shine into the garden, but New York is never really dark at night. Despite the hour, there were lighted windows in surrounding buildings, and illumination from the street lamps in front. I thought I'd go undetected, though. New Yorkers are not curious to see sights that might disrupt their routine.

The wind was high, the leaves swirling. Mr. Ulrich and I proceeded slowly out the back door and across the yard toward his burial plot. I didn't feel afraid. I felt noble and brave, a woman worth killing for.

My exalted mood was broken by a toddler's shriek of delight coming from the dark house next door. Scalded by dread, I strained toward the neighboring deck and saw something move there. The Lego block probably sailed near me then, but I was unaware of it. I heard another shriek, a muffled gasp, bare pattering feet. Most toddlers would not be awake at two in the morning, fewer would be out of their cribs, and fewer yet would have managed to find a way outside. This, however, was Titania.

I put Mr. Ulrich down and stood still and quiet. Not another sound from next door. Had there been one pair of feet, or two? Even a baby as resourceful as Titania would need help unlocking the door, and I doubted she had gotten it from her parents or the *au pair*. William, maybe. Or Portia.

I left Mr. Ulrich where he lay and shrank into the shadows. As fast as I could, I scuttled toward the house. Once inside, I stayed there. I couldn't bury a dead body under the eyes of innocent and loudmouthed children.

I used the rest of the night to remove all traces of Mr. Ulrich and his demise from my apartment. In the morning, just after dawn, I took a cup of birdseed and a bowl of nuts and went into the garden.

The papers had a field day with the Ulrich case for the forty-eight hours until the next atrocity came along. Tony called, of course. He was brisk, and so was I. A lot had to be said, but it wasn't the time.

Angelo called, too. "Hey, doll. You're all over the *Post*. What's happening?"

I told him my standard version, ending with, "The police think somebody mugged him at the front door and dragged him out through the basement." This theory had been put forward somewhere, and I was pushing it.

"And are you—all right?"

"Fine, fine."

"Well, then. When should I come over?"

The relationship ended, though. Angelo was touchy and irritable, and obviously I was too preoccupied with my own concerns to cater to him. I had the police to think about. And Tony. No wonder Angelo was getting on my nerves.

During our final blow-up I called Angelo a dumb ox. He said who was I calling dumb, me who was hung up on a weatherman who didn't care squat. I wasn't wounded by the remark. I knew, knew for certain, that Tony did care squat.

In the aftermath of our shouting match, Angelo put his Jockey shorts and socks and St. Pauli Girl and pepperoni sticks into a plastic bag from D'Agostino's and slammed out. I didn't expect to see him again, and I didn't care. When he was gone I thought about calling Tony, but it was still too soon.

A day or so after Angelo's departure, while I was standing at the front windows looking out for the police, a black limousine pulled up in front of the building and a woman got out. The short silverfox jacket she wore proclaimed her indifferent to the rights of animals. She approached the door, and in a moment my buzzer sounded. The voice that crackled through the intercom said, "My name is Belinda Ulrich. Could I speak with you, please?"

Belinda Ulrich smelled of Fracas, one of my favorite perfumes. Under the silver fox she had on pencil-straight black slacks and a huge, silky black turtleneck. She was handsome, fashionably gaunt, her hair raked back in a tight chignon. She was approximately my age. When she said she was Amos Ulrich's wife and not his daughter, I understood why the sick old man had needed a Greenwich Village hideaway. Belinda looked capable of wearing a person down.

She had come, she said, to go through her husband's apartment, but she wanted to stop and say hello to me. "I understand you found Amos's body," she said.

"Yes."

"It's such a strange, awful thing." She touched her temple with her fingertips and shook her head. Her nails were faultless.

I agreed that it was strange and awful, and assured her that I was as baffled as the police seemed to be. She watched me avidly, her curiosity almost palpable. I saw her notice my jeans, my fisherman's sweater, my Nikes, my hair, my hands. Her scrutiny was so intense, I stumbled over my words, but not, I think, in a guilty way. At the end of my declaration she nodded. She didn't ask any questions. When we parted I watched from my doorway as she climbed the stairs, skinny black legs scissoring upward, Maud Frizon shoes noiseless on the worn carpet.

I heard her coming down again later, and opened the door to say good-bye. She was carrying her jacket, but was empty-handed otherwise. "There's nothing worth saving up there," she said. "I'll probably give it all to the Salvation Army."

"Good idea."

She nodded. Her mind, I could see, was already on her next appointment. "Since you're always here, I can tell them to buzz you when they come, can't I?"

"Yes."

"Good."

She was moving toward the door, having consigned the disposal of Mr. Ulrich's possessions to me, a total stranger, when I said, "How do I reach you if there's a mix-up?"

"I'll give you my number." She searched in her purse, a slim black leather envelope, and produced a slip of paper and an inelegant red plastic ballpoint. Watching her scrawl a number, I saw that the pen bore the legend "WNYB Is Great TV." She handed me the paper, dropped the pen back in her purse, and gave me a "so long" waggle of her fingers. The limo was gone by the time I reached the front windows.

Three

I called Tony. He was slow to return my messages, but I finally got through to him at the station. He sounded fairly friendly.

"I thought it was time we talked," I said.

After a short hesitation he said, "OK. What's on your mind?"

I told him. I told him I understood why he had done what he did, and I had covered for him as best I could. I realized it had been a misunderstanding, he had thought Mr. Ulrich was Angelo, and I had been wrong to —

"Ulrich," he said. "The old man whose body you found?"

"Right. The one you thought was my lover, and—"

"Rebecca." His throat had closed. Even over the telephone, I could hear it in the timbre of his voice. "Rebecca, don't say any more."

"But—"

"No. Don't say a word. I was in Westchester that night. I was toastmaster at a Rotary Club banquet."

"Tony—"

"My speech was covered in the *White Plains Reporter-Dispatch*, Rebecca. Go look it up. And then promise me that you will never, and I mean never, say one word—"

I hung up.

I started thinking, then, about Belinda Ulrich. Her curious stare. Her knowing I'm always here. The WNYB ballpoint in her purse. That WNYB promotion had taken place four years ago, at least. The only place those pens are still in plentiful supply might well be my apartment, where they're available to anyone, a meter reader for instance, who happens to come in.

I don't make a production of telling people I never go out. I never told the police, for instance. Tony knew, of course. So did Angelo. Sorting through it all, I went on to take what seemed a logical next step.

I had never had Angelo's phone number, so I called the personnel office at Consolidated Edison. Without a tremendous amount of trouble, I learned that the company had never employed an Angelo Fiore, as a meter reader or in any other capacity. Anybody can buy a uniform, for the right price. And who has a better excuse than a meter reader to hang around a building until an old man shows up far from his usual haunts?

Mr. Ulrich was a sick man. He wouldn't have lasted long, but I suppose waiting, especially when sex and money are involved, can be terribly difficult. When you see a chance in a lighted window, it's best to get in there and bash away (with a heavy-duty flashlight?) and be done with it.

The skein unraveled. Tony hadn't been watching the house, Angelo had. Angelo wasn't my lover, not really. He was Belinda Ulrich's. She, not I, was a woman worth killing for.

I tried to call Belinda Ulrich. A maid answered and said Mrs. Ulrich was in Cancún and hadn't set a date for her return. I picture her and Angelo on a terrace, in brilliant sun. A blue-tiled tabletop, blue sea beyond. I can't imagine why they would ever come back at all. Can you?

I don't go out, except to feed the birds and squirrels. When I hear the voices of the children next door raised in squabbles or play, I wonder whether, some day soon, Portia will talk about what she saw that night. If she saw anything.

I wonder how I will explain, if anyone asks.

A body is found traveling in gaslight New York . . . but where did its journey begin?

Joyce Harrington

The Elevated Elephant-Hunter

Timothy Crane wanted nothing more than a hot toddy and a chance to take his boots off. But at three in the morning, Satan's Circus was still going strong, and daybreak a good three or four hours away.

He stood on the pavement outside the Cremorne, on 32nd Street just off Sixth Avenue, his ears freezing under his leather helmet and his nose as red from the cold as any reveler's stumbling out of the notorious dance hall to join the boisterous street crowd in search of further distraction. Through the constantly opening doors of the Cremorne, he caught glimpses of the ruddy, sweating face of Don Whiskerando, the walrus-moustached manager of what was surely the most abandoned dive in the city. He knew that if he went through those doors, Whiskerando would treat him to a toddy and even a quarter of an hour warming himself in a curtained cubicle with one of the young waiter girls, but if he took advantage of those favors, he could lose his position. Not because such largess was frowned upon, but because the Cremorne's delights were the jealously guarded privilege of those with more seniority.

Crane had been on the force only a few weeks. He'd paid all the required tribute, from the Superintendent on down to his supervising Roundsman. His uniform was still new and stiff, and the leather helmet sat awkwardly on his head, the more so whenever one of his former associates derisively dubbed him "Leatherhead."

A Hell's Kitchen lad born and bred, Timothy had himself often shrieked the insult at a passing policeman and then scampered away into the warren of tenements that housed his family and thousands like them. But young Timothy had seen his best friend's father thumped on the head and carted away by a pair of those same Leatherheads for stealing a barrel of oysters from a shipment bound for Delmonico's.

"You couldn't call it stealing," the guilty party protested. "They was standing there neglected, and I was just givin' them a good home."

The two burly policemen disagreed, and it was off to the Tombs with the oyster thief. But before they all departed in the paddy wagon pulled by a team of sleek chestnut horses, Timothy noticed that the oyster barrel had been breached and its contents seriously depleted. Indeed, what was left was scarcely worth taking along as evidence or returning to its owner. The urchins of Hell's Kitchen had feasted on the leavings.

After Timothy had swallowed his share, he fell to thinking about the policemen who had eaten most of the barrel and the thief who had looked on with hunger in his stomach and misery in his eyes. It didn't take much thought to decide which side of the law was better fed. From that moment, it was young Tim's ambition to join the despised ranks of Leatherheads. He had learned to read and write, and had measured himself weekly until he had attained the required height of five feet seven and one-half inches, and a bit more. He'd saved up the money he'd gained from picking pockets and snatching purses and muffs on the Broadway streetcars until he had the three hundred dollars needed to buy himself a place on the Metropolitan Police Force.

Now that his dream had come true, Timothy Crane was as hungry as ever, and cold into the bargain. True, he'd been given a plum assignment to the Tenderloin, where, his fellow patrolmen assured him, there was plenty of opportunity for "honest graft," but so far his only opportunities were the dubious invitations of raddled and diseased night-walkers who looked old enough to be his mother, and the occasional swig of turpentine disguised as whiskey from the greasy keeper of one of the countless grog shops that rubbed shoulders with the flash establishments. He had no plans in his future for a dose of Venus's Curse or the barrel fever that had made loonies of half the men and many of the women in his home streets.

His job seemed to be to look the other way when certain rough-looking characters decoyed a drunken elephant-hunter—Fifth Avenue swell or out-of-town yokel—into an alley to relieve him of the burden of his cash, and to break up any fights that threatened the peaceful accumulation of profit in the dance halls, concert saloons, gambling hells, and bordellos that lined Sixth Avenue under the El and spread east and west along the side streets.

Crane turned back to Sixth Avenue to finish off the rest of his round. From 34th Street to 23rd Street and back up Seventh Avenue, with stops at the Egyptian Hall, the Haymarket, the French Madam's, where he'd heard that street women would dance naked for a dollar at private parties, and Buckingham Palace, where he'd seen masked gents in their fancy dress mingling with the cheap spangles of actresses and harlots.

There was money to be made in the Tenderloin, legally or otherwise, and Timothy meant to make some of it his own before too many more tours of duty had elapsed. The only obstacle was getting himself taken up by a person of influence. Boss Croker was said to favor stalwart Irish lads, paying them well to serve as bodyguards and strong-arms in their off-duty hours and arranging for their rapid advancement in the force.

He sighed and trod his frigid beat, his new boots creaking and raising Cain with the blister on his heel. A steam locomotive had stalled overhead, showering him with soot and sparks, but the noise and falling embers scarcely distracted him from his reverie of heroic deeds that would bring him to the notice of the Grand Sachem of Tammany Hall. He would save Mrs. Astor from the path of a runaway horse. He would scale a burning building to rescue a help-less cripple from the flames. He would hunt down and bring to justice a ring of dangerous anarchists. His picture would appear in all the newspapers, artistically rendered in delicate lines and shadows. Surely then Croker would no-tice him, or if not Croker himself, some other notable per-sonage in the Wigwam's hierarchy would ease the path to modest riches for him. He didn't ask for much. Just enough to find a decent place for his mother to live away from the street gangs and saloons of Hell's Kitchen.

He was ripped abruptly from his dream by a shriek followed by a spate of profanity uncommon only in its being delivered in well-bred female tones. He looked about for the cause of the commotion but saw nothing up and down the avenue apart from the ordinary throng of disorderly habitués.

The noise continued unabated and unnoticed, it seemed, by anyone but him. A sudden crash and a shower of broken glass on his helmet and on the sidewalk around him drew his attention upward. There, at a third-story window of a small hotel, a woman stood framed in broken glass, screaming into the night.

"Help!" she screamed. "Murder! Police!"

"Here I am!" Timothy shouted back. "What room?"

The woman glanced down and seemed about to say something when she disappeared from the window and the profanity resumed.

Timothy burst through the etched-glass doors of the hotel, followed by a panting horde of onlookers who had scattered from the shower of glass but clustered again at the prospect of imminent bloodshed. He strode toward the staircase, pausing for a moment to apprise the desk clerk that he had Police business upstairs. A feeble old bellboy came racing down the stairs to stop him and find out what the matter was.

Upon reaching the third floor, he had no difficulty discerning which of the several brass-numbered doors sheltered the heinous crime in process of being committed. Here, the woman's voice was accompanied by loud thumps, bumps, and bangs, as if the furnishings of the room were being dismantled by a team of wreckers.

He tried the door of room number 32, only to find that it was securely locked. "Police!" he shouted. "Open up!"

Silence fell behind the door, but it remained closed. And locked.

He placed his ear against the door and heard not even a whisper. If the woman was quiet, he wondered, could it mean that she was dead, murdered? So much for his glorious rescue of frail womanhood.

"I'll have to break it in!" he roared at the door. "Stand

back!" he admonished the crowd that filled the narrow hallway. They inched back barely enough to give him leg room, and a voice cried out, "Go to it, Leatherhead! Show us the body!"

Timothy applied the heel of his boot to the door once, twice, thrice before it gave way. There in the gaslit chamber he beheld the woman who had cried out to him from the broken window. She was huddled on the bed, staring at that same window, and shivering in the cold blast of winter wind that swept into the room, causing the gas flame to flicker in its naked wall bracket. Her plump white hand was raised to her throat, and her mouth worked dryly, but no words came.

There was no one else in the room.

"What's the trouble, ma'am?" Timothy asked.

The woman sat and shivered, but she didn't answer him, except for a low moan that escaped from her parted lips that glowed red with rouge in her ashen face.

"Are you hurt, ma'am?" Timothy asked. "Is there some injury, perhaps, that I should be looking at?" As it was, he couldn't take his eyes from her swelling bosom, her narrow waist, her blooming hips, all encased in gleaming scarlet satin. She seemed young, about his own age, but Timothy knew that paint and powder could do wonders for even an ancient hag of thirty.

The woman sighed and turned her tragic dark eyes toward him. "Gone," she murmured. "But he'll be back. He'll find me. And then he's sure to kill me after what I did to him."

Timothy was sure that the voice was the same that he'd heard screeching foul epithets inside the room. Now it was soft and pleading, and the words were those of a well-bred young lady, although their meaning was such that no coddled shakester would ever conceive. And her costume, though as stylish as any seen in the fashion parade on Fifth Avenue, betrayed her by its garish color as one of the night brigade.

The crowd in the hallway, disappointed in their quest for blood, began muttering and drifting away, but not before one hooligan in a plug hat shouted, "Ask her about Maggie the Monkey, why don't you."

The young woman shuddered at the sound of the name.

Timothy had heard of Maggie the Monkey, but had never set eyes on her. She was known throughout the Tenderloin as the keeper of a brothel that she staffed through a team of procuring agents who scoured the entire Eastern Seaboard for talented young ladies who spoke well, behaved politely, and knew how to pour tea. That the tea was often laced with brandy and chloral hydrate was known to all but the flat sams who drank it.

Maggie the Monkey had gotten her nickname not only because she resembled the agile little beast, with her long, thin arms and her wizened face in which a pair of quick little eyes were embedded. In her long-ago girlhood, so the legend went, Maggie had preyed on Central Park strollers by swinging from tree branches and dropping down on them, relieving them of their valuables and then shinnying back up into the overhead foliage. It was even rumored that her habitual black bombazine concealed a long, hairy tail that whipped into a frenzy when she was enraged, but no one had ever seen it.

Timothy could not believe that the young woman staring at him in the wrecked room was one of Maggie's geese. To give himself time to gather his thoughts, he attempted to right an overturned chair but gave it up when he found it had only three legs. The other leg was lying on the tumbled bed, half concealed by a scarlet fold of the young woman's skirt.

"And what might this be?" Timothy asked, picking up the splintered piece of wood.

The woman cringed and buried her face in her hands. "Don't hit me!" she cried. "Please don't hit me!"

"Ah, sure now, I won't be hitting you. Is that what happened to you? Did some bingo-boy try to beat you with this? And what did you do to earn such punishment?" He tossed the chair leg back onto the bed.

"Nothing, I swear, Sergeant." She raised her tear-stained face and reached out to clutch at his arm. "Oh, this is a terrible city. I wish I'd never come here. There is no one more unfortunate than I. No doubt you heard me berating my companion. That's what it's come to with me. Foul speech in a despicable resort of criminals and worse. Can you help me?"

"Now, now," Timothy consoled her. "It's not so bad if you know the right people." For some reason, he failed to correct her impression that he was a Sergeant of Police. Perhaps he would be soon enough if she turned out to be what he thought she was—one of Maggie's girls, stolen from a good family and trying to run away and get home again. Returning her to Maggie's protection should earn him notice in the right quarters.

"Are you the right person?" she asked, favoring him with a tentative smile even as a final tear rolled down her cheek.

Outside the window, the stalled train, with a hoot and a rumble, got under way, making conversation impossible until it passed on down the line.

When it was gone, the young woman rose from the bed and requested Timothy to turn his back while she adjusted her disheveled clothing. Timothy was pleased to oblige, dreaming all the while of the great reward that would be his when he appeared at Maggie's establishment with the runaway in tow. Maggie would surely put in a good word for him with the men of influence who were her patrons.

Timothy knew what hit him. He saw it coming in the cracked mirror of the vandalized dresser from which he was trying, with only modest success, to avert his eyes so as to afford the young lady her privacy. He whirled too late to stop it and bring his own sturdy locust club into play, being somewhat loath to bounce it off the head of a woman. The chair leg caught him just over the ear, knocking his helmet off. The first blow sank him to his knees; the second brought him sweet oblivion.

He awoke with his head cradled in the fusty lap of the ancient bellboy. "She cracked you a good one, didn't she, didn't she?" the relic cackled. "Coulda told you, but you wouldn't have listened. Wanted to be a hero, didn't you, didn't you? He-he-he."

Timothy groaned and sat up. "How long . . .?" he muttered.

"Not long," said the ancient one. "But you'll never catch up with her. She's a fly one, is Miss Dandy Dover. She's gone these twenty minutes, and that's time enough for her to disappear from the face of the earth. What I'd like to know is what happened to the lush she was rolling. I seen him come in with her, but I never seen him leave. Ah, well, it's none of mine. But I was thinking, it might be worth your while for me to forget what happened here."

Timothy was about to tell the fellow to go hang himself from the elevated tracks, but sober second thought produced a revelation. It would do him no good for word to get around that he'd been konked on the idea pot by a woman, and a lush-roller at that. He groped in his pocket for some loose change. Finding a disturbing absence of clink, he went on a search for his wallet. Gone! And with it the ten dollars he'd collected on his rounds that night to be passed on to his Roundsman. And how was he going to explain that?

He retrieved his helmet and got to his feet. "I'll see that you get a reward," he muttered to the bellboy, who was still kneeling on the floor. "I'm not carrying any cash right now."

The bellboy cackled. "Cleaned you out, too, didn't she, didn't she? Well, that's OK. I'll trust you for it, but no longer than tomorrow night. After that, the word goes out and every active citizen in the district will know what a billy-noodle you are. I won't be hard on you. A finnif will do the trick." The old man leered up at him ingratiatingly. "Now give your grandfather a hand and help me get up. My old bones ain't what they used to be."

Timothy hauled the codger to his feet and stumped out of the room and away from the scene of his disgrace. The old man's cackle followed him, ringing down the hallway. "Just chalk it up to experience, me boy. Everybody gets smart from experience. See you tomorrow night. Just ask for Albert Dooley, Bert the Barber to me friends. He-he-he."

As he tromped down the stairs and out of the hotel, Timothy realized that he was very, very lucky, despite the loss of his wallet and the shame of being bested by a woman. If the old bellboy was, indeed, Bert the Barber, he was lucky to have escaped without having his throat slit. Bert the Barber was famous for his nasty habit of giving extremely close shaves to people he didn't like. And if Miss Dandy Dover hadn't lifted his wallet, Bert likely had.

Somehow, he'd have to come up with the missing ten for his Roundsman and another five for the bellboy. This being a policeman was turning out to be very costly. Sadly, he resumed walking his beat, vowing to come to no more rescues of ladies in distress.

The following morning, an alarm was telephoned in to Police Headquarters in Mulberry Street. An early-rising tenant in a block of flats at Sixth Avenue and 47th Street, while taking a bracing breath of fresh morning air at his fourth-story window, had seen something on the roof of a passing train that suspiciously resembled a body. The word went out on the police telegraph, and soon patrolmen and detectives were deployed up and down the line, stopping all trains and searching them, inside and out, to the outrage of the passengers thus deprived of their speedy delivery to their destinations.

Timothy Crane was not one of the deployment, being at that hour at home in bed in the tiny, windowless room he shared with his elder brother, James. But Timothy was not asleep. He lay staring into the darkness that inhabited the room at all hours of the night and day, nursing a fierce headache while trying to keep in place a chunk of ice chipped from the melting block in the icebox and wrapped in an old undershirt. Beside him in the lumpy bed, Jimmy snored and emitted stale beer fumes.

Jimmy Crane's business kept him active in the dark hours of the city, too. He was a member of The Gophers, the acknowledged ruling gang of Hell's Kitchen, and some thought him in line to become its leader if and when One Lung Curran coughed his last.

Although Jimmy bore his brother some slight ill will for having joined the Police, he was an intelligent lad, and softhearted when it came to girls and family. "It's all the same, isn't it?" he would often say to fellow Gophers in defense of his brother. "We knock heads and so do the Police. We collect our share in our territory, and so do they. What's the dif? There's plenty to go around."

Unable to sleep, Timothy kicked his brother under the

covers. Jimmy groaned, snorted, and belched. Timothy kicked him again. "Say, Jimmy," he muttered. "Can ye lend me twenty?"

"Bugger off," Jimmy mumbled, rolling over and taking most of the covers with him.

Timothy yanked them back, leaving his brother exposed to the chill. "It's life and death, Jimmy," he persisted. "Ye wouldn't want to find me with me throat slit, now would ya?"

"Now what on earth did you do to deserve that, ye silly sucker?" said Jimmy, hauling back his share of the comforter.

"Nothing," Timothy mumbled. "I just need it."

"Ain't you getting your share of the spoils? What's wrong with you?"

"There's nothing wrong with me that twenty dollars won't cure. Come on, Jim. Don't you want to save your only brother's life?" Timothy hated the wheedling tone he adopted, but he knew the way to his brother's soft heart.

"Tell me what your trouble is, and I'll give it to you."

Timothy was loath to tell anyone of his shame. He considered inventing a tale of bail needed to save an innocent neighborhood girl from prison. But Jimmy was long accustomed to his fanciful imagination and always cottoned to his stories. He decided on an abbreviated version of the truth.

"I . . . ah . . . I owe some money to Bert the Barber."

"Oh, is that all," said Jimmy. "Well, me and the boys'll take care of that. We'll break his legs and bite both his ears off and carve him up a little. That's more than we usually do for twenty dollars, but you're a relative. Now kindly shut up and let me get some sleep." Jimmy rolled over and began breathing rhythmically.

Timothy kicked him again. "That's not it!" he howled. "Just give me the money and I'll take care of my own problem."

"Okay. Okay. I'll give it to you when I wake up. I was only kidding, anyhow. Can't you take a joke?"

"Give it to me now," Timothy insisted. "Otherwise I'll never get to sleep myself."

"Go look in me trousers," Jimmy mumbled. "And don't take a penny more. I know exactly what's in me pockets."

Timothy got up and groped in the darkness for a lucifer to light the gas. He found his brother's trousers in a heap on the floor and from one pocket pulled out a wad of bills that made him gasp. He felt a pang of envy. His brother had had a busy and profitable night, while he had shown himself a fool. Never again, he promised himself. He would find Miss Dandy Dover and get his own back and a little bit more.

He peeled off two fives and a ten from the fat roll, stuffed it back into Jimmy's pocket, and with the bribe money and an extra five for himself secure in his fist, returned to the bed to sleep the sleep of the pure in heart.

While he slept, a frozen body was removed from the roof of one of the cars of a Sixth Avenue elevated train at the Eighth Street station in Greenwich Village. It was the body of a young man in evening dress. He was not identified since his pockets had been completely cleaned out, his shirt studs were missing, and whatever jewelry he might have worn was gone as well.

He was carried off to the morgue at Bellevue Hospital to thaw out and await further developments.

When he reported to the station house the next evening, Timothy handed over ten dollars to his supervising Roundsman, who praised him for his diligence. "Keep it up, me lad, and there'll be a little something extra for you at the end of the month," the officer confided.

Timothy thanked him politely, even while calculating the Roundsman's daily take from all the patrolmen under his jurisdiction. Not as much as Jimmy had amassed in one night, but the Roundsman's haul was steady, and Jimmy's was hit or miss. The thought comforted him that he'd made the right choice in joining the force, and steeled his ambition to rise in it.

He set off upon his rounds, always keeping an eye out for the white face and scarlet skirts of his nemesis, and made an early stop at the hotel, where he found Bert the Barber dozing in an armchair in the minuscule lobby.

"Did ye hear about it?" Bert inquired as he pocketed the five.

"Hear about what?" Timothy inquired.

"The body that was found on top of the train. Now that's a real mystery. The police don't know who he is or how he came to be there. I was thinking you might have some idea."

"Me? How would I know? That's a job for the detectives."

"Sure enough it is, isn't it? But a smart young copper like you, wouldn't ye like to get in ahead of 'em?" Bert stared up at the ceiling as if examining it for cobwebs or possible leaks from the upper regions.

A warning went off in Timothy's brain. Why should Bert want to be helping him get ahead? He still half-suspected the bellboy of having lifted his wallet. Nevertheless, he guilelessly asked, "How could I do that?"

"Well, if you don't know, I'm not sure I should tell you." Bert grinned at him, showing spacious gaps between the yellowed snaggles that remained in his mouth.

"Tell me what?" Timothy asked earnestly. "You've got your finnif. What else do you want from me?"

"Ah, now, don't get brave with me. I can be a good friend to you if I take a mind to it. Here, let me show you something I found." The old man went to a door set under the staircase that led to the upper rooms and laid a gnarled hand on the knob. "Did ye not wonder," he smirked, "whatever happened to the lush she was rolling last night?"

"He left," said Timothy. "Before I got there. If he was ever there at all."

"Oh, he was there, all right. And how, may I ask, did he leave?"

"Why, in the usual way, I suppose," said Timothy.

"What? With you barreling up the stairs and a pack of rabble close on your tail?"

"Well, then he went up to the next floor and hid there until I went away."

"Did he? And I suppose he's still up there, waiting for the Fourth of July?"

Timothy turned and started up the stairs, but the old man grasped his arm and yanked him back. "Don't be such a cabbage-head. The pigeon flew, but not through the front door. I'd have seen him go. Bert the Barber never sleeps, not when there's things to be seen and thinking to be done."

"Then how?" Timothy asked in bewilderment. "Is there a fire escape?"

"Not yet, there isn't. And there won't be as long as the Fire Department keeps happy. Enough of this. I want to show you something. Though what you'll do with it is up to you."

He opened the door and revealed a closet full of satchels, trunks, carpetbags, and odd bits of clothing.

From a shelf, he grabbed a silk top hat and handed it to Timothy. "What do you make of that?" he asked.

"It's a gent's topper. Did someone leave it here?"

"It was in that room, under the bed. I found it after you left. Take a look inside. Do I have to tell you everything?"

Obediently, Timothy looked inside the hat. "There's a label in here," he announced. "Martin G. DeW. Shaw. That must be the owner."

"Now you got it," the old man crowed. "The rest is up to you." He retrieved the hat and stowed it back on its shelf. "I'll just hold on to this, for safekeeping, until you need it."

Timothy's brain was whirling. The hat, the body on top of the train, Miss Dandy Dover. Had murder, indeed, been done on his beat, and right under, or over, his nose? This was worse than anything he could have imagined. He'd never be able to redeem himself if this got out. Unless . . . unless he could bring the criminal to justice single-handed and before anyone discovered what had happened here.

But he hadn't quite lost his senses. "Why?" he asked. "Why are you telling me all this? What's a little murder to you?"

"Who said anything about murder?" exclaimed Bert the Barber in real or feigned astonishment. "I know nothing about any murder." And then his eyes brightened with intelligence. "Oh, you mean the body on the train. You think she did it? Well, it wouldn't be the first for her. I could tell you things about Miss Dandy Dover that would shock even you." He patted Timothy on the arm and led him toward the front door. "Just remember," he cautioned. "You didn't hear anything from me."

Before leaving, a few more questions occurred to

Timothy. "Why are you ratting on her? What's she done to you?"

"First place, though you may not think so, this is a respectable establishment. I don't hold with croaking on the premises. It gives the place a bad name."

"What's it to you?" Timothy interposed. "You're just a bellboy."

"So it may seem," Bert responded. "And that's the way I like it. But the fact is, I own this place. You could call it my retirement home. And I don't want my old age disturbed by murder and the like. Second," he went on, "Miss Dandy Dover owes me. She was supposed to hand over my share of her gains, but she hared out of here without so much as a wink. That's no way for an honest thief to act. So find her, young Leatherhead, and we'll all be merry."

With that, he pushed Timothy out the door and into the cold.

By midnight, the Police had still not been able to identify the corpse that had been found on the train, but he had thawed sufficiently for an autopsy to be performed.

The doctor found that he had frozen to death after having swallowed enough chloral hydrate combined with a sufficient quantity of brandy to knock him out for a week. It was actually enough to kill him, but he had died before the lethal combination had had a chance to do its final work.

One thing was certain. This was no Hell's Kitchen or Tenderloin ruffian. His soft white hands and his well-groomed, glossy hair, as well as his expensive evening dress, proclaimed him a member of the upper class, if not a scion of the mighty Four Hundred. Inquiries had already been instituted, up and down Fifth Avenue, and among the new mansions, apartment buildings, and row houses of the Riverside Avenue and the high-numbered streets between it and the Park. They had been halted at supper-time, but would continue on the morrow and as many morrows as it took to discover the corpse's identity and how he had come to his elevated and frozen end.

Meanwhile, detectives converged on Sixth Avenue and the streets bordering the elevated tracks, seeking information from anyone who might have seen a drunken man climbing by himself or being assisted to climb on top of a train. They were particularly attentive to the denizens of Satan's Circus, where the administration of knockout drops was a common practice.

Though murder was a consideration, the official view was that the man, groggy from drink and drug, had died by misadventure or in trying to escape from the gang of thieves who had doped and robbed him. The detectives were instructed to pursue this line of inquiry, but to be alert for any indication of even fouler play. There was no point in needlessly disturbing the businessmen and women of the Tenderloin, who were so cooperative in other respects, with suspicions of murder.

Timothy passed a number of these detectives on his rounds, but he recognized none for what they were. They blended perfectly with the crowd in their dark-colored, anonymous ulsters and stiff bowler hats.

When he came to 27th Street, he turned off the avenue and stood for a time outside the tall brownstone that housed Maggie the Monkey's establishment. He had remembered the advice shouted out in the hotel hallway the night before, and he determined to find out what he could there about Miss Dandy Dover. But how was he to gain entrance? What pretext might he use to get past those carved doors and see for himself whether or no the lady was within? Maggie, he knew, was well protected. It was rumored that she paid thousands each year into the coffers of Tammany and the Police Commissioners alike.

As he stood there, gazing up at the lighted windows and listening to the faint tinkle of ragtime piano, he rejected ploy after ploy as being too feeble, too easily seen through. After about five frigid minutes of this, the iron gate guarding the lower entrance creaked open and a half-grown girl, wrapped in a shawl, crept out.

Timothy tipped his helmet to her and said, "Good evening, Miss. It's a cold night to be out in. Have you far to go?"

She eyed him warily and shook her head.

"Perhaps I'll walk along with you for a bit. The night streets are dangerous. Which way are you going?"

"Ach, only a little vay, I hope," she whispered, her words strongly tinged with the Germanic stamp. "They ran out of cream for the syllabub, and I must find some or lose my position. Do you know where I might find fresh cream this time of the night?"

"That I might," said Timothy, racking his brain for the unlikely prospect of a dairy in this region, let alone one that would be open for business. "Walk along with me, and we'll see what we can find." He began walking in a westerly direction, the girl shivering along beside him.

"And what is this position of yours," he asked, "that you are so fearful of losing?"

"Ach, sir, I'm only a scullery maid, but I daren't lose my place. I'd have nowhere to go."

"So you live in that fine house. That must be grand for you."

"It's a grand house, ja," she agreed, "but the mistress is hard. But my poppa died last month and now my momma is sick in the hospital, and for the rent I had no money, so

I must work here and hope she don't die also. I think I am lucky to have this job." She spoke phlegmatically, as if these misfortunes were only to be expected.

"Tell me a little about your work," said Timothy. "What is it you do in that house?"

The girl looked up at him, searching his round, open face for any sign of mockery. Apparently satisfied that he would not jeer at her lowly status, she began to chatter. "I wash the dishes and clean the rooms. And then, I help the cook. She's nice. She always lets me taste what she cooks. The part I don't like is taking breakfast up to the ladies. They never want to wake up, even though it's almost night again, and their rooms smell funny. Oh, I know it's just perfume and old champagne and the sweet stuff they smoke in their little pipes, but it gives me a headache."

She would have gone on chattering, but Timothy interrupted her. "Tell me about the ladies. How many are there?"

"Twelve," she answered with certainty. "The mistress has always twelve ladies living there, but not always the same ones. And then there's the cook and me. The doorman comes at five o'clock. I don't like him. He's always asking me when I'm going to graduate to the rooms upstairs. And then, of course, there's the mistress."

"Is there any lady there that wears a bright red satin dress?" Timothy asked.

The girl giggled. "They all do," she said. "And purple and green and blue. But never black. Only the mistress wears black. They're so beautiful. The ladies, I mean, not the mistress. She's ugly and old."

Timothy felt he was getting on swimmingly with the girl, but he still didn't know if Miss Dandy Dover was in residence. "Tell me their names," he demanded.

"Well, there's Fritzie and Mitzie, they're sisters. And

then there's Dolly, Marie, Eleanor that they call Sidesaddle, and Gussie, who has a tattoo on her chest . . ."

Timothy stopped the spate. "Is there no one there named Dandy?"

"Oh, you mean Miss Dover? She comes only once in a while, and always the mistress takes her upstairs to her office. She's nice. She gave me an ivory fan once with pictures of cupid on it. She was there last night, but she left with one of the guests."

"Do you know where she lives?"

"Oh, no, sir. Just that she comes there sometimes."

They were walking up Seventh Avenue by then, and Timothy spotted a restaurant still open where he was known to the proprietor. Perhaps he'd be able to get a pint of cream there. "Wait here," he said. "By the way, what's your name?"

"Elsa Muller," she said. "Will you be long?"

He noticed that she was shivering in her thin shawl. "Not long," he told her. "And with any luck, you can go right back to your nice, warm kitchen."

The proprietor was accommodating and even offered Timothy a glass of schnapps, which he downed gratefully.

Back on the street, he hurried Elsa Muller home to Maggie's brothel. It wouldn't be long, he reflected, before she did graduate to the upstairs rooms, perhaps not at Maggie's but at some other, less particular establishment. She was pretty enough, with her blonde braids and her fresh, rosy cheeks, but she lacked the polish that was required of Maggie's girls. He guessed her age at about ten or eleven. By the time she was thirteen, she'd, no doubt, be an accomplished tart.

The information Elsa had given him was useful. He knew that Miss Dandy Dover turned up occasionally at Maggie's and that she had left there last night with an elephant-hunter, probably the same one that was found frozen on the train. But he was no closer to finding out where she might be located. He couldn't spend the night lurking outside the brothel in the hope that she might appear. It looked as if he might have to lose sleep if he was to beat the detectives to the criminal.

He resumed his rounds, making his collections, carefully ignoring certain activities, and breaking up a fight or two before the gaslights paled in the gray, cold light of dawn.

No one, it seemed, was missing a young gentleman in his mid-twenties, five feet eleven inches tall, 157 pounds, brown eyes, dark brown hair, with a three-inch scar on his left forearm and a mole on the back of his neck over which he had let his hair grow. The detectives, wearying of the search, dreaded the prospect of extending their inquiries to the City of Brooklyn, or even to Westchester or New Jersey.

They met at Police Headquarters early the next morning to discuss the case, and agreed that before searching farther afield, they would investigate the hundreds of Manhattan hotels and boardinghouses, descending into the areas of questionable respectability if necessary.

The detectives who were working the Tenderloin had met with a stone wall of ignorance wherever they turned. They were intuitive men, however, and they had the feeling that something was known but no one was talking. "We may have to pound some heads," said one of them.

"Not until we know who the victim is," cautioned another. "If he turns out to be nobody, we could all lose *our* heads if we ruffle the wrong feathers. You all know the drill."

Meanwhile, Timothy Crane, off-duty at last, and somewhat refreshed by a cup of hot tea, a splash of cold water in the face, and a shave, decided that the best place to start looking for Mr. Martin G. DeW. Shaw was the city telephone directory. But where to find one? No one he knew had a telephone. There was one, of course, at the station house, and a directory to go with it, but the day Roundsman or the Sergeant-in-Charge would surely want to know what he was up to.

His mother was already busy at her washtub and scrubbing board, and the wash boiler was steaming away on the coal-fed kitchen range, making everything cozy and warm and damp. The place smelled, as it always did, of hot starch, bluing, and the strong soap that ate up her hands and left them raw and scabbed. "Are ye not going to bed now, Timmy, darling?" she asked.

"No, me old dear. I've got important work to do." He couldn't resist boasting a little to his mother. He knew she was proud of him, but it wouldn't hurt to give her something else to be proud of.

"What is it, then?" she asked.

"Secret," he whispered. "And don't you go blabbing to anyone about it or you could spoil it all for me."

"I'm sure I don't want to know." She turned, tight-lipped, back to her washing.

"You can help me, though," Timothy cajoled. "Who do you know who's got a telephone?"

"Nobody." She continued scrubbing away at the hem of a fine ruffled petticoat. "Oh, the street dirt that gets on everything. It's so hard to get out."

"If I come out on top of this, you won't have to take in washing anymore. Where did you go to call the doctor that time Jimmy was so bad with the typhoid?"

"I won't take any money from you if it's dishonest," his mother said. "I don't take it from Jimmy and that's my rule. I'd rather scrub my way into my grave."

"It's not dishonest, I swear. Now, where did you go?"

"Hurley, the drug store in Tenth Avenue. He showed me how to use it. It's a frightening thing, Timmy. Cora downstairs told me it could shoot electricity into your ear and scramble your brains. You be careful with it."

"It's Cora whose brains are scrambled. The telephone is a wonderful invention, and we'll soon be having one here."

"Not while I live," his mother replied, turning back to her work.

Timothy went out into a bright, clear, cold morning in which the traffic of Ninth Avenue was already on the rumble. The clip-clop of countless horses' hooves on the cobblestones and the thunder of the iron-wheeled convey-ances they pulled created a din that certified to the amazing vigor of the huge metropolis that seemed in one breath to have grown as much as it could, and in the next, to sprout new buildings, new marvels of science, and fresh hordes of greenhorns to fill up every nook and cranny.

He walked up Ninth Avenue, bundled into his reefer jacket, happy in his youth and strength, and in the determination that he would this day find some answers to the many questions that filled his head.

In the shadows under the El, broken by slanting rays of sunlight shining through the tracks, tramps had erected rude shelters between the supporting pillars. A few of them, desperate-looking men, squatted in front of their foul nests, warming themselves at trash fires and boiling up their morning coffee in blackened tin cans, while the traffic swirled by on either side and trains roared over-head.

At 49th Street, he headed west, but before leaving Ninth Avenue, he stood for a moment gazing up at the tracks and at the building facing them, trying to estimate the open space between and guess how a body might be got across from one to the other. A circus strong man might, perhaps, heave such a weight from the roof of a building to the top of a train, but certainly not a woman such as Miss Dandy Dover. More than likely, the body that was found, which fact he had verified upon his return to the station house, had nothing to do with his problem. Bert the Barber was simply trying to incriminate the lady out of sheer meanness and revenge.

He walked rapidly over to Tenth Avenue and entered Hurley's drug store, where he found the white-coated proprietor brandishing a feather duster over his shelves of patent medicines.

"It's young Tim Crane, isn't it? And a good morning to you," Mr. Hurley greeted him. "I haven't seen you in some long time, not since you were in knickerbockers, but I'd know you anywhere. And how fares your good mother? Have you come for her ration of Lydia Pinkham's? I know she swears by it, as do many of my lady customers. It's a grand tonic, and one that I heartily recommend."

Mentally, Timothy cursed the old man for a blathering fool, but a shrewd one, ferreting out all the neighborhood gossip and dosing it out liberally along with his cure-alls and nostrums.

"She's well enough," Timothy answered. "I'd like to take a look at your telephone directory, if you please."

"Ah-ha!" Hurley exclaimed. "A wonderful book, a truly democratic book. Everyone on the telephone is listed in there, from my own humble self to the grandest of the Vanderbilts, and all in the same kind of print." He reached under the marble-topped counter and drew forth a slim volume, which he handed proudly to Timothy. "I hear you've joined the Police," he remarked. "A grand profession, and well worth the modest amount required of me each month for ease of mind and freedom from the depredations of the unruly. Is it business or pleasure you're bent on?"

Timothy longed to tell the old fool to put a sock in it, but he couldn't afford to make his visit any more memorable than it already was. Whatever he told Hurley would be blown up, embroidered upon, and purveyed to all the old biddies who came into the shop. Might as well make it good, he thought.

"Aw, it's nothing important," he muttered, insuring that Hurley would take the opposite meaning. "It's just that I've met this young lady. Well, not so young but not so old either. And she invited me to tea. But like an idiot, I lost her address. So, I thought, well, maybe she's on the telephone and I could find her that way." Timothy opened the book on the counter and began leafing through its pages.

"Tea, is it?" Hurley leered, his eyes shining with lascivious interest. "A lonely, old woman, and rich, no doubt. You're a lucky lad and I'm sure you'll make the best of this opportunity. Might I know her name? Perhaps I could help you locate her in the book."

"I couldn't tell you that, Mr. Hurley, sir," said Timothy. "It wouldn't be the gentlemanly thing to do." He continued leafing idly through the directory, prolonging the moment of reaching the appropriate page.

"Right you are. Everything confidential and circumspect. That's the way to treat affairs of the heart. But if you want some advice, don't ever let her get the upper hand. And make sure she gives more than she gets. You're only young once, and youth is a commodity like everything else in this world."

The bell over the entrance tinkled and a bevy of young

mothers with their infants in their arms swept into the shop. The druggist reluctantly went to tend to their needs for teething remedies, colic cures, and herbal teas to promote the flow of milk for nursing.

Quickly, Timothy flipped to the appropriate page and found that there were a half dozen Shaws listed, in places ranging from a cigar factory on Canal Street to an undertaker in Harlem. There was no Martin G. DeW. Shaw, but there was an Edgar F. Shaw on Park Avenue and a Miss Wilhelmina Shaw on West Eleventh Street. Both were worth looking into. The silk hat could belong to a son or a brother or a maiden aunt's nephew. He jotted down the information on a scrap of paper, which he stuffed into his pocket.

When Hurley returned, Timothy was frowning over a page near the front of the book.

"Any luck at all?" Hurley inquired.

"None," said Timothy. "I guess I'll have to miss my big chance."

"Didn't I see you writing something down?"

"Ah, it was just the name of a foot doctor that I happened to notice. I've been having some trouble with my feet and I thought I might go see him." He was about to close the directory and hand it back to Hurley when his eye was caught by a name on the page that he had been pretending to study. Danielle DuVerre, milliner. D. D. Dandy Dover. It was a long shot, but it might pay off. The address was on East 49th Street, just across town, and in a different world.

Hurley was watching him closely even as he babbled on about his corn removers and bunion relievers. "It's a terrible thing for a policeman to have bad feet. You should soak them in hot water and oatmeal every day, and take every occasion to give them a rest."

Timothy bought a bottle of the recommended corn remover, thanked Hurley for his help, and left the shop, with the druggist shouting additional advice in his wake.

Miss Dandy Dover slept until noon, as was her habit, but awoke promptly at the stroke of twelve. Her maid brought her tea and buttered toast and the morning newspapers. She turned first to *The World*, where, true to her expectations, she found extensive and graphic coverage of the mystery surrounding the body found on top of the Sixth Avenue train.

The headlines screamed at her. "Detectives Baffled by Frozen Stiff!" And "When Will These Outrages Cease?" And further, "Gentlemen Are Warned to Avoid West Side Dives." Dandy read each of the articles carefully and quickly scanned the other papers, giving more than a cursory glance to Mr. Hearst's *Journal*, which, in trying to outdo Mr. Pulitzer's *World*, often printed news of questionable veracity. But even there, the reports held nothing that might link her with the crime. Now, if only Bert would keep his mouth shut.

After all, she may have rolled the lush, that was her trade—picking up the rabbit suckers at Maggie's and getting what was left of their goods someplace else, so they couldn't complain of being robbed at Maggie's. But she hadn't bargained for the simpleton to pull a gun on her when he realized what was going on. Thank heaven the Mickey Bert had slipped into his brandy had taken effect before he'd had a chance to do any damage. Nothing like that had ever happened before.

"And it'll never happen again," she murmured. "It's time for little Dandy to go into some other line."

She reached under her pillow and drew out the small, gold-plated revolver, ornately engraved with curlicues on the barrel and eagles on the ivory grip. She aimed it at her reflection in the mirror over her dressing table. "Bang!" she shouted. "Dandy Dover, you're dead! And Danielle DuVerre is going west. This very day."

Timothy Crane raced down the stairs of the Eighth Street station of the Sixth Avenue El, and rapidly headed north. A worried maiden aunt or spinster sister, he reasoned, would be easier to deal with than a Park Avenue male relative, so he might as well start with Miss Wilhelmina Shaw. If he hit pay dirt at either Shaw residence, then he would be ready to face Miss Dandy Dover with his accusation. On Eleventh Street, he found himself outside a well-kept brownstone house guarded by an intricate black iron fence. The windows were hung with dark red velvet draperies and the front door seemed designed to intimidate the uninvited.

He mounted the stoop and twisted the polished brass bell-ring. He waited. And waited. And waited. "Nobody home?" he muttered dejectedly. He rang the bell again. This time, he was rewarded by a furtive scuffling behind the door and the sound of the lock being turned. The door slid open a crack and a pair of thick spectacles peered out at him. The spectacles were crowned by a frizz of sparse gray hair topped by a frilly white cap, and a starched white apron billowed behind the door.

"Miss Wilhelmina Shaw?" Timothy inquired.

"The mistress is not at home," a wispy voice replied.

"You mean she's not here or she's not receiving?" Timothy pursued.

"Oh, she's here, all right," the voice replied, "but not for the likes of you."

"Would she be here for Martin?"

The door closed abruptly in his face.

Left cooling his heels, Timothy was sure he'd come to the right place. The ancient maid had as good as told him so by slamming the door on him.

At length, the door opened again, not widely, but wide enough for the maid to announce haughtily, "Miss Shaw says Mr. Martin may go to the Devil for all she cares."

Before the door could close on him permanently, Timothy said, "I believe he has."

The maid gaped at him. "Wait," she murmured. And the door closed again.

But not for long. The maid ushered him into the back parlor and left him standing before a small, frail, but regal old woman who sat enthroned beside a marble fireplace in which a coal fire smoldered.

Everything about her was cold and disdainful, from her pale eyes to the tips of her polished black boots. "If you've come for money," she snapped, "you'll get none from me."

"No, ma'am," Timothy said respectfully. "But if you are connected to a Mr. Martin G. DeW. Shaw, I may have some news for you."

Miss Shaw stared at him without blinking. Timothy thought that a snake would have shown more interest. "Are you?" he asked. "Connected?"

"Out with it, young man. Whatever my grand-nephew has been up to, it is nothing to do with me. He has left my house and my protection. He has no other relative in the world, but since he seems to value his low companions more than me, let him apply to them for help."

"Have you not heard of the body that was found on the El?"

"I do not travel on the 'El,' as you call it. And it has never been Martin's habit to do so."

Timothy searched his mind for the right words to breach

the old hag's cold heart and adamant disdain. "Would you be glad, then, to learn that he has died?"

"You are impudent, young man. Martin would not dare to die without letting me know. Who are you?"

"Timothy Crane, ma'am. And I don't mean to be impudent. But the truth is that a young man has been found frozen to death on top of a train, and I have reason to believe he is your grand-nephew."

"Are you one of his evil companions?"

"No, ma'am. I've never laid eyes on him. But I have information of his whereabouts night before last, and further reason to believe that he is the same young man that the Police cannot identify. The case has been in all the newspapers."

"I do not read newspapers."

"Would you come with me to the Police to identify him?"

"Absolutely not. You may go now."

"But, miss. Ma'am . . ."

"Go!" she commanded. Her eyes closed and she seemed to be instantly asleep or in a trance. It was obvious that the interview was at an end.

Timothy backed out of the room, never ceasing to watch her for some sign of grief or remorse until the door closed and he found himself in the hall, with the maid hovering nearby.

"Is it true?" she fluttered. "Oh, poor Mr. Martin. She's a terror, she is. It's not his fault he wanted a little life and gaiety. If it was up to her, she'd have him doing nothing but taking her to church and reading poetry to her every evening." Her tears gushed forth and she ended in a wail. "Oh, the poor orphan, to be taken off in such a terrible way!"

"There, there," Timothy soothed. "Would you be will-

ing to identify him for the Police?" At the sight of her
stricken face, he added, "You'd want him to have a decent
burial, now, wouldn't you? And how can he have that if
they don't know who he is? It'll be Potter's Field for him."

She shook her head sadly. "I dare not. She'd find out.
You must go now."

As she closed the door behind him, Timothy heard a
low keening that faded with the footsteps that pattered
away into the back regions of the house.

"Lulu! Lulu, where are you?" The young maid appeared, smiling, in the bedroom doorway. "Lulu, get my
trunk down from the attic and then help me pack it."

Lulu scurried away, no longer smiling, and Dandy
began emptying her bureau drawers, throwing piles of
lacy underthings and stiff corsets onto the bed. From her
tall wardrobe, she snatched gowns and cloaks, separating
them into those suitable for her new life and those she
would never wear again. When Lulu came thumping
down the stairs, dragging the trunk behind her, Dandy
was ready to start packing it.

"These are for you," she said, indicating the heap of
scarlet satin and purple silk and black lace. "Be sure you
get them out of here as soon as I'm gone."

"Oh, but Miss Dandy, whatever would I do with those
things?"

"Well, you might consider going into business for
yourself. Unless you like being a drudge. And don't ever
call me Miss Dandy again. Forget you ever heard that
name. Miss Dandy Dover doesn't exist. And Miss Danielle
DuVerre is removing to Boston, if anyone inquires. But
you won't be here, and neither will I."

"But Miss Dandy . . . I mean Miss Danielle, where shall
I go?"

"Anywhere you like. Now let's get busy on this trunk."

Between the two of them, they had the trunk packed within twenty minutes. The jewelry box went into a secret compartment, but not before Dandy had presented Lulu with a gold locket watch. "So you'll always know when it's time to scamper," she said. "Now help me dress and then go out and find a cab."

Lulu trembled as she hooked up Dandy's dark brown traveling costume. "Won't you take me with you?" she ventured. "I can be just as good a maid in Boston as I am here."

"I can't take you with me, Lulu. You see, I'm going to be married, and my husband-to-be has already provided a fully staffed house. But I must hurry, or I'll miss my train. Run along now and hire a cab, and be sure the driver is sturdy enough to carry this trunk down the stairs."

Lulu hesitated. "Miss, will you give me a reference? Please, miss, so I can get another situation?"

"Of course. How thoughtless of me. You shall have your reference, and a fine one it will be. I'll write it out for you while you fetch the cab. Now run along."

When the maid had gone, Dandy wrapped herself in her fur-trimmed traveling cloak, perched her broad-brimmed hat on her piled-up dark hair, and lowered its veil to hide her face. All her ready cash was concealed within her corset. The gold-plated revolver was secreted within her sable muff.

When the cab arrived, she was waiting for it at the front door. She directed the driver upstairs for the trunk, and took Lulu's hands in her own gloved ones. "My dear, Lulu, I shall miss you."

"Oh, Miss Dandy . . . I mean Miss Danielle, I hope you'll be very happy in your new life, and that you have lots of children." Lulu was close to weeping from the loveliness of this unforeseen romance.

"Be sure you clear out all the clothes I've left up there," Dandy admonished. "If you can't wear them, you can always sell them."

"Oh, I wouldn't . . ." Lulu began. But Dandy had swept out the door, and the trunk was descending on the shoulders of the cab driver. She had to content herself with waving farewell from the doorway.

"The Grand Central Station," she heard her former mistress instruct the driver.

As soon as the cab had rounded the corner, Dandy tapped on the roof to catch the driver's attention. He obediently reined in the horse and slid open the trap on the roof. "I've changed my mind, driver," Dandy called up to him. "Take me to the Pavonia Ferry dock, instead." As the driver changed to a westerly course and the ferry connection with the Lake Erie and Western Railroad, she settled back, content that she had done everything she could to avoid complicity in the death of young Mr. Martin G. DeW. Shaw.

"After all," she murmured to herself, "I had nothing to do with killing him. And Bert and Maggie can just go scratch for their share of the haul."

Timothy Crane arrived at the corner of Fifth Avenue and 49th Street just in time to witness the departure of a veiled woman from a small house near the corner. His sharp eyes spied a discreet trade sign in a front window of the house. "Fine French Millinery," the sign read. The trunk strapped to the back of the cab alerted him to an imminent getaway.

"That's surely her!" he exulted, and with the agility born of childish years of hitching rides, he ran after the cab and attached himself to its rear platform, grappling himself snugly onto the trunk. He could see nothing but a broad hat brim through the oval isinglass rear window of the cab, but confident that he had come upon Miss Dandy Dover in the act of escaping Justice, he settled down to await events.

As the cab jolted west and then south, a detective arrived at Maggie the Monkey's establishment. He was kept waiting in the deserted parlor, with nothing to occupy him but the remains of the previous night's festivities only now being cleared away by the young drudge whom he had intimidated into admitting him. Her cheek bore the fresh imprint of a vicious slap, and she sniffled as she went about her labors. The detective was certain that she'd been instructed by the old harridan to keep an eye on him while he awaited Her Majesty's pleasure.

As Elsa Muller cleared away the dirty glasses and the reeking cigar butts, she contrasted the detective's stern behavior with the kindness shown her the night before by the young policeman who had helped her find the cream she needed. Last night, she had been praised by Maggie for a resourceful girl. Today, she had been slapped and scolded for an incompetent wretch. But Maggie was always nasty when her sleep was disturbed. Elsa wondered if the detective, too, was looking for Miss Dover.

When she heard footsteps on the stairs, she scurried to put a large armchair between herself and the wrath of her mistress. The detective rose to his feet and removed his bowler hat.

Maggie the Monkey strode into the room, her scowl as black as her habitual bombazine. "Scat!" she snarled at Elsa. "Before I give you another one."

Elsa sidled past her, afraid to run, but equally afraid to

get too close to those gnarled little hands that stung like fire.

When the girl had gone, closing the door behind her, Maggie's face transformed itself into a hideous smile of welcome, revealing a set of false teeth much too large for the little simian face wreathed in wrinkles. "Is something amiss?" she inquired sweetly of the detective. "Or are you here for a little unscheduled recreation? My ladies are all asleep."

"No, ma'am," the detective replied. "I am here with respect to a gentleman found deceased. You may have read about the case in the newspapers. We're canvassing all possible locations in the hope of discerning his identity."

"Ah, yes." Maggie nodded sagely. "A pitiful end for one so young. The newspaper said he was not more than twenty-five or so. But you must know that my clientele is not given to such escapades. Nor are my ladies in the habit of rolling lushes. They wouldn't last long here if they were. That's where you must search. Among the army of predatory females who ply their evil trade in the streets beyond the walls of this respectable house."

The detective cleared his throat to keep from choking on this torrent of sanctimony. "Of course," he murmured soothingly. "Nevertheless, our instructions are to make inquiries of every person who might have seen the gentleman on the night in question. Could it be possible that he spent some time here *before* venturing outside to his doom?"

"Possible?" Maggie echoed. "Anything is possible. But I doubt that he would have been so dissatisfied with the entertainments provided here that he would seek further distraction elsewhere. We pride ourselves on catering to every slightest whim. Within reason, of course, and for a price."

"Yes," agreed the detective. "But young men sometimes become unreasonable, and sometimes run out of the ready."

"Are you doubting my word?" Maggie's scowl was back in place.

"No, ma'am, not at all. But you haven't yet heard a physical description of the deceased. Will you hear it now?"

Still scowling, she nodded.

The detective reeled off the young man's particulars while Maggie continued nodding and seemed lost in thought. At length, her face brightened.

"You were correct in coming to me," she said. "I believe I can help you. There was a young man here on the night in question. He was such as you describe, but so are many young men, so I can't be certain. The one I have in mind was already inebriated when he arrived, so we offered him nothing more than a sobering cup of tea. He became displeased at this and left. Being fearful for his safety while on my property, I watched him stagger down the stoop and reel away toward Sixth Avenue. Before he had gone ten paces, he was accosted by one of those women who prey on his kind. That was the last I saw of him."

The detective, who had been scribbling in his notebook, looked up and asked, "Would you, by any chance, know the name of this woman?"

"In other circumstances," Maggie answered, "I would be most reluctant to give you that information. But murder is bad for business. On the other hand, informing is frowned upon in this district. I trust you will not reveal that I spoke her name."

"I said nothing about murder."

"True. But you and I know it was not an accident."

"Her name?"

"Your promise?"

"If anyone should ask," said the detective, "I believe I heard a name rumored about the streets."

"Is it possible that name was Dandy Dover?"

"Right you are," said the detective, slapping his notebook shut.

"And your name?" said Maggie the Monkey. "Just as a precaution, of course. Although I'm quite sure I shall have no occasion but the most laudatory to mention it to my dear friend, the Commissioner."

"Detective Johannes Schmitt, at your service, ma'am. And I'm much obliged."

"Ah, the redoubtable John Smith. I know him well. Your name is not important. What's important is that murder shall not go unpunished." The interview had ended.

In the hallway, Elsa Muller betook herself down to the kitchen quarters in haste, troubled by the lies she had heard while her ear had been pressed to the parlor door. The young man had left the house in company with Miss Dover. She had not accosted him on the street. Of that, Elsa was sure. Now the young man was dead, and the police looking for Miss Dover. Even the nice policeman last night had been looking for her. But Miss Dover could not have done murder. She was too kind. Elsa was in a quandary. She wished she could talk to her policeman friend and tell him that Maggie had lied to the detective. Surely he would know what to do.

Quiet and worried, she began to help Cook with preparations for the ladies' breakfast.

When the cab arrived at the Pavonia Ferry dock at the end of East 23rd Street, Timothy Crane instantly leaped off the rear platform and hid himself behind a large dray heaped with luggage. From there, he watched as the veiled woman alit from the conveyance and summoned a dock worker to carry her trunk into the terminal.

He followed her to the ticket office, and congratulated himself when he heard the familiar, genteel voice book passage on the ferry and thence by train to Chicago. The crowd waiting for the ferry was small; it was too early for the evening throng of commuters heading for their New Jersey homes. Timothy decided to take a ferry ride and apprehend his quarry before they got to the other side. That way, the fly Miss Dandy Dover would have nowhere to run.

He kept out of sight until the ferry pulled in, then remained at the rear of the small knot of boarding passengers, always keeping the broad-brimmed hat in his view. The lady went into the cabin and seated herself on one of the benches, far removed from any of the other passengers. Timothy did the same, a few rows behind her, and hunched himself down inside his reefer collar.

When the ferry got under way, he slid onto the bench beside her. "Heading west, are you?" he asked softly.

She peered at him through her veil and said, "Remove yourself at once, sir, or I will have you arrested for a masher."

"I'm no masher, and you know it," Timothy replied. He took off his cap and displayed his head, on which the aching knots had not yet subsided. "Recognize your handiwork?"

The woman laughed. "Serves you right for being such a dimwit. What brings you traveling this fine day?"

"To make it short," said Timothy, "I'm here to arrest you for the murder of Mr. Martin G. DeW. Shaw. And to get my wallet back."

She laughed again, in a ladylike manner but nonetheless raising the hackles of affronted pride in her adversary.

"I don't see what's so funny," he blustered. "Murder's nothing to laugh at."

"I'm no murderer," she told him, lifting her veil to favor him with her wide, innocent dark eyes. "And I didn't lift your wallet. But I know who did both."

"I know someone who says that you did both."

"It wouldn't surprise me," she said, "if we're talking about the same person."

Timothy studied her smooth white face, stared into her guileless dark eyes. Could someone so beautiful be a cold-blooded killer? If only she were ugly and misshapen, it would be easier to believe the stories Bert the Barber had told him. "You lied to me before," he said. "Why would you tell me the truth now?"

She sighed and dropped her eyes to gaze at the muff resting on her lap, both hands snugly inside it. "You're right," she said. "You have no reason to believe me. I did lie to you. But I've grown weary of this life. I thought that if I left this miserable city, I could begin again in some other place." She drew one hand out of her muff and placed it on his arm. "I've learned my lesson. You wouldn't want to stand in the way of a repentant soul, would you?"

"No." Timothy hesitated. "Let's hear your story, and then I'll see whether I believe you or no."

"I can ask for no further consideration than that," she said humbly. "It was like this. I had taken the young man from Maggie's place to Bert's hotel. That was the arrangement we three had whenever a gentleman sported a roll and seemed disinclined to leave it all at Maggie's.

"Bert brought him the usual brandy laced with what I thought was just a few drops of chloral hydrate. It must have been more or this young man suffered an adverse reaction. He turned wild and drew a pistol, threatening to shoot me. I called for help. But before Bert could arrive, the young man dropped like a stone, and I thought he had died.

"Bert said we had to get rid of him right away, using the customary method of disposal." She paused and gazed out the window at the opposite shore.

"And what, may I ask, is that?" Timothy prompted. He was finding both the story and the storyteller fascinating.

"Did you not notice the coal chute in the hallway?" she asked. "Bert has a wide acquaintance among the train engineers. Whenever he wants to shift a lush, he flies a white flag from the window of that room, and the train stops just opposite. Then out the window with the coal chute, and down the chute the lush goes. The engineer catches him and makes sure he's nicely arranged so he won't fall off the roof, and away the train goes. The lush awakes in some other part of town, too embarrassed at his foolishness to say anything to anyone."

"What went wrong this time?" Timothy asked.

"Well, for one thing," she said, "you were down there, mooning about on the sidewalk and showing no sign of moving on, just when we were ready to play chute-the-chutes. We had to do something to distract you, so I raised a disturbance. While you were on your way up, Bert did the chute trick and then ran downstairs to meet you. Then I wrecked the room and kept you occupied until the train was gone."

"And then you beaned me with the chair leg."

"I'm truly sorry about that, but I was afraid that Bert would do worse. And I didn't want to have anything to do with his cutthroat ways."

"Kind of you," Timothy muttered.

"So, you see," she went on, "if there was murder done, it was not my intention, and it was not by me. If anything, the lushes have, in the past, been revived by their ride in the fresh air. I don't know what went wrong this time."

A gentle thud reverberated throughout the ferry, and Timothy looked up to see the passengers congregating at the front end of the boat. "Just stay where you are," he told Dandy. "We're going to ride right back to the other side and you can tell your story at Police Headquarters."

"No, we won't," she said, smiling at him. "Did you ever wonder what happened to the gun I told you about?"

He gawked at her.

"It's right here, in my muff, and it's aimed at your heart. Now, get up and walk slowly in front of me. We'll be the last ones to disembark, but you, unfortunately, will stumble and fall into the river. I will raise the alarm and, with any luck, you won't drown. You're a nice young Leatherhead, and I bear you no malice. Now, upsy-daisy with you, and remember to walk very slowly. I would sincerely hate to shoot you in the back."

Timothy did as he was bid, raging inwardly at being once again bested by Miss Dandy Dover. His eyes darted from side to side, searching desperately for some way out of this predicament. He had no doubt he would survive a dunking in the river; he'd swum in it often enough from the Hell's Kitchen piers. He was not so sure he would survive the mortification.

As he stepped off the boat and onto the dock, Dandy a few paces behind him, two men materialized out of nowhere. They both wore dark, anonymous ulsters and stiff bowler hats.

"You'd be advised to come quietly," said one. The other said, "The both of you."

A sixth sense told Timothy to drop flat on his face, which he did just as a bullet whined over his head. Subsequent shots were fired, several of them splintering the raw planks uncomfortably close to his person. He tried rolling out of range, but received a sharp kick in the stomach from a heavy boot belonging to one of the ulsters.

Behind him, Dandy shrieked and swore and fired away wildly until the revolver was empty. Then she tossed it into the river. The ulsters closed in on her. She kicked and bit and scratched and screamed and struggled, but the impassive detectives would not be deterred. Within a few minutes, they had manacled her wrists behind her, whereupon she spat in their faces. They laughed at her. "Quite a little wildcat, aren't you," said one of them. "She'll do well in the Tombs, I'd say," said the other.

Gratefully, Timothy got to his feet. "Glad to see you boys," he said. "She was going to dump me in the river."

"You may wish she had," said the one who had kicked him. "I don't know who you are, but you keep evil company. We've had our eye on Miss Dandy Dover for quite a while, but this is the first time we've been able to get the dirt on her, thanks to Maggie the Monkey. We followed the two of you all the way from 49th Street. And now we'll go straight to Mulberry Street."

As the detective spoke, he fastened a second set of manacles to Timothy's wrists.

"Wait, wait!" he protested. "I'm not one of her sort. I'm a policeman."

"Yeah, and I'm Colonel Teddy Roosevelt. Whoever you are, we'll sort it all out at Headquarters."

All the way back on the ferry, Dandy and Timothy were forced to sit side by side under the watchful eyes of the stern detectives. They spoke not a word to each other, although Dandy was somewhat inclined to rest her head on his shoulder. Each time he felt its weight there, he rudely shrugged it off. His thoughts were occupied with the imminent end of his career. "Well," he mused to himself, "maybe Jimmy was right. I should have gone with him into The Gophers. I wouldn't be having this kind of trouble."

At Headquarters Dandy surprised him. She refused to speak to anyone but the Superintendent himself. When that gentleman appeared, she spoke up. "This young man," she said in her most ladylike fashion, "is not an associate of mine. He is a police officer, and a smart one. He found me before any of your detectives and was attempting to arrest me for the murder of Martin Shaw, of which murder, by the way, I am quite innocent, when those detectives interrupted and mistook him for a miscreant. He deserves full credit for my apprehension. I will tell you my story, just as I told it to him."

In the ensuing hubbub, Timothy was highly congratulated for his enterprise but warned not to exceed his responsibilities. As Dandy was taken away, she blew him a kiss and called out, "We'll meet again someday. Just remember what you owe me."

The next evening, despite his picture in all the newspapers, Timothy was walking his beat again. Bert the Barber's hotel was dark, and the windows of Maggie's house were shuttered. A small, shawl-wrapped shape huddled, shivering, on the stoop.

Timothy said, "Is that you, Elsa Muller?"

The girl looked up and through the chattering of her teeth whispered, "My momma has died and this house is closed by the Police and I don't know where to go."

"Come along with me," said Timothy. "We'll find a place to warm you and feed you. It won't always be like this in the city. Great things are going to be happening. Have you heard about the grand new subway that's going to be built? We'll all be speeding along under the ground."

"Is it true Miss Dover murdered that poor gentleman?

That's what the mistress said before they took her away."

"Well, we don't know about that, do we?" Timothy said. "I have a feeling that we'll be seeing Miss Dandy Dover on the loose before very long."

"Oh, I hope so," said Elsa. "She's a very kind lady."

"That she is," said Timothy. "That she certainly is."

*For **Immediate Release:** The Transit Authority Property Division will hold a lost property auction at 3 P.M., Friday, February 21st, at the Transit Museum on Boerum and Schermerhorn Streets in Brooklyn. Division Chief Joshua Matthews reports that among the items left by riders on the city's transit system in the past six months are: 3,728 umbrellas, 511 briefcases, 679 pairs of gloves, 138 pairs of shoes, 28 hair dryers, 3 violins, 45 typewriters, 5 hamsters, a chicken, 2 artificial legs (not a matched set), 2,341 textbooks, and the body of an adult male Caucasian, age 58.*

Judith Kelman

The Kiss of Death

I would have noticed the creep sooner, but I was thinking about Wanda Jamieson.

Since I got the call last Thursday, the impossible news about Wanda had been pressing at me like an angry mob, demanding answers I didn't begin to have.

How could it have happened to Wanda of all people? She had seemed so indestructible, so secure. Wanda was the type who smoked brown cigarettes and knew people in the Village. She was the sort who dated thin, round-shouldered boys with earrings and attended private screenings of experimental films. Wanda Jamieson was the only girl in all of Bronx Science High School who'd never shown the slightest concern about the daunting mechanics of shedding her virginity. At times I had secretly suspected she'd been born without it.

In a way Wanda was responsible for what I was desperately trying to become. My acting ambitions had been spawned during her incredible performance in the Science High senior play. It was a drama written by Iggie Stephenson, who'd gone on to become the head of the "Thinking of you" division at Hallmark cards. Bronx Science could boast many such accomplished alumni.

Determined to join their ranks by distinguishing myself onstage, I'd dropped out after two restless years as a physics major at Columbia. My folks had migrated to Florida by then, so I'd moved in with my Aunt Evelyn, who had a rent-stabilized junior four on lower Fifth Avenue with a Castro in the living room.

Ever since, I'd been making the rounds of so-called open auditions. These ritual humiliations are known in the biz as "cattle calls," but that doesn't begin to describe them. Having attended cattle auctions, I can assure you that the heifers are never called "babe" or told they need nose jobs by potbellied bald men puffing cigars.

Still I persisted, as I thought Wanda would have, sandwiching the auditions between my two jobs. Days, I waited tables at a nouvelle Mexican-Italian place on East Forty-first Street. Evenings, I baby-sat for several air-kissing rich ladies on Park Avenue when it was Nanny's night off. I was much in demand through Miss Ivy's Wee Watchers Agency. Children, even obscenely pampered children, found me amusing. I danced, sang, did stand-up. Anything to perform in New York. Anything.

In a sense, I supposed it was even Wanda's doing that I was standing at that moment on the littered Hunter College Station subway platform at half past midnight waiting for the downtown number six. Prudent or not, I always took the subway home from sitting jobs. The cab fare I saved went into my Emergency Housing Relief Fund. After a part on Broadway and a perfect man to adore and indulge me beyond the bounds of decency, what I wanted most in the world was my own apartment.

Not that living with Aunt Evelyn was all that intolerable. I had grown accustomed to her compulsive talking. And I had mastered the complex dance steps necessary to evade her killer Electrolux. What I could not bear was the State of the Ingrate report she telephoned to my parents in Fort Lauderdale every Friday at five minutes after the long distance rates went down.

Here she was doing all this for me, and I refused to eat her creamed spinach or be civil to her repugnant cat or go out on a blind date with her friend Sadie's sister's nephew from Cleveland. Here she was so wonderful to me (like a saint), and I kept worrying her to death by going out at all hours in unspeakable weather conditions without my earmuffs. And when was I going to take her impeccable advice and give up this acting nonsense? After all, who ever heard of a movie star with fat thighs and a head for physics?

When I finally snapped out of my reverie, the approaching train was a pin of light at the end of the inky tunnel. Feeling suddenly uneasy, I took a fast look around the platform. There was a sleeping street person under the waiting bench. A wino with glazed eyes sat talking to one of the turnstiles. No threat there.

Then I spotted him. Pressed in the shadows of a column on the platform was a dark man with tangled hair and a lupine face. He was staring at me with black, burnt-out eyes and a hungry expression.

Prickles of fear erupted on the backs of my arms and started scaling my spine. From the corner of my eye, I saw the creep draw his thumb over an invisible knife blade. An evil smile stained his face. I could feel his gaze, burning like acid as he moved closer with slow, languid steps.

No way out. He had positioned himself between me and the exit. And even if I managed to get past him, I couldn't think of where to run for help. The college buildings would be dark and locked. Nothing much on the streets at this hour but two-legged trouble and the devoutly uninvolved.

I decided to take my chances on the approaching train. Forcing my shoulders square, I stared into the tunnel at the looming metal worm, willing it to hurry.

With a pneumatic wheeze, the number six braked at the platform. The guy was so close now, I caught his scent: a blend of stale sweat, zoo musk, and tobacco. He mumbled something ugly as he followed me through the sliding doors.

Terrified, I scanned the car. There was an old, toothless woman clutching a bundle of clothes and an enormously pregnant young Asian with the look of a startled doe. In one corner, a teenage boy and girl were going at each other like snack food. The best prospect was a napping middle-aged man in an overcoat and fedora seated near the far connecting door.

The creep was right behind me, muttering obscenities and making lewd noises. My heart was hammering, but I refused to let him know it. First rule with animals was not to let them catch the scent of fear. I was an actor, I kept reminding myself. Delia Lamb, now starring in the performance of her life.

I strode over and slipped onto the plastic bench beside the man in the hat. I looped my hands through his cocked elbow and said, "Hi, sweetheart." Leaning closer, I rasped, "Play along and I'll never forget you. Please!"

I chanced a sidelong look at the creep. His face had changed a little, gone tentative.

"You're such a darling to meet me like this and see me safely home," I said aloud. Jiggling the man's forearm, I tried to nudge him awake.

No response.

The creep was still staring at me, sizing things up. His coal eyes narrowed.

"Love you, Sweetheart," I said. Ducking under the hat brim, I kissed the stranger's cheek.

The cheek was cold rubber.

Numb with shock, I worked my eyeballs over the man. His face was the color of damp cement, the lips blue as an old bruise. His lids drooped like broken shades. Dead, I thought dully.

Dead.

I don't remember screaming. But the next thing I knew, my throat was scraped raw and an astonishing number of people were streaming onto the train: blue uniforms, white coats. I spotted the creep making his reptilian exit in the confusion.

One man with a terrible plaid sport coat and a steno pad was questioning the other passengers. Assorted fingers pointed in my direction. The man approached, flashed his shield, and sat beside me. His voice was the gentle sing-song of bedtime stories.

He asked a lot of questions. I was able to tell him that my name was Delia Lamb and give him my Aunt Evelyn's address and phone number. The rest of the quiz was impossible: Was this my husband? Had he been sick for long? Did I understand there would have to be an autopsy? All I could manage was a stiff series of nods. My neck needed oiling.

Finally, he pressed a business card into my hand and

told me to get some rest and come in to see him at headquarters first thing tomorrow.

I watched in dull fascination as several people hefted the dead man onto a gurney, covered him with a sheet, and wheeled him off the train. There was a hard silence. But soon, the doors sighed shut, and the number six chugged out of the station and continued on its way as if nothing had happened.

Aunt Evelyn was waiting up when I got to the apartment. She scrutinized me like something on a sale rack and clacked her tongue in disapproval. Her interrogation was much worse than the detective's. Did I have any idea how late it was? Wasn't I going to ask her about the cat's appointment at the vet? Had she mentioned that Sadie's sister's nephew from Cleveland had passed his C.P.A. exam? And where was the wonderful scarf she'd given me for my last birthday?

"Don't tell me you lost that scarf, Delia. You have any idea what it cost me? A fortune, that's what. A fat fortune."

She trailed me around, talking nonstop until I opened the Castro and fell asleep in self-defense. Her droning voice went on and on, an unscratchable itch at the edge of my consciousness. It continued until I fell further asleep and started dreaming about the dead man in the hat.

He was sipping champagne at a party on the platform of the Times Square subway station. A swing band was playing the Charleston, and a pregnant Japanese woman was passing stuffed mushroom caps on a silver tray. There were bursts of laughter and the crystalline clink of happy people coming together.

Then the mood changed. The band lapsed into a slow number, and the dead man got up to fox-trot with Wanda Jamieson.

As usual, I was awakened by the killer bee sound of the

Electrolux and Aunt Evelyn hoisting up the foot of the Castro so she could vacuum underneath.

Last night's weird events hung on me like too much spiked punch. At breakfast my aunt rebuked me for not listening while she explained about treatment alternatives for her cat's periodontal disease. Inattention would no doubt be added to her long-distance litany of my sins this coming Friday.

All I wanted was to forget about last night, but I knew it would not be finished until I saw the detective and came clean. I left the apartment accompanied by Aunt Evelyn's dire warnings about the plummeting barometer and an escalating ozone level.

Sergeant Max Maxwell's office was on the third floor of the District Three, Area B, Transit Police Detective Division Headquarters at 145th Street and St. Nicholas Avenue. The building was cold, gray stone; the tiled corridors chill and echoing. My anxiety mounted as I walked to his office. Words like "perjury" and "implicated" threaded through my mind. I knocked, half expecting a masked executioner to open the door.

But Detective Maxwell turned out to be a sweetheart. He rose to greet me and settled me in the visitor's chair with the kind of care Aunt Evelyn took with her Swedish figurines. He fetched me a cup of machine coffee and tried to help me relax with small talk. How had I slept? Was I feeling any better? Did it look like snow?

Sergeant Maxwell had soft, formless features and wide puppy eyes. I warmed to him despite his hideous taste in clothes. Today he wore a striped shirt in mud-puddle tones and tan pants blighted by a spouting whale pattern.

He eased onto the subject of the dead man. "I know it's very hard to talk about this, Mrs. Lamb, but had your husband been sick? Any history of heart problems?"

I cleared my throat. "Look, Sergeant, he wasn't my husband. The truth is, I didn't know the man."

His brow peaked. "Let me get this straight. Several witnesses saw you enter the subway car, go directly over to the deceased, call him sweetheart and embrace him, but you didn't *know* him?"

"I know it sounds crazy, but I can explain."

"Yes, that would be nice."

I told him about the creep and the poor selection of potential good samaritans and how I'd certainly never intended to misrepresent myself, especially about having an intimate relationship with a dead person. I mentioned that I was an actress and that my natural instinct when menaced was to try to act my way out of the situation.

The dear man sat and listened. When I finished blathering, he nodded and offered an indulgent little grin.

"Pretty resourceful, Ms. Lamb. But I have to tell you it would be way more resourceful to stay out of the subways in the middle of the night."

"Oh, I will, Sergeant. Definitely."

"Good. I'd hate to see a nice young woman like you get hurt."

"Yes, so would I."

"If there's nothing else then. Thanks for coming in." He stood and held out a hand.

"As a matter of fact, there is one more *teeny* thing. It's about my scarf."

Before leaving Aunt Evelyn's apartment, I'd made a thorough search for the missing muffler. It was a limp, homely thing that scratched, but Aunt Evelyn would not soon forgive its disappearance.

Then, on the train up, it had come to me: a clear image of the edge of my ugly scarf poking out from under the sheet as they wheeled the dead man off the subway car. I told Sergeant Maxwell I didn't know how it had happened, but my scarf had somehow found its way onto that gurney.

"I hate the thing, Sergeant, but I *need* it."

He rolled his eyes and mentioned for me to follow him. Property was in the bowels of the building, a cavernous room packed with crammed metal shelves. Maxwell explained the problem, recited the case number, and the portly bald clerk went to fetch the dead man's personal effects.

"I'm running late," Maxwell said. "Mind showing yourself out when you're finished?"

"Not at all. Thanks for everything."

"You too, Ms. Lamb. It's been . . . interesting."

The clerk soon returned with a brown cardboard box. "You can use that table over there to go through it."

Gingerly, I emptied the contents on the pocked wooden surface. There was the tweed overcoat and fedora, an ancient Benrus with a worn strap, half glasses in a plastic case, a rumpled handkerchief, a battered pair of oxfords, a gray cardigan and matching corduroy trousers. The blue shirt had a frayed collar. A set of underwear and socks were in a separate plastic bag. Aunt Evelyn's scarf was at the bottom of the heap.

My face went hot as I lifted the dead man's things to retrieve the wretched scarf. Pulling it out, I heard something drop to the floor. Looking down, I saw a matchbook. Without thinking, I picked it up and slipped it in my pocket. It felt heavier than a matchbook should, and somehow more important.

Variety had listed an open call at ten-thirty that morning for an off-off-Broadway production on Walker Street. They were looking for a slim Latino teenager with knowledge of Brazilian folk dances, but I figured that a baby-faced Bronx woman on a diet who knew the cha-cha might be close enough.

Given the acute talent glut in the acting profession, I knew I had to do everything possible to encourage my legendary break. I was always willing to try out, no matter how improbable the opportunity. I was always prepared. Despite the dent in my right shoulder, I kept my feedbag purse crammed with about twenty pounds of emergency paraphernalia: makeup, wigs, business cards, letters of reference, assorted accessories, good luck charms, indigestion remedies. Above all, I never, ever overlooked a potential contact. The truth is, I would have dated Sadie's sister's nephew from Cleveland in a minute if he was, say, Stephen Sondheim's accountant. Forget dating, I would have *married* the guy.

But today my heart wasn't in it. After standing in line for an hour with a hundred gum-cracking girls in spiked heels, I left. No way I could concentrate on anything but the dead man. I had to know what was to become of him.

From a pay phone, I called Sergeant Max Maxwell. The dear heart was still patient and understanding. In response to my questions, he told me that the deceased had been taken to the medical examiner's office for a postmortem. If his death was found to be from natural causes, standard procedure was to release the remains to the next of kin.

"But you said you have no idea who he is."

"True, but we'll keep trying to find out, Ms. Lamb. There wasn't any I.D. on the body, but we'll get what we can from his personal effects. And we'll keep an eye on the missing person reports. Nothing's been filed on anyone meeting his description so far, but it might come in any time."

"What if you don't find any relatives?"

"I'm sure we will."

"But what if you don't?"

". . . They'll hold him at the city morgue for two months. After that, if he's still an unclaimed John Doe, he'll be disposed of at Potter's Field."

Disposed of.

The words were dark and hollow, like "breakdown," which is what had happened to Wanda Jamieson. Terrible how people could be reduced to conditions best described by landfill terms. Crumpled, wasted, tossed away. Degraded.

From what Mrs. Jamieson had told me when she called, Wanda had suffered a slow, relentless decline.

After graduating from Sarah Lawrence, she'd gotten involved with one of those cults that hand out brochures at Kennedy Airport. She'd gone from that to a militant environmentalist group, where she'd spent a year or so getting arrested for picnicking on public thoroughfares during rush hour and threatening manufacturers of polyvinyl chloride products.

Her parents, accustomed to Wanda's eccentricities, had ignored her bizarre behavior until the hysterical calls began. Wanda would phone in the middle of the night and rant about Nazis trying to break into her apartment. She was convinced that these Nazis were putting spiders in her bed and poisoning her food. There was an alarming drop in her weight. She stopped taking care of herself and lay in bed for days at a time.

Her parents had tried to get her into therapy, but Wanda failed to keep the appointments. Once, when Mrs. Jamieson showed up to escort her to a treatment session, Wanda had threatened her with a carving knife. After that, the Jamiesons had seen no choice but to commit Wanda to a private facility in Connecticut. The doctors there had determined that she was schizophrenic.

After three months as an inpatient, she'd been released with a prescription for an antipsychotic medication. Her parents had taken her home to their floor-through on Riverside Drive. They'd redecorated her room and pulled strings to get her into therapy with the top man at Payne Whitney. But less than a week later, which was a week ago Wednesday, Wanda had disappeared.

Until then, the Jamiesons had tried to keep her illness a secret. But now the important thing was finding their daughter. They were calling everyone they could think of, even old friends like me who hadn't seen Wanda in years, hoping someone had heard from her.

A tearful Mrs. Jamieson told me that Wanda had left home with no money, nothing. They'd found her antipsychotic pills in the trash. For all her parents knew, she was living on the streets in a state of complete, maybe dangerous, disorientation.

"So if you hear from her, Delia. If you hear anything . . ."

"Of course, Mrs. Jamieson. I'll call right away. And please, let me know what happens."

En route to my waitressing job, I found myself staring into strange faces, scrutinizing the masses of human driftwood that littered the city's parks and sidewalks.

Not easy. I'd been weaned on the studied indifference that was part of the standard urban survival kit. Early on, my mother had taught me to turn away from the sad and unsightly in the same knowing, somber tones she'd applied to the issue of public toilet seats.

But now I grappled with the awful awareness that each of the rag-wrapped urchins was someone's child. And worse, I realized that anyone, no matter how exotic or appealing, might harbor the poison seeds of her own destruction. If Wanda Jamieson could come to this, anyone could.

Working the lunch shift, my mind was full of Wanda and dead Mr. Doe from the subway. Not concentrating, I spilled a tray laden with Perriers, forgot to bring the water for Mr. McKwethy's bourbon, and mixed up the orders for two pizzas so that the tofu ginger pie had the sun-dried tomatoes and the black bean cilantro got the extra fennel.

My boss was not amused.

Leaving, I realized that I would not be able to function at my normal level of mediocrity until I sorted out some of the mess. All afternoon, I wandered the midtown streets, hoping to spot Wanda Jamieson or happen upon some clue to the identity of the dead stranger. A dozen times, my heart hopped at the sight of a lanky female with Wanda's square shoulders and thick Irish Setter hair. But none of them turned out to be my broken idol.

Near six, I realized I hadn't eaten anything since Aunt Evelyn's punishment oatmeal at breakfast. My feet were sore, and my eyes ached from searching, but I was not ready to quit. I decided to fortify myself with a coffee shop tuna sandwich and plod on.

Knowing that my aunt would be furious if I didn't let her know my dinner plans, I stopped at a pay phone on the corner of Fifty-fifth and Fifth. When I dug in my coat pocket for a quarter, I found the matchbook.

After I hung up on Aunt Evelyn with a promise to include servings from all the critical food groups in my evening meal, I hesitated at the phone. I considered calling Sergeant Maxwell, but I couldn't bring myself to admit that I'd pocketed a piece of the dead man's property.

I didn't know why I'd taken the thing in the first place. But as I studied the cover, I knew what I had to do. It was a simple white matchbook with a restaurant name on the back. The address was on the front: Second Avenue near Eighty-fourth. The tuna could wait.

On the way I realized that this was a long shot. The dead man had carried no cash or credit cards. His clothing had been worn and less than pristine. He hadn't looked the type to patronize the sort of chic upper east side Italian bistro I expected to find.

And I was not disappointed.

Through the polished double doors, I entered a slim, narrow space with dim, artful lighting. A dozen linen-draped tables lined the carved, panelled walls. On each was a perfect rose in a crystal bud vase.

The place was packed. No doubt it provided the combination of arrogant service, paltry portions and outlandish prices that many rich New Yorkers find irresistible.

I asked to see the owner on an urgent matter and was shown to a small office at the rear, where an oily man in a tuxedo was poring over a stack of receipts.

Leaving out the more unsavory details, I explained that I'd met one of his customers on the subway. I didn't know the man's name, I said, but he was in his fifties and wore a tweed coat and brown fedora. The man had left something behind, and I needed to find him to return it.

The owner pursed his lips. He started digging for details.

"What color hair did he have? Blue eyes or brown?"

"I . . . didn't notice."

"Did he speak with an accent?"

"I'm not really sure."

"Walk with a limp?"

"Didn't see him walk."

I left my card, though I knew it was useless. On the bus to my sitting job, I felt a sinking sense of failure. I was out of ideas, and I had gotten nowhere.

I tried to put the whole business behind me. But all evening, I was haunted by the mysteries of Wanda and the dead man. The lounge act I performed for the Weller children was a flop. Megan, the four-year-old, walked out in the middle to watch a rerun of "Gilligan's Island." Courtney, one of the two-year-old twins, fell asleep during my big number while her brother, Jason, crouched red-faced in the corner. Before the last note faded, he stood to announce a "great big poo-poo." Fortunately, I am not daunted by bad reviews.

I tried to catch a cab home, but none materialized. After walking a dozen blocks in a mizzle of frozen rain, I gave up and headed for the subway. I hated to break my word to Sergeant Maxwell, but there was no choice.

I was nervous waiting for the train and very wary during the ride. But climbing to the street at the other end, I felt almost giddy with relief. Maxwell's admonitions aside, it was good to do something I feared and emerge unscathed. I'd encountered not a single mugger or dead person. Last night had been a one-shot freak incident. I was done with it. Good.

Despite the slick of rain, I all but danced the distance to Aunt Evelyn's apartment. For the first time in a week, I did not feel weighted by Wanda Jamieson or anything else. Life was good. My senses were tingling. If Aunt Evelyn was still up, I would make a pot of cocoa and attempt to feign concern over the cat's bad gums.

I turned the corner onto Fifth Avenue. The apartment house was half a block away. With my eyes narrowed against the rain, the street was reduced to a gaudy blur. I was almost at the adjacent building before I spotted the man slouched in the dark beside the entryway to Aunt Evelyn's house. Rain was pelting him, but he stood immobile, staring in my direction.

I hesitated, confused. But as he took a step and then another toward me, I turned and ran.

I raced down Fifth and started circling Washington Square park. No one was around; no lights; nothing open. My breath came in fiery stabs, heart squirmed like a beached fish. His footsteps were an anvil strike behind me. He was closer, gaining. Fear thundered in my ears.

Pushing harder, I turned to the south side of the park and ran toward the law school. If I could get to the following block, there were a few places that would still be open.

But as I passed the blackened NYU buildings, my calf fisted in furious spasm. I stumbled, scraping my palms and right knee on the slushy pavement. I tried to stand, but before I could, he was standing over me, breathing in stertorous puffs.

I wasn't about to give up without a struggle. Rearing back, I hauled off and smacked him in the gut with my pocketbook. He staggered backward and fell with a sound like a tire deflating.

My leg was still cramped, but I managed to stand and hobble away. He was just starting to recover when I rounded the corner. I forced myself to move as fast as I could.

I thought I'd made it safely to Aunt Evelyn's building. But as I stood at the door groping for my key, a hand caught my wrist.

Reeling around, I faced an attractive, young man with sea-blue eyes and a beleaguered look. He was flushed and panting. Rivulets of frozen rain dripped from his sodden brown curls. I flailed loose and started to run again.

"Wait," he gasped behind me. "Please . . . wait. I'm not going to hurt you. It's about that man you met on the subway. I think . . . it may have been my father."

I stopped short and turned to face him. "Oh?"

"Late fifties, tweed coat, brown fedora, gray corduroy pants? Was that the man you saw?"

"Yes, that's him." There was an awkward lull while I searched for the words that didn't exist, the easy ones. "Look," I said finally. "I'm afraid I have bad news. Can we go somewhere and talk?"

Three blocks away, we found an open coffee shop. We were both drenched and frozen. I ordered hot cocoa, he asked for his with extra marshmallows.

He listened without visible reaction as I told him about his father. When I finished, a cloud of sorrow crossed his expression.

After he composed himself, he told me that his father had suffered from Alzheimer's disease. He'd tried to keep an eye on the old man. But every so often, his dad would wander off.

"Pop was a brilliant man, a history professor. But he'd deteriorated to the point where he didn't remember the simplest things. I had to remind him to brush his teeth, to eat.

"He was living in the past. My mother died five years ago, but to Pop, she was still the twenty-two-year-old he married. He'd put on his oldest, rattiest clothes and go riding on the subways. That was the way my folks used to get around when they were newlyweds. The first few times he disappeared, I called the police. But he'd always come back on his own in a couple of days. Until now . . ."

He told me his name was Daniel Bradshaw. His business was selling fine produce to New York's poshest restaurants and caterers. One of his accounts was the Italian bistro where I'd left my card. Later, the owner had remembered Daniel talking about the subway disappearing episodes. He'd made the connection and called to give Daniel my address.

"Sorry about your dad," I said.

"Thanks. Me, too. But I know he'd be glad it's over. Damned illness stole what he was."

The conversation veered onto more neutral ground. He asked what I did, and I talked about my two jobs and my professional aspirations. He was an excellent listener, very cute ears. Cute everything.

"You're interested in acting? That's great." He told me that his produce business had accounts with the catering operations for several major stage and screen producers. On a regular basis, this man rubbed elbows and apples with the likes of Jerome Robbins. Andrew Lloyd Webber was crazy about his raspberries. Joe Papp had his pineapples flown to out-of-town openings of Broadway-bound shows.

Daniel insisted on paying for the cocoa and walking me back to Aunt Evelyn's. The rain had softened and the air bristled with a rare sweetness that made my eyes water. At the building door, he thanked me and promised to let me know when he'd made the funeral arrangements.

Over the next two days, I thought often about Daniel Bradshaw and resisted the urge to call him. Several times, I looked up the listing for D.B. Produce in the yellow pages and the residential listing for Daniel A. Bradshaw on Seventy-eighth between Madison and Park. In my fantasies this adorable, caring, successful man with incredible connections was home agonizing over what would be a decent grieving interval before he called and admitted that he'd fallen madly in love with me at first sight. I imagined him planning our first real date. We would go to a romantic little Italian bistro, sip Chianti, twirl pasta, and finish with a dish of Andrew Lloyd Webber's favorite berries.

By the time he called, I had worked myself into a frenzy. Daniel told me that the funeral, a simple graveside ceremony, had been planned for day after tomorrow. In the meantime, since I'd been so nice, he wondered if I'd be interested in a possible job opportunity. It would be great if I could come up to his apartment right away and meet everyone. He was sure I'd be perfect.

Aunt Evelyn followed me around the junior four as I dressed in my serious possibility outfit: sexy black heels, a demure but alluring red cashmere sweater, the slim black skirt that advertises my cute little knees while keeping the grand piano thighs a secret, my mock Hermés scarf.

By the time I arrived at Daniel's address, I was a frazzled mess. I rang the buzzer for Four D and tried to compose myself with slow, deep breaths. When I was calm enough, I took the elevator up and rang at the door marked Bradshaw.

Dry, Daniel looked even cuter. He led me into a lovely, sunken living room and took my coat. I sat on the plush tan sofa and gave him an expectant look.

He eyed his watch. "They'll be here in a minute. Want anything?"

While he was in the kitchen getting my glass of water, the bell rang. My throat constricted. Could it be Joe Papp? Jerry Robbins? Whoever it was, I vowed to appear self-assured and unfazed. I was an actor, after all. Delia Lamb, a breath away from the big break.

I heard Daniel at the door. There was a flurry of voices, and steps approached the living room. I gazed toward the bay window, not wanting to appear too anxious.

They were at the entrance to the room now. Daniel's voice wafted toward me. "Delia?"

"Yes?" I turned and was startled by the sight of a flushed moppet and a graceful reed of a woman with lemon silk hair and perfect features.

"Delia Lamb, I'd like you to meet my wife, Betty. And this is Jeffrey, our son. I told Betty all about you, and she said you sounded like a terrific sitter. I have to tell you it must be fate, my meeting you. We've been desperate for someone reliable." He put a hand on the child's shoulder. "Say 'hi' to Delia, Jeffy. Remember I said she was coming to see you?"

The little boy approached and gave me the once-over. "What's your name again?"

"Delia Lamb."

"Dwilla Wham?"

"Right."

"Hi, Dwilla Wham. I'm Jeffy. Wanna see my big boy bed?"

"Sure. Wanna see my Ophelia?"

The child giggled and held out a set of chubby fingers. I took his hand and allowed him to lead me to his room. It was, after all, the best offer I'd had in quite some time.

Aunt Evelyn was full of news when I returned to the apartment. The cat would not need any extractions after all. Sadie's sister's nephew from Cleveland had gotten engaged. And Mrs. Jamieson had called to say that Wanda was back home and fine.

Seems Wanda had spent the week sailing the Caribbean on the sixty-two-foot yacht of a wildly successful investment banker she'd met at the Connecticut asylum. He'd been in for a *teeny* spell of depression, and he'd naturally fallen like a brick for Wanda. The happy couple was tan, rested, and planning for a June wedding. Things could not be better.

"But you said she threw away her medication."

"My mistake, Delia. Turns out she had it refilled before she left."

"But she took off without telling you."

She chuckled. "Finally, my Wanda is back to herself again: impulsive, inconsiderate. Isn't it wonderful?"

As I hung up, Aunt Evelyn squinted at the wall clock and bustled toward the phone. It was five after five on Friday, and she looked anxious to put in her regular call to my parents. I opened the new issue of *Variety* and sprawled on the Castro. Given the week I'd had, this call was bound to be a long one.

*The body was found facedown, but in the final analysis,
did anybody really care?*

Warren Murphy

And One for the Little Girl

"It's a well-known fact that in the winter everybody in
Scandinavia commits suicide. Which maybe isn't so bad if you
figure they all live in a place that doesn't exist.

"I mean I know all the real places there. I know about Finland
because the Finlandias all look like herrings, and Sweden is where
the people look all right but are the worst degenerates on the face
of the earth. The Norwipudlians all have square heads and . . .
right, Denmark's the last one, I know that, but I don't know
anything about the Denmarksmen, never having slept or fought
with one.

"But Scandinavia? What does that mean? Was there a place
once called Scandin or something? You won't find it in any
encyclopedia. I think we take too much stuff on faith. Probably
some guy got all liquored up on glug one night and said let's
invent a place, like Oz, and we can call it Scandinavia. People are
always trying to get over.

"What do you mean, what am I talking about? I am talking,
dear heart, about the reasons for staying indoors because of all

those goddam Scandihoovians jumping out windows and maybe landing on your head. You know, they do it because there's no damned sunlight over there in the winter and that makes people depressed and then they go gobble the gas. And now New York City is going the same way. The buildings are so high that there are places in New York that never get one single solitary little quantum of sunlight. This is absolutely correct. Madison Avenue, for instance. It's a scientific fact that on Mad, from Fortieth to Forty-ninth, there has not been one ray of direct sunshine in the last twenty years.

"You think all those advertising people jump out the windows because they just lost the Gallo Wine account? Hah! It is to laugh. They take the dive because they finally go batpoop from never seeing the sun. And don't tell me they all go home to Westport and they can see the sun there. The sun never shines in Westport either. Don't ask me how I know.

"So that is why I spend all my time in this gin mill, because it's too damned dangerous out there on the streets. That and your bathrooms."

"What about my bathrooms?" the bartender said.

" 'Cause you have the only bathrooms left in New York that have the words men *and* women *printed on them. All the other bars have those damned pictures painted on the doors and I can never tell one picture from another picture and so I always wind up in the lady's room looking for a urinal. That's what I like about this place."*

"And here I thought it was my sunny personality," the bartender said.

"That too. You're my only friend."

That's the way he always talked. Three-Bags was just the funniest guy. You know, lady, you run a bar like I do and you get all kinds, and, hey . . . you know where they held the funeral for Sammy Davis Jr.? Congregation Beth

You Is My Woman Now. That was one of Three-Bags'
jokes. He was always telling stuff like that.

One day he was in here and he was talking about some
hungry Arab actress who was always asking for bread,
and I didn't know what the hell he was talking about and
what he was talking about was Bette Davis. 'Pita, pita,
pita.' Three-Bags thought she was talking about bread. Or
maybe he didn't, but he acted like he did.

Yeah, we get a lot of them.

Three-Bags? I don't know. He said he got the name
'cause he was like the black sheep in the family. You know
. . . baa, baa, black sheep, three bags full? His brother was
like a doctor or something and he had a sister that played
symphonies somewhere and his folks were rich and he
went to college but he never worked. He was always
trying to get some kind of an edge on things. If he worked
as hard at working as he worked trying to get *out* of
working, he would have been rich. Instead of what he is.

It's a long story. You want another one of those? You
know, we don't get many pretty girls like you in here.
More of a ball-and-a-beer trade, you know?

Oh, yeah. Well, one day Three-Bags comes in and asks
me if I got a million dollars to spare.

"Sorry. You're fifteen minutes too late," the bartender said.
*"I just put my last million on Diplodocus in the fourth at
Aqueduct."*

"Your loss," Three-Bags said. *"I was going to make you rich."*

"I'm rich already because I'm surrounded by my true friends,"
the bartender said.

"You mean these cretins?" Three-Bags said, *waving an arm
around the bar.*

"Who you calling a cretin?" asked the man on the next stool.
"I'm a Sicilian."

"You're a moron. How the hell smart can you be watching Phil Donahue?" Three-Bags *said, waving at the television before glancing at the bartender.* "Phil Donahue has to have the stupidest clappers I ever saw in the audience. He gets people on this show and then somebody on the stage says something like 'Respect. First you have to have respect and then everything else will follow.' And then everybody claps. They clap for anything. But 'you got to have respect and everything else will follow.' What does that mean?"

"What it means, Three-Bags, is that if you got more respect, you wouldn't have to come in here trying to con me out of a million. The money would be part of the everything-else-that-follows."

"Maybe I can borrow it from Phil Donahue. He must get paid a lot to find so many imbeciles for his audience."

"Just why do you need this mill so much?" the bartender said.

"To win the lottery. I've got a plan."

"Everybody's got a plan but nobody wins the lottery," the bartender said.

"Every week people win the lottery. You always see their pictures in the paper saying how they're going to use the money to send their kids to college and they're really thinking about how much they'll have to give up in alimony when they divorce the old bag."

"They win 'cause they're lucky. You're the unluckiest guy that ever lived."

"Not anymore," Three-Bags said. *"Not anymore."*

Well, I didn't think any more about it 'cause Three-Bags was always filled with get-rich-quick schemes. He was telling me one night that when he was rich and retired, he was going to invent a special kind of mirror that you could hook up on the back of your car, like a laser mirror, and when some guy followed you and wouldn't put down his high beams, you could focus this mirror and aim his own lights back at him and then press the laser button and burn out his eyeballs.

Jeez, he was a funny guy. But like I say, he always had a scheme. Then one night, oh, a couple of weeks later it was, he comes in. I remember 'cause Marcel Marcel, you know, that mimic guy who wears black pajamas, was on somebody's talk show, Carson I guess, and Three-Bags just walks over and turns off the TV before he sits down. He always sat right on the stool where you're sitting. I said, hey why'd you turn that off and he said why the hell should he pay good money to see some guy pretend to walk up the stairs? He said if he wanted to see somebody walk up the stairs, he would go to the subway station on the corner because people were walking up the stairs there all night long and that was the real thing. What's excitement when you watch a guy pretending to walk up the stairs, he's gonna make believe he trips?

And so he leans over close to me like he always did when he wanted to talk serious, and he didn't have to because there was nobody else in the place, and he says that he thinks he's finally got a backer for his lottery scheme.

I said something like you're still jerking around with that, and he said that I was going to rue the dismal day when I missed my opportunity to invest.

So anyway, Three-Bags hangs around all night and we close the place. Nobody even came in except this one guy with a gimpy leg that's always hanging around the neighborhood and I call him Stork 'cause he kind of lunges around like one and once in a while I load him up on the cheap 'cause it's always a big laugh to see him get drunk and stagger around. But this night I chase the freak out of here and me and Three-Bags talk around most of the night.

And the way the lottery thing goes is like this. Of course, I don't have the numbers memorized the way Three-Bags did but maybe you'll get the idea.

"Did you ever play the Delaware lottery?"

"Who the hell cares about the Delaware lottery?" the bartender asked.

"You will, if you just listen," Three-Bags said. *"In Delaware, they got a pick-six-numbers-out-of-thirty-six Lotto. You know how many tickets you got to buy to make sure you win the top prize?"*

"No, but I guess you're gonna tell me."

"Less than two million tickets. That's how many you need to make sure you play every combination of six numbers. At fifty cents a game, it wouldn't cost but a million to make sure you're the top prize winner."

"Great. Now if we can just scrape together a spare million dollars, we'll be rich. I got it, I'll hock my bowling trophy with the plastic fag on top."

"Too late. You had your chance. I'm after the big money-men now. Anyway, what you do in Delaware is wait until the top prize is big when nobody hits it for a while. Say, eight million dollars. Then you plunk down your million bucks and you win the eight million. Guaranteed."

"Yeah, unless somebody else wins it with you," the bartender said. *"Then you only get a piece of the prize."*

"That's why you wait until the prize gets up to eight million. Then you're still going to show a profit. The only way you'd lose is if you had like eight other winners and there's never been that many winners at once in Delaware. So it's a pretty small risk."

"You know," the bartender said, *"for a pretty smart guy, you can be pretty stupid. Even if you won eight million, you don't get it. They pay you like four hundred thou for twenty years."*

"Right. They annuitize it."

"So how do you win?"

"Because you invest a million and get back four hundred thousand a year for twenty years and if you invest your winnings . . . say, at just twelve percent . . . you'd wind up with twenty-nine million dollars," Three Bags said. *"That's the best investment in history."*

"You got everything figured out," the bartender said, *"so try this. How the hell are you going to buy . . . what, two million lottery tickets?"*

Three-Bags grinned. *"You know, there's a whole class of people around like you who just keep saying no to everything. Your problem is you keep trying to shoot down dreams."*

"And there's a whole class of people like me who've got a couple of bucks in the bank because we don't fall for every half-assed scheme that comes chugging down the Harlem River Drive."

"Half-assed, huh? Well, consider. In my room, right now, I have two hundred thousand lottery cards . . . you know, the kind of things you feed into the computer . . . all made out, ten games on a ticket so that every set of numbers is covered. The winner is in there."

"Two hundred thousand computer cards? That must have taken you an hour or two."

"Not me. I wouldn't trust myself. With my luck, I'd make them out and get them wrong and leave out one damned card and those'd be the numbers that would win. No, old buddy, I went over to Jersey City."

"Great," the bartender said. *"A lot of real smart people in Jersey City. You must have been right at home there."*

"And I got this mathematics professor and he rigged up one of the college computers and I gave him all the blank lottery cards from Delaware and he ran them through the computer and when they came out, every possible set of six numbers was covered. All inked in, nice and neat and ready to roll."

"I don't believe it. You live in one skanky room and now

you've got it filled with a couple of hundred thousand worthless
lottery cards? Where the hell do you sleep? In the sink? Do you
have a sink?"

"I got a sink and when I win this money, you can use it to soak
your head," Three-Bags said. "I tell you, the next time the
Delaware lottery gets to eight million, I'm going to be in it. With
the winner."

"Look, you got two hundred thousand computer cards. That's
not the same as two million lottery tickets. Who's going to sell
you the tickets? If you stand in line at some goddam candy store
in Wilmington and say I want two million tickets, you're gonna
get a lot of people pissed off when they're standing in line behind
you and they wanna buy one ticket and get home in time for
supper."

"I've got that all worked out too," Three-Bags said.

It was the bartender's turn to shake his head. "You got it all
worked out. How come, if you're so smart, you're not rich
already?"

"My life has been spent in preparation for this moment. I'm
going to be rich," Three-Bags said.

Well, that's the way he was, you know. Like I said, he
always had some kind of scheme for beating the horses or
something and he'd come in at night and read the damned
income tax manual that the feds put out and tell me about
ways, legal ways he always said they were, to cut your
income taxes to zero. And I used to tell him, you don't
make no money, you don't pay no goddam taxes. Your
taxes are already zero 'cause you don't work. Why do you
waste your time with such crap?

But it was like a game with him, like he wasn't happy
until he was finding some way that nobody ever thought
of before and . . .

"Yeah, Rambo, good night. Don't let the bedbugs bite."

That was Rambo. He gets some kind of Army pension 'cause he's like half a nut and he always sees bugs in his sleep, so we always say that, Don't let the bedbugs bite. Someday, I figure I'm gonna open up and Rambo won't be here anymore 'cause he's gonna jump out a window some night when the bug dreams get too bad. He's always good for a laugh around here. Sometimes, some guy'll catch a roach and drop it in his drink and he'll start screaming and sweating and crying. Like a circus some nights. Rambo's real funny to have around. We love it. I sent him a box of flies last Valentine's Day.

Where was I? Right. Three-Bags. So I don't see him for a while, you know, and I figure he's gone off to Las Vegas or something to make his fortune playing roulette or something like that. Anyway, one night he comes in again, with a grin like one of my juiceheads gets when I blow-back a drink, and he says he's solved the big problem, and when I say I don't remember exactly what big problem because his whole life is a big problem to me, he says . . .

"The million dollars. I got it."

"You mean for that lottery bullshit? Who the hell would lend you a million dollars?" the bartender asked.

"It's not a loan. It's an investment. Partners. I do the work, my partner puts up the money, and we split the winnings. I get a million, he gets the rest," Three-Bags said.

"Ask your partner if he'd like to invest in a saloon," the bartender said disgustedly. "I'll give him a ten percent share for only a million dollars."

Three-Bags was looking at the late night news on the television set behind the bar. "You ever notice?" he said.

"Notice what?"

"You got to be a rebel redneck to say 'thow the ball.' Because they can't pronounce their r's or something. That's from getting

chitlins stuck in your teeth when you're young. But all the New York sports guys on TV say 'thow the ball' too and they're all Jewish and they never got any farther south than Southampton. Why is that?"

It turns out that Three-Bags' partner is a dothead. You know, some Arab or Indian or something. You sure this isn't boring you? It's not often we get somebody here pretty like you and I'd hate to be putting you to sleep with this story.

Okay, so, like I said, some sand nigger who's over here chasing women and back in the desert, the oil pumps are going chug-a-chug-a-chug day and night and night and day, making the bastard richer, he turns out to be the one who's going to put up the million so Three-Bags can beat the lottery. You ever hear anything dumber in your life? I mean, I must have laughed for five minutes when I hear this. Here's Three-Bags, who's smart but a nitwit if you know what I mean, and he gets some other nitwit and they're gonna beat the lottery, as if intelligent people with real brains hadn't tried to do that already.

But Three-Bags was just looking at me when I finally stopped laughing and he said something like the game is a foot, or something . . . I never really understood what he meant by that 'cause how can a game be a foot? But he said all he had to do now was to wait until the Delaware lottery went a few weeks without a big winner and then he would be ready to strike. Like a well-oiled machine. That's what he said. Like a well-oiled machine.

And I was thinking, suppose this noodle *does* win a share of a couple of million dollars, well, that's pretty disgusting because he never does any work or anything and here I am, busting my buns all the time, and sometimes things don't work out fair. I hate people who win the lottery. I hope they all get killed when their new Cadillac runs into a freight train.

Yeah, you're right. He was sort of my friend, but there's a limit to friendship, you know what I mean?

So where was I? Oh, the dothead. Another jerk who got rich 'cause his family screwed in the sand, and underneath the sand the oil's going bubble, bubble, bubble. There's something wrong in the world when a guy gets rich just by being born with sand in his butt.

Especially this one. Three-Bags is telling me how dumb this guy is. He explains everything to him, how he's got cards to play almost two million games, and that covers every possible combination and the Arab grabs a paper and pencil and writes down six numbers and says make sure to play these. And Three-Bags explains it all again, and he's trying to smile, we're going to play *all* the combinations and Dothead just smiles and says yes, play these. Can you imagine that, sweetheart? Here's a guy going to put up a million dollars and he doesn't even know what the hell he's putting it up for. He doesn't even understand what Three-Bags is talking about.

So we're talking, soft like Three-Bags always talked, but there's always somebody around who's on the earie so this guy, Jitter, comes down a couple of seats, he's shitfaced, and sits next to Three-Bags. He's a guy hangs around here sometimes, got a bad case of the shakes, so I like to give him a free plate of French Fries once in a while because it's a big hoot to watch him try to pick them up with his fingers. But I remember that night, Jitter just come and busts into our conversation.

"There's three rules I follow in life," Jitter announced.

"What are the other two besides get other people to pay for your drinks?" the bartender said.

"And butting into private conversations?" Three-Bags said. Jitter ignored them like a man on a roll. "These rules are from some writer. He said don't ever play cards with a guy named Doc. And don't eat at no restaurant called Mom's. And don't sleep with no woman who's got more problems than you got. That's my advice too. To both of you."

"Who wrote that?" the bartender asked.

"Nelson. Nelson something," Jitter said. His face screwed up as he thought. "Nelson Aldrich," he finally said triumphantly.

"Nelson Aldrich. That was Rocky," Three-Bags said disgustedly.

"Right. Nelson Aldrich wrote Rocky,*" Jitter said. "I told you he was a writer."*

"Not that Rocky. Rockefeller, you jerkoff," Three-Bags said. "Nelson Aldrich was Nelson Aldrich Rockefeller and he was vice president. You're thinking of Nelson Algren. He was a writer." He covered his face with his hand. "Why do I bother?" he said. "Look, if I buy you a drink, Jitter, will you go away?"

"How far away?"

"Just down the other end of the bar," Three-Bags said. "We'll still be able to see you if you have an attack."

"I'm leaving now."

When he was back in his old seat, the bartender said, "You're really going to do this, aren't you?"

"Absolutely," Three-Bags said. "I've got everything worked out and now I've got the money for the lottery tickets. This is a no-lose situation."

"You know all these years, you come in and we talk crazy talk and you're always figuring out small scams and hondles and none of them ever work and that's okay, but now all of a sudden, you're trying to play with the big guys. What's the reason right now that you're looking for a big score?"

"Things have changed," Three-Bags said.

"How so?"

"I'm in love and I'm getting married, and I'm going to start all over again. So let's start rooting for nobody to win the Delaware lottery. Let's get that prize up over eight million." He paused and grinned. *"How will you like me as a millionaire?"*
"I hate you already," the bartender said.

The way it was with Three-Bags was sometimes I'd see him every night for two weeks and then he wouldn't come around for a month, maybe two. And now if he had a girlfriend, well, then I probably wouldn't see him much at all.

I started looking at the paper to see what was happening with the Delaware lottery but the answer was nothing. It seemed like there was a winner every week and the top prize never went anywhere, like nickels and dimes compared to New York, so I stopped watching after a while.

Just another half-witted scheme that wasn't going nowhere. I remember I said that one night to Shrimps.

Shrimps? Well, his real name is Rocco. Rocco Scampi so everybody calls him Shrimps, like Shrimps Scampi you know, except not to his face 'cause he'll have your ears taken off with a chain saw. He's a connected guy . . . you know . . . yeah, that's right . . . the mob but nobody calls it that no more. He comes in once in a while, this is like his old neighborhood, and he always buys a drink for the house and then he sits around and imitates Marlon Brando. He makes me nervous. He sits here and he says, "So what's going on?" and you tell him and he doesn't have no reaction at all and you just wait a minute and then he says all over again, "So what's going on?" like he didn't even hear you the first time. So you try something else and the same thing. He listens and doesn't say anything and then he says, "So what's going on?"

It's like when you tell a joke and nobody laughs, you feel like a moron, so you keep trying to find a funnier joke and that's the way I was with Shrimps, feeling like a moron, so finally I told him about Three-Bags' asshole scheme and how funny it was.

But I don't know, he didn't seem to think it was real funny. A lot of Italians are like that, you know. They don't have any real sense of humor. So he says, "So what's going on?" and so I told him that this was a real good one, because after Three-Bags and the dothead beat the Delaware lottery, they were coming after the big lottery money . . . in New York and New Jersey and Pennsylvania. I said it just like to keep him amused, but he didn't crack a smile. Like I said, Italians . . .

"Yeah, Horsefly, goodnight."

That's Horsefly. We call him that 'cause he works on a garbage truck. You get it? Horsefly, always around garbage? He's okay. Minds his business. Once in a while he eats in here and sometimes we put his hamburger and fries on a garbage can cover when we give it to him. Everybody laughs. What a joke. He don't laugh much though.

Yeah, right, Three-Bags. So this one night, I look in the paper and I see the Delaware lottery doesn't have no winner and it's up over four million dollars. Now, I'm starting to get interested and wouldn't you know, that same night, Three-Bags comes in. I haven't seen him in more than a month.

"Quick. A double Scotch," Three-Bags said.

"What's the matter? I thought you were in love," the bartender said.

"I am in love and I'm the happiest clam in the world and I'm going to make this big score and then go buy a farm somewhere

with my honey. And what happens to me now? The goddam Mafia is on my case.''

"What are you talking about?'' the bartender said.

"Shrimps. You know that guy . . . he wants in on my lottery action. How the hell'd he find out what I'm doing?''

"What difference does it make?'' the bartender asked. "So you got another partner. What's so bad about that?''

"What's so bad is that the pot don't get any bigger. Whatever is the top lottery prize is the top lottery prize and that's all. You cut it more ways, but it's still the same jackpot. So if I get another partner, my share's going to get smaller. I can see it coming.''

"Then tell that to Shrimps. He'll understand.''

"I tried, but those wise guys don't understand anything when they smell money. He said that my share stays the same. And I use the Arab's money. He said he'll make his deal with the Arab.''

"Then why worry? You're out of it,'' the bartender said.

"It's not that easy. It doesn't smell right. Shrimps has got some damned plan and it's making me nervous. I don't like having them for partners. I want to bail out after this and Shrimps is talking about us taking on all the big lotteries, here and Jersey and Pennsylvania and I just don't want to be his business partner. Why me, God?''

"Why don't you just take off now and forget the whole thing?''

"I want to get married,'' Three-Bags said. "I told you that. And this is a nice girl and I'm not going to start off our marriage with an envelope filled with food stamps. I need this million.''

"Then do what Shrimps says.''

"Those bastards will never let me get away with a million. They'll get their mitts on it someway.''

"Then hope that the Delaware lottery never gets above eight million so you're home free.''

Three-Bags drained his drink, ordered another, and shook his head. "I'm not that lucky. You watch, this goddam lottery is going right up to eight million dollars and I'm stuck with it.'' He *lowered his head until his forehead touched the bar. "Can you believe my luck? I've got this foolproof scheme for winning a bundle and I got one partner who's so dumb that every time I see him, he writes out his lucky numbers for me, and I can't explain to him that we're going to play them all, and I got another partner, if he gets his hooks in me, I'm dead forever."*

"You just hang out with a low class of people," the bartender said. "That's your problem."

So Three-Bags tells me that things aren't going so good—sometimes that guy just didn't have any luck—and then I watched and sure enough, don't you know it, the Delaware lottery goes up to eight million dollars top prize.

So this is the big moment. Three-Bags explained it to me a long time before. One time he was missing for a couple of weeks and when he came in, he told me he was down in Delaware going around to stores that sold lottery tickets.

See, the problem was getting so many tickets printed on these computer machines that they have in the stores in time for the drawing. What he did was hire a lot of guys who ran stores and make a deal with them, so that when he came in with his big bunch of tickets, they would sit at their computers when *their* store was closed but while the big lottery computer was still open and they would feed in his tickets.

He said once it was going to take like fifty stores, maybe fifteen hours each, running out his computer cards to print out the tickets for . . . what'd I say, like two million combinations. He said he had to give them some money up front, but only a couple of bucks because they were going to make a commission on all the tickets they sold. And what he said was that not only was he guaranteed the big first prize, but he'd have like a hundred and eighty winning tickets that picked five numbers and maybe like another six thousand or so that picked four winners. And his idea was to give all those six thousand small prizes to the store owners who used their machines to punch up his tickets.

So it sounded pretty complicated, but I got to say this for the crazy bastard, he seemed to have it all worked out and he said it was doable, and I'll tell you the truth, after going this far with him, I was beginning to believe. Maybe if I had a spare million, I would have come in with him at the start. But what the hell, who knows how things are going to work out? Especially when the guy's a nut. So it was probably all for the best.

Hey, the place is empty. Just you and me now. I didn't even notice. I guess that's what they mean when they say time flies when you're having fun. No, you don't have to leave. You're so pretty, you don't ever have to leave.

Just a joke. I'm not some kind of lounge lizard that you have to worry about. I'm a little old for you actually. Well, thanks, that's nice of you to say. Freshen that for you? Yeah, I'd be glad to have one with you. Thanks.

What's that? You're really interested in this story, huh? It *is* a good story, isn't it? No, it didn't make a lot of the papers and I guess there's only a couple of us who know the whole thing. There just wasn't any reason for it to be a big story. It wasn't like he was a big shot or anything. Nobody cared about Three-Bags.

But it was weird and I guess it'd be sad if it wasn't so damned funny. He was a funny guy.

The Delaware lottery gets up to eight million and Three-Bags is out there with his thousands of computer cards, buying up a million dollars worth of tickets with the dothead's money.

He hadn't stopped back in to talk to me, so I didn't

know how he was making out with Shrimps. But I guess
Three-Bags knew what he was talking about—those gang
guys never want to put up any of their own money. But I
don't think he had any idea of what Shrimps' guys were
going to do. Three-Bags was sort of a jerk that way. You
got to be careful in this world, 'cause everybody's your
enemy.

Anyway, comes the day of the lottery drawing. The
prize now is up to almost nine million and the more I think
about it, the more jealous I get of Three-Bags because I
don't see how he can lose. That's if he gets his bets in, but
the way he explained it, it looks like a lead pipe cinch.

And then that night, just before midnight it was and the
place was empty and I was thinking about closing early,
and Three-Bags comes in and I don't think I ever saw a
man look worse in my life. I'll never forget that expression
in his eyes. Sad but really comical too . . . I poured him a
drink before he even said a word and he spilled half of it
on the way to his mouth.

*"What's the matter with you? I thought you'd be celebrating
by now, millionaire."*

*"I'm in deep trouble," Three-Bags said. "I've got to get out of
town."*

"What's the matter? Didn't you win?"

*Three-Bags looked up. His eyes had the fatalistic, confused look
of a crippled deer dropped into the middle of a hungry wolf pack.
"You don't know, do you?" he said.*

*The bartender shook his head and Three-Bags pulled a news-
paper from his pocket and tossed it onto the bar. The other man
opened it and saw a large Page One photo and a headline:*

ARAB FINANCIER DIES AS PRIVATE JET
EXPLODES

The picture showed a body facedown, partially covered with a blanket, lying on the tarmac of the airport in Wilmington, Delaware. Spread out behind him was the twisted, exploded wreckage of the small jet aircraft. The only part of the plane that seemed to have escaped the full force of the explosion was the wedge-shaped tail section, covered with numbers, that served as a silent, eerie backdrop for the dead man's body.

The bartender looked up at Three-Bags, who said, "They killed him. Shrimps' crazy bastards killed my money man. They put a bomb in his freaking plane and blew the poor sonofabitch up. I knew this was going to go sour as soon as they got their paws in it. They said they were going to make a deal with him. This is their idea of a deal. Just blow the bastard up and take over."

The bartender shrugged. "Well, I didn't know him," he said, "but I'm sorry about the dothead. But so what? Did you get a winner in the lottery? If you did, what's the big deal? Cash your ticket, take your cut, give the rest to Shrimps and get out of here. Did you win?"

Three-Bags began to laugh and stopped only when it turned into a fit of choking.

"Sure, I won," he finally managed to gasp out. "I told you, it was foolproof. I had every combination of numbers. I couldn't lose."

"So?"

"So? Remember I told you how the Arab wanted me to be sure to play his lucky numbers?"

"Yeah?"

"Well, his lucky numbers . . . they were those goddam numbers on the tail of his plane." He stabbed the newspaper photograph with an index finger. "Those there," he said. He recited the numbers without even glancing down at the page.

"Six, thirteen, twenty-seven, fourteen, three and eighteen. His lucky numbers. From the freaking tail of his freaking plane."

"I don't know what the hell you're talking about," the bartender said. "So what?"

"So those dopey, kill-crazy bastards murdered this guy this afternoon and some photographer was out at the airport and he took this picture of the plane and it showed on all the six-o'clock news. And everybody in all of goddam Delaware saw the picture on TV and saw those numbers on the tail of the plane and went running off to the candy store to play them in the lottery. And guess what came up?"

He stared at the bartender, who did not answer.

"Yeah. Six, thirteen, twenty-seven, fourteen, three and eighteen. There were a thousand first-prize winners. First prize was worth eight thousand dollars. Eight and a half million dollars sliced a thousand ways. We bet a million to win eight thousand dollars. All because of these dopey bombnut bastards. I'm a dead man. I should have known I was dead as soon as Shrimps stuck his paws in."

"I think you're overreacting," the bartender said. "So the Arab is dead. But he's the one who's out the million. Shrimps can't be pissed at you for that. You didn't have anything to do with it. Just tell Shrimps, next time he puts up the money and you'll run the play and you'll both cash in big."

"It doesn't work that way," Three-Bags said. "Shrimps is going to figure he's due a couple of million in winnings. As far as he's concerned, it's already his. He already killed somebody for it and he doesn't understand it any better than the Arab. When he sees there are a thousand winning tickets and he knows we bought two million tickets, he's going to say they're all ours and when I don't give him eight million in winnings, he's going to take it out on me. I'm dead. How did that bastard ever get on to me? I'm dead."

The bartender tried not to agree, tried not to nod, and finally settled for just looking away across the room at the silent jukebox.

"I need to borrow some money," Three-Bags said.

"What for?"

"I want to get my girl and me out of town. Go someplace else and start over, before Shrimps' guys come after me. All I need's a couple of thousand. You know I'm good for it."

"Gee, Three-Bags, I'd like to help, but . . . well, I just don't have it right now. Maybe I could give you a hundred."

Three-Bags nodded to himself and then stood up at the bar. "Well, that's the way it goes," he said. "I think I'll be moving along." He went to the door, then grinned back at the bartender. "Don't do anything I wouldn't do," he said. "But if you have to, make sure she's pretty."

Then he was gone.

Jeez, he was a funny guy. So I tried to help him out with some money, you know, but it didn't work, you know, and, well, about three days later, they found his body laying facedown on some old pier up on the East Side. He'd been all carved up and the cops couldn't identify him, but then there was this report that the corpse had this lottery ticket for a stinking eight-thousand-dollar jackpot stuck inside his shoe. So I read that and I went up to the morgue and identified the body as Three-Bags. I tried to tell the cops that I was his partner on that lottery ticket but they said they had to give the ticket to his next of kin. They never got the guys responsible for it. Just another unsolved crime.

Well, naturally, it was Shrimps. Who else could it have been? But nobody knew that and I sure as hell wasn't going to say anything. Open your mouth and that's how people get killed.

I guess maybe his family buried him. I kind of lost track. I'm surprised you didn't see it in the paper. Too bad. He wasn't the worst guy but he just got in with the wrong crowd, you know. And I guess he just wasn't lucky. But he *was* funny. He told me this story once about this blue pigeon and how . . .

What's that? Yeah, I guess you're right. It *is* time to close the place up. We don't get women as pretty as you in here very often, time just kind of slipped away on me.

Say it again?

You want to go home with me?

You sure? You know, I'm not a rich guy or anything and you . . . no, no, I didn't mean that. I know you're not like that. Sure, come on, we'll even grab a cab.

The bartender had never realized just how dismal was his little two-room apartment until he opened the door and stepped in ahead of the beautiful young brunette.

He flipped on the light, turned and spread his arms, grinning sheepishly.

"Well, here we are," he said. "Sorry for the look of the place."

"Somehow it's you," the young woman said.

She lingered only a step inside the closed door and they looked nervously at each other across the small room.

"I'll make you a drink," he said, and walked off to a sink littered with dirty dishes, where he fussed around, cleaning a glass. "A drink makes everybody relax," he said. "Old Three-Bags used to call it the 'no-worry.' Boy, he was a funny guy."

The woman had not moved from her spot by the door.

"Turn around," she said.

When the bartender did, he saw she had a small gun in her hand. It was pointed at his belly.

"What . . ."

"Remember when he said he was going to get married?"

"Not you?"

"Yes. Me."

"Oh, gosh. I'm sorry. But . . ."

"Not as sorry as you will be," she said.

The small gun barked twice, echoing sharply inside the dirty room. One slug took his stomach; the other got him in the chest.

The bartender felt a sudden outrageous pounding in his temples, but it began to subside as he slumped down to the floor, then fell forward on his face.

He lifted his face toward the woman, then shook his head. "Some people got no sense of humor," he mumbled before his lips froze open and his head sank again.

The corpse was found the next afternoon, facedown. No friends or relatives came forward to claim the body, and he was buried in Potter's Field.

A body is found on a famous publisher's carpet. In its hand is a recently fired thirty-eight revolver. The body is mine. The gun is not.

Justin Scott

Katherine's Faces

The first time I saw Katherine Farnall she was wearing what I came to call her public smile. My agent and I were pitching a book to her husband, a publisher famous for being famous, editing the famous, and occasionally making some unknown plodder like me famous, too. Jeff had published my last novel, a flawed attempt to break out of sea stories into mainstream commercial fiction, which had capsized in hardcover and sunk without a trace in paperback.

It wasn't the happiest of meetings. Jeff was at his desk, little hawk eyes indecipherable behind his tinted glasses. Behind the desk were photos of him with famous people and a glass gun case containing an arsenal that a *GQ* or *Esquire* profile had dubbed "a gentleman's collection of firearms." I perched on a leather and chrome chair. And occupying the greater part of a couch against the wall was Roland, my literary agent of ten years, silent as a bear in winter.

Two things Jeff was not famous for were a long attention span and loyalty, so I was regaling him a little desperately with a new idea about a Ted Turner–type TV mogul who sponsors a single-handed round-the-world sailing race. That was when his wife walked in.

Jeff Farnall had a lot of qualities that made him easy to loathe: he was a cocksure, arrogant son of a bitch who just happened to be a wonderfully talented editor, wealthy by his own hand, and a successful writer himself of high-glitz crime novels he researched by cruising Manhattan with his friend the Police Commissioner. But it was hard to dislike a man who looked so genuinely delighted to see his own wife.

He started skipping around his office like a happy little kid, bounding up to kiss her cheek, bouncing back to admire her outfit, apologizing that he hadn't known she was free for lunch, and introducing her proudly to Roland and me. I'd have been proud, too. She was a perfectly lovely-looking woman, somewhere in her thirties, with pretty blond hair, a hint of a splendid figure inside all that expensive silk and linen, striking blue eyes that could tempt a 747 to try a landing, and that public smile—half innocent, half aware, and one hundred percent proper.

She apologized, in faintly Virginian accents, for interrupting our meeting, and explained something about being stuck in midtown and having to use Jeff's telephone to call her parents, who were traveling abroad. She was so fresh and clean, I hated to imagine her touching a public pay phone. Jeff settled her on a couch in a little alcove on the far side of his office, adjusted the window blinds to her liking, and finally returned to Roland and me, asking, with a glance at his watch, "Where were we?"

Roland said, "Dennison was describing his new novel, *Seascape*, about a televised single-handed around-the-world sailing race."

Dennison. That's me. Dennison Marker, born with a pen name. I picked up the *Seascape* story and ran with it, feeling pretty good, because I was excited by the possibilities and could hear my excitement in the telling. The thing I liked best, of the little I knew of the book so early on, was the rivalry between the Ted Turner–type's son and mistress, who I felt would fall in love even as they competed desperately against each other to win the race.

"Now, Dennison," Jeff interrupted. He seized his gold pen, touched it to his little pad, and leaned over his desk with an expression of sheer certainty. "What if Arab terrorists kidnap the front-runners?"

Arab terrorists in the middle of the ocean. Clearly Jeff's commercial instincts had run amok. I might have been more confused if a helicopter had crashed through his forty-seventh-floor window at that moment, but not much. Dead in the water, I turned to Roland.

Roland rumbled like a volcano heretofore thought extinct. Planting his feet on the floor, shifting his bulk off the couch, he rose definitively, saying, "I think we've had a productive first discussion. It's time to let Dennison go home and think."

Jeff didn't like that. A sharp, mean glare shot from his tinted glasses. I thought for a second we might be treated to one of his famous temper tantrums, but Roland's stellar client list demanded respect. Nor had Jeff forgotten the long two years Roland had stopped doing business with him for throwing an ashtray. Never a gracious loser, however, he had to have the last word: "And I'll think here how a sea story might fit our current list."

I paid Roland fifteen percent to deal with digs like that, so I looked away, right into the sapphire gaze of Mrs. Farnall, who, for one tenth of a second, let a little question travel between her eyes and mine: *What are you doing here?*

The tenth-second passed. Good-byes were made. Roland and I were out the door. In the elevator I suggested that things hadn't gone too badly. Roland's reply was noncommittal. We'd been struggling together long enough that I knew his habits. He hated postmortems. I'd get nothing more out of him about the meeting. In a few days, if he had the time, he'd start thinking up some new strategy that might get me a contract, either with Farnall, or failing that, some new house he could persuade to take a chance on me.

Knowing his habits didn't mean I liked them, and I was really feeling the need of some shoring up. So I pointed at his stomach and accused him of backsliding.

Roland had survived a heart attack the year before, and when the doctors told him to lose weight or die, we had agreed that Roland would discover whether he was fat because he was self-indulgent or harbored a death wish. His answer was to drop sixty pounds in a year, but now it looked as if he had put some back on.

"Kevlar," he said as the elevator opened onto the lobby.

"What?"

He was a man who rarely smiled and he didn't now, as he explained, "I'm wearing a Kevlar bullet-proof vest."

"You're kidding." We were not touchers with each other; we rarely shook hands, so I was not about to poke him in the gut and feel for myself.

"I'm not kidding. Jeff Farnall is a nut in a room full of guns. I wouldn't dream of walking into his office without a bullet-proof vest." Illustrating his point, Roland nodded at the heavy set off-duty NYPD cop guarding the elevators. Years ago some poor disappointed novelist had broken up Jeff's glass desk with an Irish walking stick. Jeff, who hadn't even been in his office at the time, used the incident as an excuse to post police guards and acquire a handgun permit, which is harder to get in Manhattan than rich.

"Then how come you let me go in without one?" I asked.

Roland demolished my small joke with his standard good-bye—"I'll call you," which meant within the year—and went out to get a cab down to his Gramercy Park townhouse, while I went in search of the subway. Standing on the token line, I decided I was too thoroughly depressed to take the train. I went back up to the avenue to hail a taxi and ride home in more expensive misery.

Willingness to pay for a cab is no guarantee you'll get one, of course, and I lost a few to midtowners more aggressive than I. Then a taxi pulled up, with its passenger rolling down her window. "I'm going up Central Park West," said Mrs. Farnall, "if that's any help."

I got in, and the magic rule of Manhattan life that says there is no traffic on those rare occasions you're not late went into effect. We shot uptown as if a motorcycle escort had cleared the way, chatting briefly about the QE-II, on which her parents were cruising and aboard which I had once sailed as a pinch-hit lecturer. Soon we were at the Farnall door in one of those magnificent CPW buildings where the apartments are more properly assessed in acreage than square feet.

I kept the cab. Nothing as special as the look in her husband's office had recurred. All that passed between us was her instant understanding that, for whatever my reasons, I really did want to pay for the taxi myself. And I am certain, busy lives being segregated the way they are, that she and I might never have met again.

But then Roland's wife visited her mother in Florida, leaving Roland alone for the weekend with an invitation to a Sunday brunch his heaviest-hitter client was throwing in Greenwich. He would have preferred staying home and reading, but it was a command appearance he couldn't refuse, so he invited me along, saying we could discuss *Seascape* in the car. Last-minute invitations like this went with the territory of being a reasonably successful bachelor writer who could be trusted to dip the proper spoon in his soup. Thinking I had made enough progress to talk about the sailing race story, I accepted gratefully, and Roland had a wonderful drive, poking holes in my outline.

Our host, the richest, hardest-working commercial writer

in America, greeted us in his ballroom with a scotch in his hand and his fourth wife on his arm. The story was he was a decent enough husband who just wore women out with his relentless novel writing. Wives two through four had all started as his typists. His latest, a good-looking woman who looked up to a few more books, took charge of Roland, and Dave got me. Yes, he had a ballroom with three walls of French windows onto the garden and a secret stairway to his master bedroom. I told Dave I'd been in houses almost as large, though I couldn't recall one privately owned. He gave me a generous laugh and steered me to the bar, where he told some men and women drinking champagne that I was the best writer at his party.

Katherine Farnall extended her hand. "We met in Jeffrey's office." She looked quite stunning in a simple blouse and the baggy slacks women were wearing that year. She had pulled her hair up in back. Her neck made an exceptionally pretty line Rodin would have been proud of. And Jeffrey was off in California giving a speech to the Hollywood chapter of the National Rifle Association.

Katherine and our host's fourth wife were old friends who had backpacked around Europe instead of going to college—which was as good a subject as any to start a conversation that continued on and off through a long, magic afternoon. I hadn't realized before how her face was almost heart-shaped. She had rather a mobile face, actually, animated when she spoke, thoughtful-looking when she listened, warm for her friends. When guys attempted significant eye contact, she discouraged them firmly with her public smile. We kept bumping into each other and, when the party finally sat down to eat, found our place cards side by side at our hostess's table in a window overlooking a pond full of fat, golden carp.

"I read one of your books," Katherine said all of a

sudden, and I wanted to ask, Before or after we met, but her public smile said, Don't.

"Which one?"

"*The Sea Harrower.* I'll bet you've always wanted to live on a boat."

I looked at her, a little surprised, and vaguely non-plussed. Most readers assumed from my work that I was an old salt temporarily on the beach. But Katherine had seen through my research to the fantasy that made the novel work. "You found me out."

"I liked the book."

I offered to send her another, but Jeff, she told me, would find a copy for her.

I believe in fate. Nor, with my life adrift over a fraying safety net, was I averse to the idea that sudden change could lurk around the next corner. Fate had taken me to Dave's party, and a while later fate brought a request under The National Arts Club letterhead to lunch with the New York City public school kids who were learning how to write. I have my reservations about teaching creative writing, but it seemed only fair to give these kids a shot at opportunities private school students take for granted. Nor had it escaped my notice that Katherine Farnall was listed on the project's Board of Directors.

I went to the luncheon. The National Arts Club is on Gramercy Park, next door to The Players Club and diagonally across the fenced garden from Roland's Greek Revival townhouse. I stopped there first, hoping to collect a foreign rights check, which hadn't yet cleared the agency's Moldavian bank, then ducked into The Players for a quick Bloody Mary and cheese at the bar because our neighbor's kitchen was infamous.

The National Arts was swarming with school kids, seventh through ninth graders, who had apparently never seen so much stained glass outside of church. I found three little guys wondering out the front window at the garden park devoid of drunks and crack addicts. They told me they wanted to grow up to be science fiction writers, so I steered them toward my friend Chip, whom I'd seen on the way in. Later, waiting my turn at the buffet, with some misguided child who wanted to write about boats, I felt a whisper pass my ear—"The cold cuts are the least lethal"—and Katherine Farnall swooped past with a covey of small girls.

By three o'clock the little people had all been loaded back into yellow buses and I found myself on the sidewalk with a few people, including Katherine, discussing ways to get uptown. "Share a cab?" I asked her.

She looked at her watch, the way New Yorkers do when they're surprised to discover they have an hour to spare.

"Or," I said, careful to include those standing nearest her, "if anyone feels like shooting some pool, let's go into The Players and have a drink."

Katherine waited until Chip said, "Sounds good."

"Does your club admit women members?" she inquired sternly, and when I assured her we did, she said, "Yes let's do that."

So four of us went in, down to the Grill, after we borrowed a necktie for Chip. I took drink orders. Katherine asked how I happened to be a member. I explained that writers belonged to The Players as well as actors since Mark Twain was one of our founders. She was a pretty decent pool player, and on the second round, she drank her beer from the bottle.

By then I was a goner, right over the edge, head over heels in love with my publisher's wife. In the space of two months I had met her in her adoring husband's office, chatted in a cab, enjoyed her company at a party, admired her ease with children, and was now pretending nonchalance as she stretched over a pool table, sank my ball by mistake, laughed, and raised a Bass ale to her lips with a grin that could no longer be called, by any stretch of the imagination, her public smile.

In the cab at rush hour, we sat nearly silent with Chip between us. I wondered why she had married Jeff Farnall, who was at heart, despite all the dazzle, a very serious man driven to prove himself over and over and over. He couldn't be much fun, and the thought of him in bed with a woman would freeze gasoline.

After Chip got out at Lincoln Center, Katherine asked me what I was writing. I told her I was struggling with an outline for a new book and, when she prompted me, described the relationship I was trying to work out between the TV mogul, his son, and his mistress.

"I read your last book," she said. "The one Jeff published. Your writing seemed obedient."

I guess my face fell, because she laughed. "Don't listen to me, I'm just a country girl."

At her building, with her hand already on the cab door to get out, she turned back to me, and I knew our lives hung in the balance. "May I call you?" I asked.

She shook my hand in a proper good-bye. Then, so softly that even the cabby couldn't hear, she said, "I wish you would; around noon."

The next eighteen hours crept by like centuries. When it was finally time, I dialed, my heart pounding, half expecting I had heard wrong and she would say, "You can speak to Jeff at the office."

Her voice filled the wire like honey. "Why don't we meet someplace where we can talk?"

New York is a collection of villages made up of the people you know, and one of the joys of the city is running into friends. But if you're hoping to be bad, then restaurants, bars, and the sidewalks offer everyone you've ever met the opportunity to dine out on tasty gossip. We racked our brains and finally settled upon a bench over-looking the Seventy-ninth Street Boat Basin.

Katherine arrived in running shoes and sweats and a headband for her hair. I was waiting, empty notebook in hand. The jogger and the water-gazing writer meet—by chance. I feasted on the sight of her. The sun seemed to light her eyes from within.

"I don't want to be 'accidentally' caught," she said bluntly. "My husband loves me very much and he's very . . . dependent on me. I won't hurt him. Ever. So, no 'mistakes.' "

"Promise. Just remind me now and then. I've never done this sort of thing before." Neither, of course, had she. We hadn't gotten near a bed yet, but the possibility hovered like the gulls riding the wind.

Her gaze fell to my arm and she touched me, suddenly, with a jolt that wandered under my skin. "Would you kiss me?" she asked.

But I kept my promise and said, "Not here."

We talked daily on the phone and met several more times by the river, taking things slowly. Then, suddenly, the weather gave us a break, and we had all the privacy we wanted. Manhattan is an island city, after all, and sometimes the sea slips up the river beds with a surprise. Rain that had been threatening all day arrived on a southeast gale in an explosion of wind-driven warm water that soaked us in seconds and blotted visibility to a yard or so. Inside a little private capsule we tried our first kiss, the first of many mutual surprises. We kissed like we had practiced our whole lives for this afternoon.

Hand in hand we ran out of the park and squelched into my building, recognizable only as the sole survivors of a foundered cruise ship. Into a hot shower with our wet clothes on, we gradually took them off. Later, when she asked me what I was thinking, I told her I thought I had come home, which, of course, she already knew.

We needed a place. My lease was coming due and Roland had been suggesting a move to less expensive quarters anyway, so I left my West End Avenue building with its busy lobby and eagle-eyed doormen, and rented a studio apartment in a brownstone on the north side of Seventy-fifth Street between Central Park West and Columbus Avenue, five short blocks from Katherine's place. She could approach from either direction. And while the nosy Italian landladies who seemed to own most of the houses on the block watched from their grilled windows, they were not likely to show up at many publishing parties, so we felt reasonably safe. I had my typewriter and a wall of books on one side of the room and a double bed on the other, where, in the sunlight filtering through gauze curtains Katherine brought from her linen closet, we would make love as many afternoons a week as she could steal from the surprisingly rigid schedule required to keep her husband's busy social and professional life zipping along productively. Weekends were hell because they went to the country to their Dutchess County gentleman's farm, where Jeff raised prize Duroc-Jerseys.

I tried to use those two long days to get some work done and was successful at it more often than not; I kept reworking the round-the-world race idea to try and get some thriller element into it, but nothing really clicked because it was essentially a character conflict story with no place for villains who longed to destroy the world and end democracy forever. Tacked on my cork board was Jeff's final letter on the subject—"Boat races bore me!!!!! Best wishes, Jeff."

Stuck, I started a few short stories. Roland hit the roof.
Next to Jeff's letter I tacked Roland's fax: "Authors with
private incomes write short stories."

The first time Katherine showed me one of her other
faces, we had shared an ancient Thai stick that had endured
a decade wrapped in plastic in the back of various freezers
and had just enough juice left to incite a vague buzz in a
couple of people who had last smoked dope ten years ago.
We carried the buzz to bed with us most enjoyably, and
after, while I was holding her face in my hands, marveling
down into her eyes, I saw her change. Her face became a
little rounder and fuller—a more Swedish-looking face—
which reminded me of Liv Ullman's expression of gentle
wisdom.

Her second "new" face, which crept over her features
one darkening afternoon while we shared a mug of tea,
made Katherine look a bit like Jane Fonda. I thought the
similarity came from a kind of cocky certainty, under-
scored by a hint of vulnerability.

Katherine's third face didn't remind me of anyone except
an extremely innocent and doubly erotic Katherine. That
least frequent apparition would appear quite suddenly,
and rarely for long. I called that face her sexy friend. I would
say, Your friend is here. She teased me about wanting to
make love to another woman, but she knew what I saw
was true. All three women were as real as Katherine, yet
still quintessentially Katherine. Extensions of her; they did
not signal any sort of personality change. She was still
Katherine, still with me as deeply and closely as ever. Some
weeks faces didn't appear. Once when Jeff flew alone to
L.A. to publicize his latest novel, *Cop Shot!* we stayed together and Katherine's faces paraded through the night.

I felt affection for them—not to deny the little thrill she
had deduced of having a "piece of strange," as they said

in her native Virginia. It was like living with several friendly ghosts.

But it gave me an idea for a story about a guy who became obsessed with the activities of his mistress's other faces when they're not with him. This was miles from anything I'd written before—leagues from sea stories and farther still from the circuses Roland had talked me into trying to write for Jeff.

The story kept building in my head. I started scribbling notes on scrap paper, then typing the notes, then I tried an outline—a calendar of events, really just a list. Then Jeff spirited my beautiful Katherine off to a Scottish grouse hunt for ten days, and before I fell into too deep a depression, I made myself sit down at the typewriter and run the story in rough draft. It was about jealousy and it was the cleanest copy I'd ever written. Rather than mess it about, I handed it straight to my typist. She showed it to her husband. Her husband asked if I would mind if he showed it to a friend of his at *The New Yorker*, and miracles started.

A kindly editor I could barely understand took me to lunch and talked about books I would never read. Gradually, he admitted that *The New Yorker* wanted to buy "Katherine's Faces." I told him we had to change the title, and we settled on "The Other Women." Roland, my ever supportive agent, thought at first *The New Yorker* was calling to sell him a subscription. He managed to negotiate a decent fee, and by the time Katherine came back to me, the deed was done.

I was feeling pretty good, but the real test in my mind was whether she would like the story. I read it to her. The happiest time in my life would probably always be the first time we went to bed, but the second happiest was when she loved the story. Really loved it. That afternoon I asked her very seriously if she would leave Jeff.

The agreement of our love affair had always been that we would not hurt Jeff, but too much had gone down between us, and this latest ten-day separation—as hard on her as on me—had been the worst yet. And yet, emotionally torn, she feared Jeff Farnall couldn't function without her. I knew by now that she didn't feel like a wife to him, that her love for him was more like a mother's love of an errant son.

When my story was published I got a lot of phone calls from people I hadn't heard from in some time. There was even some movie interest. And a summons to Jeff Farnall's office, late one evening when he was working late and his secretary had gone home.

I hadn't seen Jeff since the meeting when I met Katherine, and hadn't heard from him since "Boat races bore me!!!!!" I prepped for our meeting by reading my various notes and many outlines for the round-the-world-race story. In several versions, I must admit, I actually tried to work in his terrorist kidnapping idea, but it always turned comic, and Roland assured me that there was even less of a market for comic sea novels than straight ones. Roland was encouraging me to write *Seascape* still, because he thought the television mogul idea would open it up. He declined, however, to come along to the meeting, which was fine with me. He could sell a story, but he couldn't write it, and at this point, I was the only one who could convince Jeff Farnall that I could make a sailboat race exciting.

If the key lay in the TV business, then I intended to propose that the TV mogul's empire was facing bankruptcy, in hopes that Jeff would leap in with some bright ideas of his own that would lend drama to the business side and get him personally involved and excited at the same time.

My week of *The New Yorker* was lying on his desk, the

cover a readily recognized Gahan Wilson cartoon of a
sleeping dog, an anxious cat, and a prehistoric animal
sporting many teeth.

Jeff got right down to it.

"Read your story."

"And?" I asked, after a long silence.

"There's only one woman in New York with those two
faces, you son of a bitch."

I almost corrected him, three, but he did it for me,
saying, "You must have made the third one up."

I wasn't surprised he had missed that face. I said, "I
don't know what you're talking about, Jeff."

Jeff reminded me of the pecking order in the publishing
industry. "I'm not giving my wife up to some damn
writer."

"Your wife?" I echoed. "Wait a minute. What are you
talking about?" What else could I say? What would you
have said?

Jeff reached back into his gun collection and selected an
enormous revolver. Holding it in two hands, bracing his
elbows on his desk, he leveled it at my chest.

"Jeff."

Jeff Farnall fired once. The bullet threw me out of the
chair and halfway across the carpet. I landed flat on my
back, unable to move. I had some vague idea about trying
to stand up, but my arms and legs wouldn't budge. Jeff
was on me in a flash, tugging a second gun from his
pocket, a little revolver, which he pressed in my limp right
hand. Working my finger around the trigger, he raised my
hand, pointed the gun at the gun cabinet, and jerked my
finger. This shot, which put a clean hole in the glass, was
a lot quieter, or maybe my hearing had died. He dropped
my hand, walked calmly to his desk and hit a speed dial
number on his telephone.

"Jeff Farnall for the PC, please. Tell him it's rather important . . . . Ed. No, I'm not. Ed, some crazy writer just tried to kill me. Took a shot at me, missed. I got my piece out and blew him away. . . . Yeah, I'm all right, but I've got a body in my office Homicide's going to want to look at. I just thought I'd call you first. Should I dial 911 or—you'll do it? Thanks, Ed. Thank you. . . . Yeah, I'm okay. Right. See you."

He hung up the telephone, laid his gun on his desk, edged past my body and went to the window, where he stood smiling grimly at Manhattan.

I finally managed to lift my hand, and that accomplishment gave me courage to try my voice.

"Jeff?"

He whirled in disbelief, gazed down the barrel of the little gun he had given me, and gasped.

"One question, Jeff. Did you hurt her?"

"But—"

"My agent told me to wear a vest. Did you hurt her?"

He had a fast mind. He took in the new situation, and seemed to weigh the distance between his gun on the desk against my condition on the floor.

"Did you hurt her?"

Hungrily he gazed at his gun until I said, "Even not knowing how to use this thing, I could put three shots inside you before you reach it."

This information he accepted reluctantly. "Did you hurt her?" I asked him again.

"Of course not," he whispered. "How could I hurt her?" And then he started to cry.

I had mixed feelings, lying there. Jeff's oversize bullet, while it hadn't pierced the Kevlar vest, had thrown me eight feet. I hurt from my neck to my waist, and a very sharp stab of pain whenever I tried to breathe suggested a broken rib or at least the biggest, blackest bruise in the history of bruises.

On the other hand, I was alive. And when it came to bruises, who could minister to them more lovingly than my Katherine? For she was my Katherine, in her heart and soul, while the poor son of a bitch who had just tried to kill me was going to lose her, if not today, then tomorrow. But I had promised we would never hurt him accidentally.

Sirens howled forty-seven stories down the street, and Jeff, abruptly realizing what trouble he was in, hastily dried his cheeks. Then those little hawk eyes settled again on his gun. Before he got any notions, I dragged myself up to my feet and staggered, half bent over, to his desk, where I picked up his gun and put both guns back in their cabinet. I turned the key, removed it from the lock, and dropped it into a little slot in the air conditioning.

"Before the Commissioner gets here, there's a couple of things you and I ought to get straight: First of all, I think you're a bit confused about your wife. The woman I wrote about was a girl I knew in college."

"Really? Was her name Katherine, too?"

"I changed it, you dummy. She's married now, but sometimes we get together when she comes to New York."

"Really?" He bought it. He even gave me a little macho smirk of approval, man to man. No problem, as long as it's somebody else's wife.

"However," I said, "you've got some explaining to do. Two guns have been fired, and your friend the Commissioner told the Homicide boys I'm dead, which I'm not."

I sat at his desk and picked up his gold pen. "Now, Jeff, I'm looking forward to your input on *Seascape*, of course, and I'm confident your personal support will secure it a place on your current list. But maybe you ought to run *your* story by me first, before you try to sell it to the cops."